FRANK FACES OF
THE DEAD

Dedication to . . . . .

Most of those who have died in the Northern Ireland 'troubles',
whether they be soldiers, I.R.A. men, policemen, U.V.F.
men. . . Catholics, Protestants or non-believers, Unionists or
Nationalists bear the common identity of the working class. It
is the working class who fill the jails, who kill and are killed,
who torture and are tortured. This book is dedicated to the
hope of their speedy realisation of their class commonality and
their reasoned action to relegate class - and the violence it
produces - to the dustbin of history. May they soon learn that
war does not make heroes; it makes fools.

RICHARD MONTAGUE

FRANK FACES OF THE DEAD

NEW HORIZON

ISBN 0 86116 074 6

Printed and Published by
New Horizon
5 Victoria Drive
Bognor Regis

CHAPTER ONE

Charlie Comes In

"Come in, Johnny! Didn't know if you'd got the message ... bloody daft bringin' ya over here t'night. No ... first left - into the parlour. Did ya hear the racket below?"

The four men had their faces turned expectantly as Johnny entered the room. Charlie Shields said, "Hello! Glad to see you, Johnny." Danno McAvoy: "A'ha! It's yourself, then!" The accent was in keeping with the brown Aran sweater and both were out of place in back-street Belfast. The other two men nodded: "Hello," "Hi!" They moved closer on the couch and Johnny said "Hello, lads. Not a good night for travelling," as he sat down beside them.

Fred Caffrey, who had opened the door for Johnny, limped into the room. There were many accounts of how 'Red Fred' had earned his limp - Fred favoured the one about Bilbao, when he'd fought with the International Brigade - some even said it was a wholly cultivated affliction, but Fred bore it heroically. Now he ambled across the room, "Aye, Johnny, well ... see anything down there?" and manoeuvred himself awkwardly into an easy chair beside the fire.

"I cut across Cavendish Street," said Johnny. "We had a meeting at Byrne's and Roger met me when the rest had gone and said the Op was on and Charlie wanted me here. There's no sign of fighting on the other side of the Falls but there's a fair number of Brits on the perimeter of the area and, just as I was coming up the street here, I heard three bloody great bangs - nail bombs, probably; and there's the din of a hell of a row in the Lower Falls. I didn't hear any firearms, though."

Shield's had returned his gaze to the fire after greeting Johnny and the latter's comments came through only dimly to him. He was with his own dark thoughts ... silly bastards! Hughes must have taken a turn for the worse ordering this sort of silly bloody operation ... wants to compete for glory with the bloody Provos ... Astride the arm of his settee chair, across from where Caffrey sat, he simply acknowledged Johnny's information with a nod of his head: the nod said, 'Jesus Christ!' and 'bloody madness!' and confirmed what he already knew of their purpose in being here.

Charlie Shields looked tortured. He was small and stocky and, though his dark hair and agile movements did not advertise the fact, he was past the middle years. His suit was good in quality and cut, and cuff-links, tie-pin and other incidentals of dress set him aside, socially, from the others. The torture sat on well-formed features and his mouth, even as it now staged a conflict of impatience and indecision, was set in a strong jaw.

It was the same as before, he reflected. The same as those three years he had spent in the I.R.A. in the Forties - before he was interned for nearly five years in 'D' Wing of the Crumlin Road Jail. He'd prised a hundred quid out of the Green Cross Fund after his release in 1946. Kearman, the cheapskate M.P. who ran the Fund, offered him forty; "It'll buy ya the necessary tools to take up yer trade again." Christ! In the service of Ireland at a fiver a year! Who the hell would give an ex-jail bird a job now that the war was over and good Protestant joiners were being laid off from the shipyard? He argued his case with Kearnan and, later, with the Fund Committee: he could go into partnership with another ex-internee, Chris Cullen, but he would need at least one hundred and fifty. They'd given him a hundred.

He'd never paid Chris the other fifty pounds but he had built the business. He had kept Cullen out of the pubs long enough to canalise his skills and worm his way into the bank manager's confidence. With workable capital, he'd given Chris his head and let him drink his way into the sale of his share of the business for two thousand quid. Anna's father had lent him a thousand. That was six months before he married her. When Chris had died of T.B. in Whiteabbey Hospital in 1953, he had given Mrs. Cullen a hundred pounds and had never quite forgotten Anna saying "I don't see why YOU should have to look after them after what you done for HIM."

That was nineteen years ago. Nineteen years during which he had built the business into a healthy medium-sized and reputable shop-fitting concern. Anna had given him five children; one was now at St. McNissi College - curiously, Anna did not want him to become a priest - and the second eldest was following him through St. Malachy's. Anna had got her split-level bungalow on the Glen Road, the double garage and the 'daily woman' to ease her chores and burnish her social standing; she'd controlled her plumpness, too, and taken the edge off her accent enough to conceal her years of childhood in the wee streets around her father's pub in the Lower Falls. Only sometimes, now, and then vaguely, did Charlie find in Anna's voice or smile a faint memory of her earlier attraction.

When the I.R.A. commenced their campaign in the North in

2

1956, Charlie had been angry. Times had changed. Wh
hell did they want to start playing political cowboys agai
He did not even take issue with Anna's puerile denuncia
and he accepted Head Constable Hewitt's assurance, when
they met in the home of a mutual acquaintance, that "These
bastards are not the same TYPE at all as you boys were,
Charlie; they're bloody reds, man!" as a compliment. Times
had indeed changed.

Charlie had been largely indifferent to the rise of the Civil
Rights Movement - until August 1969. His Catholicism, in the
theological sense, hung lightly on him; but, politically, he was
still a Catholic. During the nights that he spent in his
comfortable television lounge, following the carnage of the
fourteenth and fifteenth of August, watching on the big screen
the aftermath of the riots, the rows of burnt-out Catholic
homes, the pitiful plight of the refugees - and all within three
miles of where he lived - he found his teeth chafing his lips
and his fingers tightening on his glass.

He readily conceded to Father Maguire's request to join an
'aid' committee and, later, to get involved in the Citizens'
Defence organisation. Father Maguire wanted to see business
and professional people at the helm - "You know, Charlie,
those hooligans down there don't want a return to normality.
They want to keep the barricades up! I.R.A. dupes and
Communists ... It's up to every Catholic man of standing to
wrest the initiative and give the community back its self-
respect."

In the months that followed, as the committees and commissions set up by the Government to investigate the whys and
wherefores of the Northern Ireland troubles began their hear-
ings or completed their reports, Charlie began to see the
events of the previous August as a blessing in disguise.
Moderate opinion had been outraged by the burnings and the
killings; the British Government, too, had awakened to its
responsibilities towards Northern Ireland and had sent in the
British Army to ensure that it would not happen again - as well
as forcing changes in the narrow system of government that
had provoked the situation. Most of all, Charlie felt, the
entire responsible and moderate community - the decent
people on both the Catholic and Protestant sides - was conscious of its sins of omission towards the victims of the August
pogroms; they were even prepared to allow the ghetto
Catholics to work off their anger for a time, in their own
areas, without the previously-ubiquitous evidence of the hated
police presence. The great majority of Protestants were

3

genuinely shocked by what their minority of extremists had done and their trauma was a real guarantee for the future.

But the 'moderate's' sense of shock had been acquired from the news media; it was a mere nine-day talking point - a teacher's tolerance after the cane had inadvertently struck an erring boy's eye: all right! We didn't mean to hit you LIKE THAT but YOU know you brought it on yourself! By all means let them have a moment in tears for their dead, their momentary pique for their terror, but ... FOR GOODNESS SAKE, LET IT BE OVER AND DONE WITH! Authority had got to be re-asserted - even if it was the same authority that had promoted the terror and led the mob.

Victors and victims just had to be pushed back into 'moderate' normality.

The ghetto Catholics, on the other hand, had got their shock in the flames that burned away their homes, and in their dead. It lingered with them in the actuality of Mary and her husband occupying the back room with their four kids; it mocked them from the blackened shells of yesterday's homes and found relief in whitewashed clarions of defiance on bullet-marked walls. Unlike the comfortable 'moderates', the material basis of their normality had literally gone up in smoke and they were determined that they were not going to rebuild their future on the foundations of yesterday's political combustibles.

All the time the legend makers were at work. The cruelties gained gravity in the unfolding of greater, real or imagined, premeditation - a premeditation that still lurked in the shadows, gathering vigour and awaiting opportunity. Conversely, among the Protestants, the balm offered by the notion that the Catholics had burned their own homes and made their own dead, found increasing acceptance, and fringe remorse became anger.

All the time, Charlie was busy. He organised relief work and was the mainstay in building a flexible organisation to meet the needs of most exigencies in the area. On a number of occasions he appeared on television to explain the role of some deputation that had gone to see the Security Committee or the General Officer Commanding the British Forces. He became quite friendly with a number of army officers and had Major Windley-Smyth spend a week-end leave with him at 'Charanna', his home on the fringe of the city.

Anna was seeing less of him but she was compensated by his television appearances and the frequent mention of his name in the news media. Charlie, for his part, was back among the people he knew and understood, where language was unguarded and inhibition absent. Some of his I.R.A. acquaintances from the past again became known to him. Some remained openly connected with the I.R.A. The movement was growing rapidly and though Charlie was very careful to avoid any direct knowledge of those involved, he was obliged to acknowledge that there appeared to be better organisation now than he had known when he was a member in the Forties. The faint smell of success was bringing back the schoolmasters, and Charlie was convinced that that solicitor fellow from Tyrone who was on the Committee with him, was connected.

Inevitably, contact with the personnel of the growing Republican movement began to erode Charlie's contempt for the I.R.A. and pave the way for argument. He did not dispute their end but he took issue with their view of its means of realisation. Violence was unnecessary ... was self-defeating. The Unionist Government had always maintained power by means of a corrupt political apparatus aimed at keeping the people divided along religious lines. But the Unionists had overplayed their hand and the British Government was now guaranteeing that that corrupt apparatus would be dismantled. Unionism without religious bigotry and corruption would atrophy within less than a decade and the working people of the North, with their strong trade union tradition, would bring in a Labour Government. That would pave the way for an awakening of Labour in the South and, with a Labour Government in Britain, there would be no impediment to an independent Ireland, with a left-of-centre government, freely co-operating in an Anglo-Irish partnership within the European Economic Community.

It was the reasonable thesis of a reasonable man but, by July 1970, the basis of all remaining reason was dead.

In June the British Conservative Party had won a victory in the British General Election and immediately there followed a discernible change in British Government policy in Northern Ireland. Under the previous Labour administration, the Northern Ireland Government had not been allowed to forget that they were on probation. In the Catholic heartlands, despite growing conflict between some politically-conscious elements, exploiting local problems in their efforts to forge the beginnings of a citizen army, and the British Army, the latter had continued to maintain a more-or-less friendly policing role designed to ensure that further conflict would not occur between the residents of the Catholic and Protestant slums and, at the same time, very gingerly, re-introducing the allegedly-reformed police force.

Now, with the British Tories back in office at Westminster, the picture changed; the Ulster Government were their blood-brothers and ideological heirs and their years of service as voting fodder in the House of Commons was to be rewarded with full, uninquisitive trust.

All the time the growing body of Protestant extremism within the Unionist Party was increasingly voluble in its criticism of the Unionist Government's submissiveness to the British Government. The absence of the para-military police from some Catholic areas became the big pressure point of the Unionist dissidents intent on overthrowing the Party leadership and they succeeded in canvassing sufficient support within the Unionist Party to convene a special meeting of the governing Standing Orders Committee in mid-July. A motion of censure, based on the Government's alleged failure to enforce 'law and order' in the unpoliced Catholic areas, was to be put to the meeting and the probability that the leadership would be brought down could not be dismissed.

The new British Tory Government opted to support the Unionist Government by the dramatic use of the British Army to remove the basis of the censure motion. The Army would attack the most prominent of the Catholic districts and would assert its authority over the populace in such a way as would silence the Government's severest critics.

On a Friday evening, five days before the meeting at which the Government was to be censured by its rank-and-file supporters, the Army, in an obviously well-planned operation, turned an arms raid on a house in the Lower Falls area - and its predictable sequel - into a display of brutal strength aimed at demonstrating to the ghetto Catholics and the Government's Protestant critics that Authority would stand no further nonsense.

The people of the area arranged a hasty defence but this was swept away by mechanised units as thousands of over-wrought troops, angered by the night-long sounds of pockets of continuing resistance, wreaked a path of death and destruction through the area. The troops remained in constant, blanket occupation of the district over the week-end; they confined the residents to their homes, refused to permit them to procure supplies of food and systematically searched the houses, breaking furniture, walls and ceilings and imposing indignities on the people. Every indignity, every stick of broken furniture, every religious ikon smashed was a resounding victory for the tiny group of Republican fanatics concerned with building what was later to become internationally known as the Provos.

Violence had resolved controversy in favour of the men of violence; argument and reason were dead.

When the trouble commenced, Charlie Shields was in his office near the centre of the city. He replaced his 'phone, left a few instructions and hurried to his Rover Two Thousand. He was stopped at an Army barricade at Townsend Street. The sergeant was courteous: "Sorry, Sir, some trouble up there; you'll have to follow the diversion to the left here, Sir."

As far as Charlie's eyes could see there were army riot vehicles lined along the pavements facing the direction of the Falls Road. Soldiers in riot gear, some standing with their S.L.R.'s at the 'high port', some squatting on the pavements with their gas guns and clubs, occupied the area between the vehicles and the buildings.

Charlie explained to the sergeant that he was an officer in the local Citizen's Defence group and wanted to use his influence to help to restore calm. He was rebutted by the sergeant's hardened tones: "My instructions, mate, are ..." He tried names: Captain Garrett? Major Windley-Smyth? The sergeant enquired if he'd like to be arrested and the demeanour of some of the soldiers who closed tighter around the Rover convinced Charlie that the sergeant's was not an idle threat.

Angrily he rammed the car into gear and turned left. At John Street, he parked the Rover and crossed over Durham Street in an attempt to make his way behind Divis Flats. A small elderly man, wearing a cap, shouted at him, "Watch your step, Mr. Shields, the bastards are everywhere!" Charlie made towards the man, a little pleased at his recognition. "How bad is it?" The flat staccato of a Thompson, somewhere in the distance, echoed off the walls of the Flats. "Christ! They're shooting!" Charlie spoke aloud, unconsciously; consciously he was reflecting that everything had seemed to go quiet before the Thompson started - almost as though the lesser sounds of anger and conflict were acknowledging the entry of this, more lethal, phase.

"Look, could you tell me how ..." Charlie saw the upraised baton-wielding arm before the flak-jacketed form impinged on his consciousness. The baton fell quickly and the small man started to fall even with the first blow, but the rapid movements of the baton followed him down. Charlie got a blow on the back; despite the pain, he was in a panic to protect himself

7

by obvious surrender. He raised his arms, fully extended, above his head.

"Another bastard here, corporal!" His behind-back assailant had not revealed himself but the grotesque, menacing face now in front of him, screwed in mockery behind riot vizor, provided new terror. The muzzle of the S.L.R. jabbed his mid-riff. "Take him!" "Move, you bastard!"

He managed to get to the opened back of the Land Rover without further prompting from the gun muzzle. The little man, partially recovering consciousness, was lifted, an arm and a leg on each side. "One ... two ... three ... oops! Now ...! That wasn't hard - was it?" The blood splattered Charlie's face.

On Sunday, after some thirty-two hours in Springfield police barracks, Charlie was brought before an officer of the Royal Ulster Constabulary. After the earlier Reports of the Hunt and Cameron Commissions, it was claimed that the R.U.C. had been reformed; officers had been given new rank designations to conform with their English counterparts and it was rumoured that a new, less military-looking, uniform was in the pipe-line; but the old faces of unquestioning authority still remained and the old attitudes still prevailed. The officer was terse and efficiently courteous; he called Charlie "Mister Shields". "In the circumstances" the Authorities were prepared to overlook his riotous behaviour; there would be no charge entered against him, BUT ... in future ... Charlie exploded. Well ... if Mister Shields "liked" they would have him before the court on a riotous behaviour charge - he could, of course, make his complaints to the judge. "You should know, though, that there are six military witnesses prepared to swear ..." Probably six months imprisonment. "Kerr, who was engaged with you in the riot, got six months at a Special Court yesterday." The officer smiled a cold, thin smile and expressed the opinion that "this sort of thing can hardly do a man in your position much good, Mister Shields."

Charlie was released later that evening - an angry man abroad in a cauldron of anger and bitter indignation in which the fanatics poached for the materials of insurrection.

On the evening of the following day he joined "C" Company of the Second Battalion of the Official I.R.A.

Now Charlie Shields sat astride the settee chair-arm in Fred Caffrey's dingy parlour lost in the loneliness of his own dark mood: I was wrong; the I.R.A. has not changed in the years between. More members, yes; a sprinkling of "intellectuals" - probably more "stuff". But the old "Webley Complex"

8

still abounds. These people never really learned - the helicopter and the transistor had passed them by ... they don't play
to win but simply to lose grandly. They are the pale ghosts of
yesterday in the heroic prelude to martyrdom. The reward
they willed on themselves was a place in Ireland's monoto-
nously-long gallery of remembrance with, perhaps, a ballad to
their name to shake the timbers of such places as where
drunken patriotism acknowledges the memory of the dead who
died for Ireland.

Here they were, planning rebellion in a grotty parlour of
the home of Fred Caffrey. Shields peeped through his fingers
at the room; the worn linoleum and the threadbare mat, the
tired rexine suite and the ancient round-backed dining-room
chairs, the small brass candlesticks between the delph dogs on
the mantelpiece above the black cast-iron fireplace. Jesus! It
was fitting! Their thinking was as modern as the decor! "Red
Fred's" ... the bloody place had always been a favourite spot
for police visitors ... probably the hallowed ground of many
such gatherings as this, tonight - even the bloody, faded-
yellow papered walls seemed to bear unchanging testimony to
the memory of the dead - and, if those same dead rose, Red
Fred's fucking door would never stop knocking!

Three months in and already Company O.C. Why? Because
he was an old hand? Christ! he'd never fired a shot in anger in
his life! No ... because he lived in a big house and had a few
quid, more likely - God, how they hated wealth and how bloody
obsequious they were to its possessors! Maybe - and there was
little comfort in the thought - it was simply because he was no
LESS competent than the others. Christ help us!

Their conversation intruded on his thoughts and, again, his
gaze wandered around them. Fred was obviously in his
element; for over forty years his claim to fame was his
peculiar concoction of Irish and Russian nationalism - in a
United Ireland he would have died of boredom. The other two
lads on the couch were brothers, Liam and Phillip Gallagher -
moved in recently from "A" Company. Not too much imagination but good workers; unquestioningly followed orders - good
volunteer material. He noticed that both were well-dressed
and clean - they'd probably changed their underwear for the
possible benefit of the doctor or the undertaker and, likely,
both had been to confession.

Danno McAvoy. Poor Danno was a dedicated I.R.A. man
and a lousy soldier! Danno thought too much about his possible
victims: "God save the poor bugger - sure he's some poor
woman's son!" Charlie knew that Danno could kill no living

9

thing; he could only hate in the abstract - he'd be a better man on the other side! If Danno's father had left forty acres, instead of twenty, both he and his brother could now be happy in Tyrone. As it was, Danno carried bricks, mixed cement, lived in Mrs. McCann's back room, sang patriotic songs in a fine, fresh-water-tenor voice and dreamed dreams of a free-dom that was echoing glensides and rivers where fish cavorted among rushy leaps; a free land where the ugly cities of brick and concrete and policemen would leave with the vanquished foe.

Johnny Cairns was different. He had, against almost impossible odds, literally thought himself into the movement. For one thing, he was a Protestant - a rarity in the I.R.A. He was well-read and thoughtful - and sufficiently cautious to keep his impatience with the continual bungling in check. Cairns, in his late twenties, had served his time as a motor mechanic in the British Army and now eked out a livelihood in his own back-street workshop off the Shankhill Road. Despite his insistence that his military training was not the sort to fit him to command, he had quickly become a volunteer officer and was now Charlie's Company Adjutant.

Shields had more confidence in the quiet advice of Johnny Cairns than he had in all the edicts of the movement's pocket field-marshals.

He laughed absently, relieved by the fervent, subdued chatter of the company. The meat of events, real and imagined, was being dissected and 'analysed' by Fred. "Don't forget the whole country's undergone a traumatic experience as splendid in its way as 1916." Fred spoke slowly but without commas and the words that he imagined to be in keeping with his role of political philosopher were drawn out for emphasis and effect.

"The people in the South are catching on, too, to the shenanigans of their bloody politicians and the gombeen bas-tards they represent. Events in the North could sweep Sinn Fein into power in the South - no - no! Don't forget they laughed at the I.R.A. in 1916 too. Aye, and if Sinn Fein got power in the South we ... by Jasus we'd show Britain - an' without firin' a bloody shot!" Fred's voice lowered perceptibly, taking on an almost eerie quality - as though it were simply recording events that he could see; "We'd repudiate the Anglo-Irish Free Trade Agreement ... not too hard to find grounds there ... naked aggression against the nationally-minded people of Ireland will do ... then we'd do a deal with the Warsaw-Pact countries - man there's a market for you!

10

An' all lookin' for our beef cattle an' agricultural produce! Puts the bloody E.E.C. in the shade! An' in order to ensure a good deal we could throw in the lease - for ten years, say, with one-way options - of the Irish Atlantic Ports guardin' the Western Approaches. That would outflank Nato strategy, put Britain in queer with the Yanks and the countries of Western Europe. Christ! Could you see the Germans or French gettin' all worked up about a clatter of bloody Orangemen in Ulster who haven't looked at the clock since sixteen-ninety? Jasus! They wouldn't be long tellin' the Brits what to do with their army!"

Fred continued to talk in exclamation marks and had progressed to a distinction between Ireland and Cuba when Connor and Burns arrived. Their presence, and new information about the rioting in the Lower Falls, enlivened the conversation and, a few times before Grogan arrived, Charlie had to warn them to keep it quiet.

Just after nine the sound of a car stopping outside brought a hush to the conversation. Fred answered the knock and Speers, Boyle and Hagan crowded into the room. The new arrivals had a Thompson sub-machine gun, two M.1. carbines, a Mark Eight Lee Enfield rifle and an assortment of hand guns, including a long-barrelled Luger and a clean, but rust-pitted, Mauser semi-automatic.

Shields was talking. The weapons had been distributed to all but Danno and Fred - Fred was too old for operational work and Danno was to act as field courier. Ammunition was being swopped, checked and stowed in outer pockets and Hagan, who had the Thompson, was binding the bodies of two magazines together with sellotape, the platforms of each facing opposite directions. Movement was tense but unhurried.

"Our object is two-fold." Charlie had vigorously protested the hastily-conceived plan and felt it less distasteful if he passed on the orders in the exact manner in which the Battalion Adjutant ('that bloody bread-man, Greer') had passed them on to him. "The British Army have, as you know, been running amok in the Lower Falls for weeks now. The Provisionals, who provoke the situations that give the Brits a pretext for their activities, offer them only token resistance and encourage the civilian population onto the streets to confront the soldiers with bottles and stones. Apart from the fact that it is normal Provo lunacy to encourage civilian confrontations with the soldiers, they hope, by their armed presence on the streets of the area, to draw support away from us. Our purpose, therefore, is to go into the area - the

Adjutant will give details of the actual operation - give the Brits a short, sharp lesson - the sort that the Provos have failed to give - and, thus, re-assert our authority with the people so that in future we can keep them off the streets.

"Number one, then, is to inflict maximum casualties on the British and, two, by the success of the operation - that means withdrawal of our section without casualties or prisoners - to discredit the Provos. Right, Johnny, you can carry out your briefing."

Cairns outlined the strategy to be employed. By ten-thirty, local volunteers, already in position and unarmed, were to move among the rioters in the street where the worst of the confrontations was taking place; a courier would be briefed to meet them at Sorrella Street and advise them where this was. The unarmed volunteers would move among the rioters and tell them that the I.R.A. was going to engage the Brits, and that it was in their own interests to clear the immediate area and that those wishing to help the I.R.A. should re-form on the two main roads bounding the area, in order to disrupt the movement of military vehicles and impede attempts to encircle or contain the attacking party.

Three members of the attacking party, including Hagan with the Thompson, would commence the attack from a perimeter position which would be decided at the assembly point on the basis of the courier's information. This preliminary engagement would commence at twenty-three-twenty hours - after the rest of the section had taken up their positions.

The initial attack would have the advantage of surprise and was likely to leave the British position exposed in the direction from which the main party of I.R.A. would attack on the O./C.'s whistle blast.

The British party would be too large and well equipped for them to aim at its destruction or surrender. It was important, therefore, that the attack should be pressed home with speed and decision, allowing for the greatest concentration of fire. No attempt must be made to cut off the Brit's main option for retreat. The essential thing was that casualties be speedily inflicted in an effort to panic the troops into a hasty and discrediting retreat and that such retreat should be unhindered lest the enemy was forced into full and indiscriminate use of his superior manpower and weaponry.

If the British broke in retreat, then the I.R.A. party would not pursue; they would assemble as a single unit and, as a public gesture, march out of the area before breaking up.

He had deliberately left gaps in his briefing in the hope that questions from the section would reveal weaknesses either in the plan or the understanding of it. He asked for questions; Yes, Volunteer Connor, in the event of the O./C. considering it necessary, for any reason, to break off the engagement before they had achieved their objective, a red flare would be used - whistles may be used by the enemy for signalling, after the commencement of our attack and it would be dangerous to leave our emergency plans open to misinterpretation. Good point, Speers; the O./C. would give, not one, but three quick sharp blasts as a signal to press home the main attack.

There were a number of other questions from the volunteers and then Cairns asked first Hagan, and then Burns, to cover the salient points of the briefing.

"Now, comrades, I want you to hold out your weapons and ammunition for inspection. I will pair you off now; as you are paired, you will produce your weapons for the O./C. and leave the house as quietly and inconspicuously as possible. On the way to the assembly point you will maintain a steady walking pace and each pair will keep those preceding it within view. In the event of running into trouble you will attempt to get away without using firearms - these may only be used to avoid capture. Should any pair get into difficulties, those following or preceding it must not attempt to render assistance. The important thing is that we all arrive at the Sorrella Street rendezvous and that we remember our orders. Right ... good luck, lads! First ..."

Danno was excited; at last they were going to hit back! He, of course, would not actually be shooting. He knew he was not afraid but, all the same, he was glad that he did not have a gun.

CHAPTER TWO

Paddy Quinn in Command

Quinn was the O.C. of the Company now. After Tarno had been shot dead, in June, he had become Acting O.C. and, though he knew some members of the Battalion Staff didn't like him, his appointment was confirmed by H.Q. in August. He had gained a reputation; to his comrades in the Provisional I.R.A. - and a widening circle of hangers on - he was known as a "hard man" and a "man of action"; to those of the Official I.R.A. who knew him, he was "Killer Quinn" or "Windbag Quinn".

Paddy Quinn was a vainglorious, swashbuckling character. He had been a volunteer in "G" Company before "the Split" and, unlike so many of his comrades, he had no trouble leaving the "Official" I.R.A. and becoming a member of the Provisional movement.

The I.R.A. had commenced a campaign against Northern Ireland in 1956. At that time the movement was probably stronger and better equipped than at any time from the mid-Thirties. They won the opening rounds of the campaign with a number of daring arms snatches; the first, brilliantly conceived and carried out, the second a well-planned operation that failed without reflecting any discredit on the movement. Eventually, however, the campaign subsided into a series of raids on police stations during which machine-gun and short arms fire peppered the walls of the station until police reinforcements arrived and the I.R.A. beat a hasty retreat over the Border to the Irish Republic. Finally, the campaign petered out in such activities as cutting down telegraph poles and issuing "communiques" accepting responsibility for these "commando" activities.

The movement had been recruited mainly in the south and in the traditional strongholds of republicanism in the north. Belfast, the graveyard of so many republican dreams in the past, was avoided. Officially, the I.R.A. claimed to be concerned lest operations in Belfast might set in train events that could lead to a religious confrontation between Catholic and Protestant workers; actually, the reason was because such elements of the urban proletariat as traditionally sided with the I.R.A. in Belfast were unreliable and more prone to become engaged in internecine strife among themselves than waging war on the Unionist police forces.

By 1962 the pathetic battles were over, the I.R.A. were beaten and the great inquest on their military failure had commenced within the movement.

One thing was evident to the most intrepid Republican: the people of the North had failed utterly to respond, one way or the other, to the military posturings of the I.R.A. True, the old songs were sung and the martyrs revered but the hard realities of exported British welfare capitalism were more tangible than the glorious mystique of the Celtic twilight. Cathleen Na Houlahan could not be called upon a Tuesday morning to deliver up the Children's Allowances and, while the tedium of poverty in the slum or on the farm could be relieved with the slogans of yesterday, slogans which gave ready solace to the flouting aggression and mindless parading of Orangism, they did not affect the material conditions of the impoverished nationalists. Ireland's dead were fine but Northern Ireland's living were in immediate need of their welfare handouts. If the people were to be blamed for their failure to respond - which from the point-of-view of the I.R.A., they were - it was more for their excusing denigration of the movement ("They're not all all like the old I.R.A.") than for "selling their heritage for a mess of pottage".

The leadership decided that they could capture the support of the Northerner - some were optimistic enough to believe that this would include the Protestant workers - by non-violent extra-parliamentary action against some of the grosser social and economic problems existing in the North. The men of action, those more concerned with the means than the end, were restrained for a time and the movement gave itself over to fringe constitutional action.

As the I.R.A. leadership developed its thinking on social and economic problems, as it tentatively plumbed the depths of each separate issue, it began to realise that the struggle to which it was lending itself was against some of the effects of the system and not the system itself. Accordingly, there began to emerge from the movement an economic philosophy compounded of "left" labourism and Leninism with its attendant growth of bolshevik political thinking.

The men of action were in a panic. It was bad enough that they should be asked to use their brains instead of their trigger fingers but now they were being asked to stomach an economic doctrine that militated against their Catholic upbringing. It was anathema - the curse of intellectualism - it was Communism! Worse - it was dull and exceedingly unromantic!

The movement was strained to breaking point.

Meanwhile, success was abundant elsewhere. The Civil Rights Movement which had,largely, been spawned by the new philosophy of the I.R.A. and which the republicans had backed to the hilt in Northern Ireland might have petered out but it was given life by the bungling and bigotry of the Government and its conspiracy-orientated para-military police. Meetings which would have attracted hundreds were banned by the police or the Government - and attracted thousands. The employment of police strong-arm tactics, flashed on television throughout the world, crystallised anti-Government emotions and the Catholic nationalists of the North were united against Unionism for the first time in five decades.

But, ironically, this success brought its antithesis and an end to any hope that the I.R.A. may have nourished of bringing about a peaceful solution of the "Irish Problem". Inevitably, the Civil Rights movement accused the Government of dis- crimination in favour of Protestants and, predictably, the struggle developed along the lines of a squabbling match concerned, not so much with the inadequacies of the system, but more with the distribution of these inadequacies along religious lines. The Protestant workers, too, became united behind the promoted fear that what little they had they might be forced to share with their Catholic neighbours.

Sectarian conflict was inevitable and when, in August 1969, hundreds of homes in the Catholic ghettoes were burned out by Protestant extremists and a number of Catholics shot dead, the stage was set for another religious pogrom along classical Belfast lines.

The police were identified along with the Protestant mobs. Never popular with the Catholics because they had for decades been at the beck and call of an authoritarian government in the enforcement of its dictates, their role as a civil police force was now finished; they were no longer acceptable in the Catholic ghettoes and, such was the new unity of the Catholics, any attempt by the police to enforce their will would have resulted in a grim blood-bath that would have been the prelude to civil war.

All semblance of law and order had broken down and, bitterly, the Catholics, who had refused to help the I.R.A. a few years earlier, were asking "Where was the I.R.A. when our homes were being burned and our people murdered?"

And the Quinn's of the I.R.A. were asking the same question of their Dublin leadership; "Where were the guns when we needed them? Why were we left naked before

16

Protestant aggression? Give us back our guns!" The I.R.A.'s official apologia was reasoned; the I.R.A. did not exist to fight Protestant Irishmen but to fight British Imperialism. Religious division is a British weapon - if we respond to it, we help it.

The widening split in the I.R.A. was now no longer a theoretical difference on tactics between the conservatives in the movement who said "Let's drive the British out and thereafter decide our economic policies" and those who claimed that servitude could be overcome only by achieving an independent Ireland AND an economic policy of state capitalism. Now the argument was being resolved behind the barricades with the immediacy of the situation on the side of the conservatives. When the I.R.A. officially decided to continue its neo-constitutional struggle for political and economic change the conservative elements broke away and formed their own "Provisional Army Council" and Volunteer movement. Ironically, the conservatives then became known as the "Provisionals" while the exponents of the new thinking were dubbed "traditionalists" and "official".

It was a bright season for Quinn - "Now we'll have a bit of action instead of all that bloody bullshittin'!" As an old hand in the movement he was looked up to by the growing intake of young men whose notions of "British Imperialism" were the British Army, the police and "those Orange bastards across the Shankhill!"

The Company had been active enough when Tamo was O.C. He had been the "mad bastard" of admiration; a leader from the front in the uncomplicated sorties he engineered with the enemy. He had been on his own when he died in Albert Street. Probably he had been stopped for a routine search by a British Army patrol - though legend had it that he attacked the patrol. At any rate, he had killed a soldier and wounded two others and no one was surprised that time had redeemed its mortgage on Tamo's life.

Quinn had immediately organised a reprisal raid on the army post at Albert Street for the following evening and had himself taken part in the raid. Some seventy rounds of ammunition had been fired at the heavily-sandbagged emplacement. The soldiers did not expose themselves to return the fire and, after a time, the attackers withdrew and the street urchins replaced them to follow up the attack with stones and bottles.

Young Frankie Phillips had eluded his mother on the pretence that he was going upstairs to do his homework.

Instead he had crept back into the street and made his way hurriedly down Albert Street to join in the fun. Bottles and stones were flying from all directions when Frankie arrived and he availed himself of the ready supply of stones lying around to pelt the sandbags. But Frankie's thirteen years of undernourishment had not equipped him physically for the task; all the time he had to move closer if he was to find his target. He was in the front row of the crowd when the petrol bombs came whizzing over his head and the base of the wall, to the right of the sand-bagged post, became a sea of flame as the fire-bombs burned themselves harmlessly out.

Frankie noticed a petrol bomb strike the sand-bags immediately in front of the post. The wick had gone out in flight and when the bottle struck the sandbags it failed to break and rolled back down the repose and along the roadway, gurgling out its volatile contents. Frankie's eyes fixed, fascinated by the rolling object; a real petrol bomb that now belonged to no one! He ran forward to retrieve the bottle.

As his fingers clutched on the prize, a wave of sound engulfed him - a thundering, hellish wave of derision, catcall and hate provoked by the rising form of a soldier from behind the barricades.

Frankie had raised the almost-empty bottle above his head. He half turned, ready to seek the anonymity of the mob, and he looked up. Their eyes met, the fear-crazed eyes of the steel-helmeted youth with the rifle and the mocking eyes of the boy.

The crack brought its moment of silence as Frankie Phillips died.

Quinn set down his glass, "Can't stay more'n a minute. Just left the lads long enough to arrange a bit of a divershun." Sally Higgins was obviously impressed but her friend, Quinn's sister, Nora, sat tight-lipped.

"The whole bloody Lower Falls is out! I'm tellin' ya we'll fix the bastards the night!" Sally giggled. Nora said, "Are we allowed to enquire how many people will die in the 'fixing' and what the benefits will be?" She raised herself in her seat and adjusted her dress in the action of diversion from argument.

"I've told ya, Nora, you can't make omelettes w'out breaking eggs. You see, Nora ..."

"Whoever told you that really completed your education, didn't they, Paddy?"

"Oh, of course, I'm no intellectual like yer Prod boyfriend, Cairns. Yer great with yer fine, fancy talk, both of ya - Ah think it's mabbee him who's got yer bloody head turned. No, Sally," he turned his attention to Nora's companion, "don't let her kid ya, luv; it takes dead soldiers to win a war! Isn't that right, girl?" Sally looked at Nora apprehensively and giggled.

Nora stared at her brother; his big frame, his self-satisfied smile, his stupidity ... him! She had long since overcome her filial affection. Her voice was laden with contempt, "Unlike you, Paddy, I don't follow a leader. I don't agree with my 'Prod-boyfriend', either in the matter of religion or politics - but, at least, he's not a ... a mere gunman."

"Spare me the 'mere'! No, Johnny Cairns is no gunman; he's like the rest of his yella crowd ... hasn't the bloody guts. I wouldn't trust the Orange bastard an inch - probably a bloody spy! I think ..."

The cup and saucer smashed on the lino tiles. Nora was on her feet, her hands shaking, her dark eyes black with anger. "You think! Think! That's your trouble, Paddy, you were never guilty of thinking in all your life. Your ignorance is your saving grace. You, and your kind, don't care if you leave us a graveyard, as long as the tricolour flies over it! Forget about the eggs and omelettes - we're talking about PEOPLE! About WORKING PEOPLE who live on the Protestant Shankhill and the Catholic Falls. People whose prejudices and bigotry have been deliberately promoted to serve the needs of their COMMON oppressors. Can't you understand? It's important, Paddy, when you are playing with guns. For Christ's sake ... can't you make even a little effort to understand? Our enemy is not the Protestants - not even the soldiers or the police. It is poverty, Paddy, and the system that gives rise to it and we endure it because we are ignorant. Ignorance, Paddy; ignorance, IGNORANCE! That's the enemy of both the Catholics and the Protestants - so-called Nationalists and Unionists. Ignorance - and you can't shoot that out of people ... you can only help them to understand - and that means that, first, you must learn yourself. I don't agree with Johnny Cairns or the Official I.R.A. any more than I do with you. Nationalism, like religious bigotry, even if it is embellished with revolutionary phrases is just another link in the chain that ..."

"Shit, girl! Plain s-h-i-t! But you look luvly when yer cross! Don't worry, Nora, Cairns won't leave you a widda!" Quinn was on his feet; he grabbed Nora with exaggerated roughness and kissed her forehead. "O.K. Truce! I haven't got time for yer silly arguments."

As the outside door slammed, Sally giggled her relief. "Your Paddy's a terrible man - but it's a good job we have the likes of him."

CHAPTER THREE

The Battle Commences

In Leeson Street and the adjoining concrete carpets of slumdom's avenues the rioting raged to and fro. It was compounded of a hundred little epics the history of which would diminish or gain in gravity in accordance with the stamina, experience and intensity of hate of the front line historians.

The military occupied two positions on opposite sides of Leeson Street where it intersected with McDonnell Street. A number of Saracen armoured vehicles were nose-to-tail in a tight semi-circle at these points while, across the bottom of Leeson Street, at the Grosvenor Road side, the main party of military were entrenched behind five armoured vehicles, each facing towards the missile-throwing rioters. The troops were in an awkward position - Sandhurst training provided no basis for street strategy and the peculiarities of each separate conflict were not amenable to the thinking of the sands-table. The positions at McDonnell Street were unplanned and defensive and each locked in a trained "snatch" squad of riot troops cut off from the parent unit at the end of the street.

Earlier in the day, Lieutenant Clements had contacted Command with the information that something was afoot for the evening. Clements was attached to Intelligence and had got the information in an Albert Street public house that afternoon. He had met his informant in the bar and, arising out of comments on an item in the "Irish News" concerning military brutality, had got himself involved in conversation. In keeping with his "cover" Clements had remarked that he had to sign at the dole at 2 p.m. "The bastards watch down there, you know, an' they pull y'in if they've got your smudge" he said - implying that "they" had his "smudge". His new acquaintance had become quite animated about the death of a five year-old youngster the previous evening as the result of an accident involving an army scout car. "The bastards are supposed to be bringing us law and order and they themselves break every law in the friggin' book. Ah believe the bloody tank came flying roun' the corner ... flyin'! The poor wee thing didn't have a chance ... dead when it hit the road!" Clements mock-winced and tut-tutted, "The cows have done that, of course, all over the world ... Malaya, Palestine, Cyprus ...

Aden ... Oh, I know about it alright! I'm ashamed to say I was in the British Army myself - I'm in the Catholic Ex-Servicemens' Association." Clement's admission drew the other's interest and, after a while, the contact was regaling Clements with his opinions of the situation. He was typical of so many in the area; no love for the I.R.A. but active hatred for the Army. "And now these cowboys roun' here are goin' to have a go at them t'night again - more for the jail, the 'ospital an', mebby the bloody graveyard!"

Clements suppressed his interest.

He might have learned more after the two younger men joined in the conversation but he had already stressed the urgency of his visit to the dole and it was almost two.

He drank up and left them.

Major Hickson had put his mobiles on patrol and, inevitably, these had provoked minor skirmishes of stone and bottle throwing at various points in the area. Mindful of Clements' report, Hickson had tried to hold his main force at base but as more reports came in he was increasingly pressed to send reinforcements to assist in minor confrontations. It was one of these latter which was now obviously escalating into the main bout of the evening.

A patrol had reported a minor skirmish in Leeson Street. "Blue ... one seven to Control ... fifty people, mainly youths, throwing stones and bottles. Mob getting bigger ... request reinforcements to break them up ... over." Command had dispatched four Saracen armoured troop carriers and a number of Land Rovers each carrying a complement of riot-clad soldiers.

When the reinforcements had arrived the mob had retreated up Leeson Street in the direction of Falls Road. Members of the "snatch" squads lined up behind the armoured vehicles and followed at a cautious distance, all the time braving a hail of broken flagstones, masonry and bottles.

Private Adam Charters and Corporal Buick stood sentinel over two of the Land Rovers parked in the middle of the street - a few yards in from Grosvenor Road. The rioters, retreating before their comrades, held their attention -distance giving them safety and the comfort of non-involvement. The two men moved closer together and exchanged conversation yet keeping their eyes in the direction of the action.

When Charters looked around they were already in the street behind him. They had not been accompanied by the usual fanfare of riot and, obviously, their emergence from

Grosvenor Road was deliberately quiet. There were at least twenty of them in the street now, all young men, but the women were behind them and, now that the surprise was revealed, the amazons were providing their terrifying tribal chants. Charters hesitated; he saw Buick standing at his right with the quietness of stupefaction and fear and he knew that he must make the decision in action.

He saw the petrol bomb strike the Land Rover; then the second Land Rover belched flame. He took to his heels and ran. "Fucking Jesus!" Buick said as he drew level with him. Ahead of them the main body of troops had been alerted by the flames and the roar of the rioters whose numbers were increasing now in the street behind Charters and Buick. The "snatch" squads at the rear of the Saracens had now turned about and, to the accompaniment of the noisy engines of the reversing vehicles, were retreating down the street.

Without purpose or design the beleaguered troops had split into two distinct groups and, under cover of a discharge of rubber bullets, had formed two defensive positions, at the corner of McDonnell Street, behind their armour. It was from McDonnell Street, too, that the shot was fired as Private Carter was making for one of the hastily-formed positions.

He was conscious for perhaps a minute after he hit the ground. A terrible thing was in his chest. It didn't hurt, just filled him up and squeezed the air from his lungs. Loud noises everywhere in the distance ... long legs running around ... it was an exercise ... a play ... he would laugh at it! He kicked wildly and the laugh shrieked its horror.

The crowd fell back to allow him to die.

When the report came through Hickson moved up his main force to the Grosvenor Road end of Leeson Street. The five heavy armoured troop carriers were moved into position to block the end of the street and provide a protective screen for the new arrivals who were busily engaged preparing defensive positions.

The battle was now at close range. As far as the rioters were concerned, frenzy had conquered fear. Men and boys, girls and women, roared their defiance within feet of the army positions. Hatred, revenge, frustration and terror crystallised into a terrible cacophony of directionless intent. Decades of subservience were being cast off in the intense minutes of mindless rebellion – a splendid orgy of degradation and vulgarity was being unleashed on the agents of an authority whose answer to grief, insult and misery was "control yourselves ....

proper channels ... law and order." Fifty years of control, of acceptance, of subservience, of other-cheeking unleashed its energy to the arm of the stone-thrower and the throat of the slogan shouter.

Hickson was concerned about his improvised and beleaguered outposts surrounded by the mob at the corners of McDonnell Street. As matters stood, the mob was opposint them with stones, bottles and abuse but no mob general had yet appeared to canalise their energies and direct the physical overpowering of the outposts. It was only a matter of time, surely, before the thought was brought home to the rioters that they could capture the two army positions.

Time ... in civilised conflict the movement of men and machines and some comprehension of the options open to the enemy, gave a rough indication of the margins allowed for move and counter move. The enemy was controlled by one's opposite number, making decisions, largely on the basis of the known possibilities; it was known what the enemy wanted to achieve and, at least, some of the things he could not do in pursuit of his purpose. With a mob it was different; there was no collective comprehension, no set purpose, no sense of time - no readily-discernible counter-strategy.

Given time, the mob could grow and gain vigour and menace by throwing up a leader. Given time, a mob could find restraint in the horror of its own excesses. Time could bring consciousness of morning-after responsibilities. Hickson even remembered time bringing about disengagement in a particularly nasty riot in the same area some months earlier; the mob had thawed out and melted away quite mysteriously before ten o'clock on that particular night. The dramatic closure of the conflict had caused him concern at the time as he had read into it direction and a portent of some new evil. Later, at H.Q. the mystery was revealed - an Ireland versus Scotland soccer international was being telecast on "sportsview" that night, at ten!

Should he try an advance up the street? He had the men and equipment to do it but, as matters stood now, the mob was set on three targets; his own position and the two outposts at the McDonnell Street intersection. If he pushed them into a tight retreating mass would their forced retreat coalesce them into a solidity that could overcome one, or both, of the more vulnerable posts? Again, would he be exposing the flank of his advancing forces to the gunman, or gunmen, who had fired earlier from McDonnell Street?

His decision was disturbed by the sight of a young rioter

who, in his anxiety to find a target, had approached the line of vehicles on the run, slipped, and careered into the narrow space between two of the Saracens. He was instantly seized by one of the soldiers and impelled to the rear of the armoured vehicles, then he was immediately surrounded by a knot of soldiers; they closed tight around the fallen youth and a melee of boots, batons and rifle butts clouded Hickson's view of the victim.

The man writhed, bucked and kicked in a desperate effort to avoid the blows and all the time his piercing screams transcended the oathful anger of his assailants. Hickson's shouted commands went unheard and when finally he did physically break through the ring of attackers the young man lay silent on a spreading carpet of blood.

Johnny Cairns reported back to Shields at Dunville Park. The men had all turned up safely at Sorella Street but couriers from the adjoining streets had advised them that it was proving difficult to get the people to break off their engagement with the troops - now solely concentrated in Leeson Street. Members of the Provisional I.R.A. were urging the people on and some confusion had resulted. It would be dangerous to bring the Section in now and their task would be almost impossible without the co-operation of the people in clearing the streets. Cairns had moved his men into a friendly house in Sorella Street.

He went in the direction of Quinn's house. Nora, Paddy Quinn's sister, was a staff nurse in a local hospital but Johnny knew that she was on a fortnight's leave and had been prevented by the troubles from leaving Belfast on holiday. He also knew that Nora made a point of not knowing anything about I.R.A. business, but he wanted to see her and deceived his sense of duty into the notion that she might know something of the Provisionals' involvement in the Leeson Street rioting through talk overheard in her home between her brother and some of his friends.

He had never been in Nora's house but had left her at her door often when they had been out for the evening. Now he knocked the door, timidly conscious that Nora was not anxious to have him in the house she shared with her brother lest Paddy should make such a visit the occasion for a dispute. He knocked louder and waited but, though the living room light showed through the window blind and the sound of the television could be heard distinctly, his knocking went unanswered.

The outer door responded to his pressure and he stepped

into the short hall. Again, his knocking on the vestibule door went unanswered so he turned the handle, gingerly, and put his head into the living room.

Johnny had never met the man seated on the easy chair across from the window but he had heard of him from Nora and there was no mistaking her description of him. The man was John Hegarty. The T.V. flickered its changing patterns on the glass of the china cabinet opposite, its harsh music filling the room. Hegarty's wild eyes turned their welcome on Johnny while the brain of the madman moved his right arm clumsily and distended the thumb in an upward gesture.

Poor Hegarty! He greeted everyone like this but he seemed to know no one but Nora for whom the limits of his comprehension stretched in dog-like adoration. No songs for Hegarty; no emotive prose to tell the tale of his living martyrdom. Yet John Hegarty HAD died for Ireland and his memory was perpetuated only in this monument in lunatic flesh - this vulgar obscenity of manhood with the burning eyes that locked out the memories of love and bitterness.

CHAPTER FOUR

Interrogation

"I'm in nothing!" said Hegarty, showing for the first time in the interrogation an indication of determination. "I tell you, sergeant, I'm in nothing," he repeated, "sure I know some of them that was caught - I can't help that, can I?"

Cooper put disbelief into the idleness of running his thumb and forefinger along his pencil stem, alternating the movement by pushing first one end and then the other against his desk.

"You're in nothing, John." It was neither question nor statement - more penetrating than either in its indecision. Cooper's anonymous expression did not change and his hand maintained the methodical movement with the pencil.

Somewhere outside the office, the impersonal staccato of a typewriter; within, only the quiet chopping of time by the relentless pencil. Cooper was wise at the game; he knew the value of silence. He knew that talk was the defender of Hegarty's thoughts - force him to think his silent thoughts! Let the stream of his mind meander along its guilty course! Hegarty may have many thoughts but, in silence, they were all concerned with the subject. As his thoughts eddied along, thwarted here and there by the memory of some monstrous villainy, as he mentally ejaculated his "Jesus Christ"! at the possibility of Cooper knowing THAT, he was weakening his own resistance; preparing himself for the small admission as protection against the need for greater confession.

Hegarty was a "doer"; silence was not the material of his activities. The hurt of thinking was on him - making him restless.

Still Cooper kept his quiet. "Can I have a smoke?" - Hegarty's blurting of the question betrayed its defensiveness and the urgency of its origin.

Cooper, with absent perfection, smiled and slowly put his hand in his pocket. He fumbled for a moment, "You're not in 'G' Company, then John?" He drew out a crushed packet of ten, withdrew a cigarette; Hegarty was staring. "Honest to Christ, Sergeant, I ..." Cooper killed the denial by gently thrusting the cigarette into Hegarty's opened lips.

"You know, Sergeant Cooper, if I was ... "Hegarty took the cigarette from his lips, flicked his tongue at a straying strand of tobacco, "Sergeant, I'd tell you. Sure I'm no bloody hero -

what would I be doing in the I.R.A.?" He paused and then added conversationally, and, he hoped, cleverly "Mind you, I'd be tellin' a lie" - as though he avoided the practice - "if I didn't admit that theo-ret-ically - in some ways - not shootin' people and all that sort of thing - I could nearly support them - that is, in theory, like. After all I'm an Irishman and the majority of the Irish think England has no right forcing her will on Ireland. It's not illegal to say that, Sergeant - suppose, theo-ret-ically, of course, I do support the AIMS of the I.R.A. - so does the President of Eire." He smiled his satisfaction at his remark and looked at Cooper to gauge its effect. "But I'm not for killin' - and even if I was, I would only have the conviction, Sergeant; I'd never get the courage." He laughed his pleasure at the double indemnity and yet, in the silence that followed he was embarrassed, conscience-stricken by his phoney confession to a bastard - he'd seen him belt a wee slip of a girl at a Civil Rights demonstration - like Cooper.

The Sergeant raised his lighter and bent closer to Hegarty; his thumb flicked without drawing a responsive flame. Hegarty bent closer and raised a protecting hand to the lighter. Their heads were less than a foot apart; Cooper flicked again and the flame played its contortions on their features. Cooper said - the lighter still flickering between them; "Sean Cardew was O.C. before Tamo, wasn't he?"

A hand grenade exploded in Hegarty's brain, yet he fenced cleverly with his cigarette, fobbing off the seconds, grabbing at the strength of a minute hence.

Poor, brave Sean Cardew! If he hadn't been off work, sick, that week he wouldn't have died with his own bomb ... a dedicated patriot ... a bloody fanatic. Don't think Cardew liked me ... going to call a gaelic football club after him ... died horribly but baited the peeler that sat at his death bed. Christ! What a man! I was with him and Fra Kerr when we planted the banger at ... Jesus Christ! I was there! Cooper ... does he sus...

"Fra Kerr was in your Company, too, wasn't he SHAWN?"

Hegarty read significance into Cooper's broad gaelicisation of his name - it lessened the latter's advantage. Cooper disdained its pursuit and looked, apparently absently, into the middle distance.

Silence.

"Sergeant, y'know I know nothin' about Cardew and Kerr than what's going 'round our district. If I lived in a posh area I wouldn't know about these things - I wouldn't be in here."

"The awful truth, John!" It was a moment of obvious

27

frankness." "But you do live in the gutter where it all breeds; you have the same background as Cardew and Kerr and the rest and you ARE in it, John! My God, man, I haven't accused you of anything YET!" – the word clanged ominously –"but don't insult my bloody intelligence, man ... don't try to make me out a bloody fool altogether! Even apart from the information I have – aye ... you don't think I had you pull'd out of your bed in the middle of the night simply on spec do you? – you, yourself have confirmed, if not admitted, that you're just another seed in the same dirty soil that breeds the I.R.A. You know bloody well – look, what about the meetings in Murdock's top bar? What about ... oh, come off it Hegarty! Show some bloody regard for my intelligence or, by Christ, lad, I'm warning you! I'll hand you over to the bloody military – you know how they'll get the information out of you, don't you?"

Cooper was tired; he was letting emotion slip in. Steady ... not using the little ammunition you have wisely ... giving him the lot! Certainly he was with Cardew and Kerr when they planted it ... three people were seriously hurt ... nothing against him but the informer's word and, of course, himself. He must be played with the skill of an angler! Let this little bastard know your limitations and that ingratiating expression becomes a protesting, demanding face showing more than a little knowledge of his bloody "rights". His ignorance of my ignorance is the weapon ... steady ... bring it back again.

"Look, John," Cooper spoke slowly, almost gently, "let's not get silly about this. We both know you're involved. The question is, have you had enough? Do you want out? Do you want to become reconciled, John, to living your young life peacefully and happily within the law? If you do ... well ... I'll help you, lad. I don't want you to give me information – I could give it to you ... honest I could ... I get it by the bucketful – aye, and from some of the men you look up to. But what test have I got of your sincerity, John? How can I tell you really want to get back to sanity other than by full confession? I know what you've been involved in – I know about you and Harry Flood, for example – and I could tell you ..."

The name struck viciously, sending its shock waves to Hegarty's arms and legs. He scurried evasively down the labyrinths of his mind and Cooper let him go – he was tired. He had behaved like an amateur – making speeches!

None knew better than he, the technique; normally he could run the whole gamut of emotion ... softly ... angrily ...

gently ... offensively ... indignantly ... compassionately - but always prodding ... prodding! Short sentences ... questions ... change of direction ... surprise! That's where you used sparingly your tit-bits of information! Drawing on the virgin thought before it was tempered in the mental mills of concentration.

It was a job; the trade he had been learning from the time he left the farm to pound a hard beat in the city. He had shown promise for the work. To his enemies he might be a journeyman bully-boy but he had his moments of pride, aye, and accomplishment, even. It was a subtle, skilful game of chess for two players and, normally, he was a champion. But today he was tired - Hegarty could savour his minute's infinity.

The broad, dour face of Harry Flood filled the full screen of Hegarty's mind. Harry Flood! Jesus! What a bastard! Harry was no idealist, no patriot; he was the very germ of violence - the muscle of revolutionary success and the sinew of reaction. "We don't need moral victories; we need stacks of dead peelers!" - the one quoted quote of Harry Flood.

It was the only time Hegarty had been involved in an action outside the mean streets that had circumscribed his military career - in recruitment, training and martial ambition. He had travelled the nine miles out of the city with Flood, a dour and taciturn Flood, neither anxious nor complacent about the work in hand, while fear and excitement played tig with each other in Hegarty's bowels.

The mission was simple enough; Seamus Mullan would have already secured the gelignite and fuses and would have them locked in the tea cupboard at the quarry workers' hut. Seamus was not an I.R.A. man but his sympathy and his employment at the quarry were more useful than his membership.

Mullan was already waiting at the end of the lane that led to his white-washed cottage on the side of the mountain. He was a short man dressed in the rough uniform of his trade.

He fell in step with his visitors even as they exchanged their laconic greetings and together they moved against the rising ground on their left. The moon was near full in a canopy of bright eyes and a fresh, frost-impregnated wind raised its quiet orchestrations through the valley.

Hegarty could not remember a challenge. Was memory cheating when it stilled the wind and brushed the moon under a carpet of cloud? He could remember the double shot trailed by a short moan that grew still before its climax and he could remember the sound in the brush as Seamus Mullan fell and lay still.

He could remember the blue flame and the sharp piercing cracks that bit into the valley as Flood, roaring incoherently, rushed past him. Hegarty had fallen to the ground unmindful of the revolver in his pocket. This was it ... the training ... the planning! Crazily, his instructions, in the setting of their origin, volleyed across the mind but still he lay motionless, not terrified but caught peculiarly in the inertia of funk while his eyes and ears audited every move.

The two peelers emptied their Webleys - but there was never a Webley to match a Mauser and never two peelers to match big Flood! The Mauser barked the end of its second magazine even after the Webleys were still, its bright blue flame silhouetting the careless gunman.

The wind returned and the moon uncovered its face to the scene. Three men were dead.

They were walking up the narrow track to Mullan's cottage. Flood's lungs puffed their protest at the dead weight of Mullan's body across his shoulders. As they reached the gravel clearing in front of the cottage, a dog, its chain clinking in the night, made the formality of protest.

Even before they reached the door, it opened emitting the dull glow of a paraffin lamp. Mary Mullan adjusted her gaze to the night as she stared out into the moonlight. As Flood crossed the tiled floor she did not cry out. Her arms were close to her breast, her hands quieted her chin; only her eyes showed bewilderment and fear.

The two children started to scream as they vacated the untidy bed on which Flood was descending with his burden. Mary instinctively drew a protecting arm across the children, then: "My God! SEAMUS! Oh Seamus! Is he shot? That was the sho ... Oh, my God! Is he much the worse?"

Flood's voice was flat, banal, "He's dead, Missus Mullan" then, practically, "You'll have to get some of the neighbours to help you - the peelers will be swarmin' 'round this place in no time."

Mary fell on her knees over her dead husband trying to pull at his collar as though death, too, was demanding of air. She cried, then, her voice ascending an octave of terror, to the accompaniment of the piteous bawling of the children.

Flood drew out the Mauser from the waistband of his trousers; already in his hand he had a new clip. He pushed the snub-nosed bullets into the magazine with his left thumb and, as the clip fell away, he said to Hegarty "Come on, let's get to hell outa here!"

Cooper was staring at him, "Are you alright, Hegarty? Do you want a drop of tea?" Hegarty shivered, cold from the air of the mountain, terrified, as the scene always left him. "I'm cold, Sergeant Cooper" he said.

The big policeman pressed a key on his desk and the noises of the various activities taking place in the adjacent office filled the room. Hegarty thought ... how the hell can you beat all this? What chance has the patriot? Progress is the enemy of the hero. In the Twenties it was a fight between men and men; even if one side was better armed and more numerous than the other, the patriot could compensate with surprise - even with superior courage. Today you were fighting bloody transistors! Communications had taken the edge of surprise and the bravest flying column was only a helicopter sprint away from superior fire power.

Cooper's voice was a mere background to the depression of his thoughts: "Tell Constable Haskell to get us two cups of tea and ... ah ... Alice, ask Fleming to bring in the Green Books." He flicked the switch, "Just a minute, John" he said, as he pulled the telephone towards him across the desk. His podgy finger turned the dial. "I just want to ring your Detective-Sergeant Murray to see if ... hello ... hello! Detective-Sergeant Cooper, here - headquarters. Is Detective-Sergeant Murray there? Righto ... How do you get on with Sergeant Murray, John?" The palm of his hand was across the mouthpiece. "Hello! Hello Dennis ..."

Hegarty withdrew the smile that was forming on his lips to indicate his relations with "his" Sergeant Murray. Murray was the political C.I.D. man in Hegarty's local police station and was, in Hegarty's opinion, a greater bastard than Cooper!

Hegarty had driven the car that day. Paddy Quinn had handed him over the vehicle which had been "borrowed" from a city-centre car park. Hegarty could see Quinn and the blue Cortina in his mind's eye. Quinn ... fat, sly pig with a penchant for keeping out of trouble yet always getting sufficiently involved to play the big fella.

At Canavan's "Westway Inn", where he had been told by Quinn he was to go, McHugh was waiting. He acknowledged Hegarty's arrival in the Cortina with an uplifted arm before disappearing into the public bar.

Hegarty adjusted the driving seat, set the mirror "spot on" and familiarised himself with the controls. Wipers ... winkers ... heater ... must be fog or spot switches ... no water in the windscreen washers. He opened the flap of the glove compartment; broken handle ... a box of Kleenex ... packet of Rennies

31

with most of the contents lying among an assortment of screws, washers and plastic soldiers. H'm ... not a bad 'bus ... radio.

McHugh emerged from the bar followed by an older man with dark greying hair. McHugh jumped into the passenger seat and the other man came around to the window at Hegarty's side. Hegarty opened his door but the man said "No - open the window" and closed the door with his knee.

He leaned far into the car, his head close to Hegarty's. John felt uncomfortable as the smell of whiskey indicated his use of the other's breath. "I'm from the Batt. Staff, John. Tamo here has been briefed on what's afoot. I've given him a nice thirty-eight Enfield for you but, likely, you'll only be drivin'. Paddy Quinn said you were the man for the wheel, lad, and I know you won't let us down. The jobs official, alright, so you don't have to worry about any come-back there. It's Murray of Springfield and sure you couldn't do an obituary for a greater bastard! Could you? Alright, John? Tamo! Good luck, lads!"

Tamo McHugh said "Right m'lad!" as John, signalled by the withdrawal of the other's head from the window, instinctively put the car into gear and moved off. Good Jesus! they were going to bump off Sergeant Murray! Quinn, the fat bastard, had recommended him! Mechanically he changed gears and steered a course through the light afternoon traffic. He seemed to be three people; one terrified ... if we're caught in a traffic jam! ... a puncture ... a bloody convoy of soldiers! One calm: driving the car ... signalling his moves ... giving answers to Tamo ... tucking the thirty-eight in his waistband. The third person, and the one that dominated his consciousness, marvelled at the ability of the second to behave rationally outside the skin of the first.

They had been stopped for only a minute or two when the young woman tapped the window on the pasenger side. Tamo opened the door, "Hello darlin' ..." but the woman only said "He's coming" and moved quickly away.

The few minutes that passed before Murray came into view humbled Hegarty. Somehow it all seemed unreal: new worlds were breaking out ... a thousand men had died and their places had been taken by a thousand and two bawling infants; a woman was earnestly intent on the important business of getting something for the family dinner; two urchins appeared from a shop unwrapping ice lollies. Everywhere were the sounds he was not normally conscious of; the noises of the city - of people moving in the tight circle of circumstance.

In a minute it would all stop as though some heavenly projectionist, frightened by a loud report, had flicked a switch; the movement around him would draw jerkily to stillness and the sounds round off and die, like a broken gramophone, to begin with even greater intensity when the dying echo of the shot renewed its power. These people were the bit actors in the great drama; their clamour and devices were but the noises off; all were setting the scene for the principals. He wondered, absurdly, if Murray was a "principal".

Then! There was the quarry! His great frame, covered from his neck to below his knees in a long, drab mackintosh, almost hid the bicycle and gave his swift progress and rapid movement of the legs a semblance of ridiculousness. A cap was pulled down on his ruddy face and the whistling pout of his lips bespoke the efforts of his movement or their musical accompaniment.

Hegarty saw Tamo running across the road in the direction of Murray before he realised that he had left the car and at that moment a large van drew up alongside the Cortina and moved forward slowly until only a few feet of its rear was in the space to the right of the car's front. Hegarty looked in the driving mirror then spun around in his seat to peer out the rear window trying to gauge the distance between the Cortina and the white Viva that had pulled in earlier behind him. He was boxed in and the position of the van blocked his view of the other side of the road - his sight of Tamo and his victim!

His panicking brain lost reckoning of time. What had happened to Tamo? To Murray? If Tamo rushed back to the car ... the car! It could be his accuser! Had there been a shot? Almost unconsciously he slipped the thirty-eight under the seat, opened the door of the car and stepped, hesitantly, into the road. As he moved around the parked van, the car that was behind the Cortina reversed sufficiently to get clearance and then moved cautiously across the road.

He heard the bang, heard the bicycle fall and saw the mackintosh settle in a writhing mass of agony. Two more bangs without any visible evidence of markmanship. Now he was part of the machine that had stopped and when he became conscious of sound and movement again he was closer to the mackintosh. Murray was kneeling on the ground, his head tucked between his knees, the mackintosh pulled close around his neck. He was shouting madly: " ... I never ... auh! Jesus Christ ah niver done the boys any harm ... oh, please! Please!

Hegarty moved back across the road, his eyes constantly returning to the yelling, writhing madness. The squeal of tyres made him stop. The Cortina rocked on the road behind the van, its body see-sawing on its creaking suspension, then it spun out and, in low gear, careered down the road its tyres singing viciously.

Hegarty saw the busy head of Tamo turned momentarily towards him and Tamo's eyes burned ominously.

"Ah no, Dennis. I think you could say that Hegarty knows that we know ALL about him; more important, he accepts the situation." Cooper put his hand over the mouthpiece. "O.K., John?" Murray's rooting for you, too, but we must have your co-operation." He removed his hand from the mouthpiece, "I know, Dennis, aye, one of the victims of that bomb could still die but I'm not even questioning John about THAT - God, Dennis, you know how he'd fare if we set him up for that! No, there'd be no fixin' that." Silence. "That's the point, Dennis, h'm ... yes ... but OFFICIALLY Hegarty'll be clean and he'll be able to walk out of here a free man. Look ... leave it with me - John and I have reached an understanding."

The voice droned on but now Hegarty's brain had contracted out. "Three people seriously hurt ... one of the victims could still die ... not questioning him ... don't want him set up." Somewhere in his mind the needle had stuck; could still die ... don't want ... not questioning ... reached an understanding. The words dinned in his brain, each acting as the artery of a dozen sub-themes on the fringe of his consciousness: mangled bodies ... harsh lights ... brown-white cell bricks, questions, questions, QUESTIONS! Here now was Cooper's case for an eternity of questioning! Here was the doubt! Bluff or reality? Here was the price of non-co-operation ... three seriously hurt ... one MIGHT STILL DIE ... not questioning him ... don't want him set up ... There was the penalty, the alternative: graduation from court to court ... a leathery old face thrusting and pitiless, its clean pinkness reflecting the scarlet of the robes. Why do they call a black handkerchief a black "cap"? "... In Northern Ireland, however, those who use murder as a political weapon have imposed on us the necessity of retaining the ultimate in punishment."

Cooper was saying "True, Dennis; the lad himself agrees that it's the social conditions where he lives that got him involved." His wink in Hegarty's direction said, conspiratorily: we've got to lead Murray on, you and I - for YOUR sake!

The door opened and a young man - Hegarty wondered if he was a detective or a police clerk - came in with three large green linen-bound books - the "mug" shots; co-operation was about to commence!   Cooper was concluding his telephone conversation: "No need to worry, Dennis; John here is going to co-operate FULLY."   As the young man lowered his burden on to the desk he turned his head slightly in Hegarty's direction; his eyes combined with his mouth in his look of utter contempt.

Hegarty had often heard that immediately after they had "broken" you they became contemptuous.   Their hatred grew with their impatience during the interrogation; they were riding to hounds, drunk on the excitement of the chase; cursing at every obstacle.   The mud ... the high gate fed their determination; each speck of mud, each change of direction, each prang, boiled their frenzy.   If their quarry made cover their anger melted into their fatigue.   "A clever bastard! Bloody clever!"   But contempt was the wages of surrender!

Cooper was tired; new anger had not refreshed him - he had got his prey without effort.   Hegarty was shit.   He was easy - a mere embarrassment on the bloody gallows.   Hegarty's eyes met the indictment of the young man as the latter turned his head before leaving the room.

Cooper was searching in the drawer of his desk.   He was a man tidying up after a simple task.   He would not even remember Hegarty.   Paper ... pen - "Here we are, John" - the confident finality of his voice!   "We're leaving the bank explosion to your conscience, boy - aye, and all the other things we know.   God, lad, we're literally letting you off with murder!   But you're not one of the hard men - you're a cut above that type - and our job is to salvage, not destroy.   But, for Christ's sake, don't talk about it to anyone!   Not even your grandchildren - though I'll be dead and gone by then, John!"

The pen was in Hegarty's hand; "I want you to write down there that you were with Thomas McHugh on Wednesday the second of February last at two-twenty in York Street.   You can say that you didn't know what he had in mind, if you like - even that you did not see him actually shooting at Sergeant Murray.   But you were with him then, and at that time, in York Street.   You understand, John, that we won't be able to get McHugh on your statement, of course but it doesn't matter.   As a matter of fact, your friend Tamo's clean now; I can tell you, confidentially, that he followed the same course as yourself.   No, lad, as far as I am concerned, your statement is simply a declaration of intent, so to speak - your resignation from the I.R.A.   And you know it's the best way, John; you're not selling your principles - simply realising that shooting policemen has nothing to do with realising those principles.

Aye, you're just showing a bit of sense, boy."

It was an almost-careless fait accompli; Cooper was not even distended. "I'll let you get on with it ... just a short statemnt, John, lad, covering the facts." He came around the desk, put a hand on Hegarty's shoulder and indicated the first line of the foolscap with his other hand. "Just put the date there ... the tenth ... and your name behind it."

If Cooper had not immediately turned away things might have been different. But he did turn away and Hegarty's mind compounded a thousand thoughts into a concentrate of steel-cold anger, indignation and defiance. Words burned their way up his throat to be killed by anger on his lips. Indignation, agner, defiance - all drew on the muscle and sinew of his brain. The room no longer dominated him ... Cooper was a decrepit old bastard - his suit was shabby and his breath overladen with decay; he was only a full-time skivvy for whatever authority would pay him - a bloody gun for hire! Who the hell did he think ...

The crack of the plastic ballpoint on the desk made Cooper turn around. His eyes fixed Hegarty but Hegarty's eyes blazed back their defiance. Cooper shifted and dropped his gaze; he knew he had lost. Somewhere in his mind he thought of anger but he had been a lifetime at the game and he knew his loss was total and the little anger that should have provoked self analysis dissipated in tiredness. He had been too eager ... misjudged his quarry ... taken short cuts. Murray would be disappointed - he'd really wanted this pair of bastards. He was tired, sick, and all he wanted now was to get this little shit out of his sight.

It was nearly twenty-nine hours later when Hegarty was released. He did not know that Cooper had forgotten about him until the police officer in charge of the cells had enquired about procedure at the end of his statutory forty-eight hours detention.

To Hegarty, despite the discomforts of the police cells, the time was a mere prelude to his inevitable release during which he could savour to the full his victory over Cooper. The bastards had nothing on him; they had been bluffing! Next time - if there was a next time - he'd be big league - beyond the incompetence of that silly old cow with his crude psychology, his infantile telephone tricks, his stupid confidence. They had all been bricks in the wall of contempt - Cooper's contempt! The silly old shit! What was he? A bloody paid hatchet-man for the big-time political con-men - a mere professional thug who accepted the rules without the incon-

venient confusion of facts. What a cause to dedicate a life to!
- and the doddering banality of that life would treat him,
Hegarty, with contempt!

He was brought to the police office for the return of his
property. As he waited he watched the various functionaries
going about their allotted tasks. A girl, fairly pretty, too,
incuriously arranging documents in a filing cabinet; an elderly
Casanova perched on the edge of a desk chatting up a young
bird; the young man who had brought in the Green Books to
Cooper's office; a middle-aged woman manipulating the keys
of a telephone console. These were the boffins of "law and
order" - the tools of their trades were mere appendages to the
grosser business of violence for peace.

"One cigarette lighter, one pocket wallet, bunch of keys,
one single key, religious medal, contraceptive packet" the
pale-skinned sergeant failed to get the attention he hoped for
from his louder emphasis of the latter items" and forty-two
pence ... here ... sign here." Hegarty felt heat on his cheeks as
he bent over the desk to sign his name.

As he was going out he turned his head slightly and caught
the man who had brought the Green Books into Cooper's ofice
staring at him. He slowed his movements to prolong his
returned gaze but, even so, the other continued not only to
stare but, now, with a movement of his lower lip, to draw
concealment from his contempt.

That cow doesn't know that Cooper failed! Hegarty closed
the door. That's what evens the score for us against their
numbers, their organisation, their electronic weaponry; it's not
our call on surprise or our greater resources of guts - its
THEIR contempt! That's what makes men into heroes! That's
the built-in weakness of their strength ... their superiority.
Their stupid, bloody contempt.

He would have to be careful that he was not being
followed. Why? He was only going home. Home was now his
mother and young sister - a strip and a wash-down - a feed!
He would see the Company Intelligence Officer later ... make
them all laugh with his recounting of Cooper's stupid attempt
to get him to nail Tamo for Murray!

But he didn't simply want to make them laugh; he wanted
them to recognise him for what he had become during the last
two days. Before then he was like most of the others; he
talked about ideals but it was really all a big fling. The
regime was so rotten that bumping its hacks was not morally
reprehensible, but they all knew they couldn't win. But they

could win! He knew it! Their contempt had shown him the way. They could build a whole campaign on it ... spread that contempt among the people - move the people! Get the people going!

It was the soft purr of slow-moving tyres that attracted his attention. He looked around at the red Viva that had drawn level with him. The passenger-side window was being lowered - Quinn! Tamo was driving! Hegarty lowered his head to laugh his recognition. "Tamo! Paddy!" Tamo was staring at him and laughing. Quinn wore a strange, strained, look. The muzzle of the gun was shaking on the window frame. Quinn's shoulders were hunched and his head lowered into his neck; both hands held the gun. Tamo's bloody jokes! Quinn ... Quinn looked scared! "Hi, Paddy! Tamo - you old ..." Tamo's eyes kept their merriment, then, "Now Quinn! NOW!"

They were the last words John Hegarty understood and they were etched into his dwindling consciousness with the double flash of the two shots.

*

CHAPTER FIVE

The Soldiers

Adam Charters had only been in the army for four months and had now been in Belfast just under two weeks. The evening after his arrival in the city his Section had been attacked towards the end of his first patrol. The men were moving up Northumberland Street, away from the Falls Road, in extended file. They had slogged the area for almost two hours and were returning to their billet in the commercial complex at the old mill. A sandbagged position had been erected at the gateway entrance to the mill and, on the approach to this, three barriers of wood and barbed wire had been placed at intervals along the road. Each barrier measured about half the width of the road and they were placed about fourteen feet from each other with those on the extremities extending from the left pavement and the intervening barrier extending from the right pavement, forming, thus, a sharp chicane through which traffic had to slow down and perform a sort of Z pattern.

The old black Cambridge had passed Adam's Section and gone through the barriers. It had stopped then and a tall, fair-haired man got out and, with audacious deliberation, raised a tommy-gun to waist level and fired a quick volley in the direction of the troops. The man lowered the gun and appeared to stand for a second looking for evidence of marksmanship before getting into the car again and being driven off.

Adam knew why HE had not fired back at the attacker; he was scared - not, he told himself, with some justification, so much by the bullets as by the sheer unexpectedness and cheek of the action. He felt he could not be so badly surprised again and he wondered if this was a new method of attack by the I.R.A. because none of the others, all of whom had considerable service in Northern Ireland, had fired back either. Even when they were inside, he did not raise the matter - if the officer said there were civilians in the street, well ... perhaps there WERE civilians in the street.

Nothing happened to him during the three nights following. Now he walked around the mean streets of the area with his comrades. The people were sullen; generally they did not look in the direction of the soldiers but they knew they were there.

Old and young, men and women, even the children, avoided them; sometimes an eye responded to Adam's nebulous smile but, usually, it sent hate at him. As always, the soldiers were in extended file along the pavements close to the walls; at street intersections the man in front covered the street they were crossing while his comrades, still in extended file, crossed the mouth of the street, crouching and at the double. The faces of the people greeted these tactics with obvious sarcastic amusement and, when Adam's turn came to make such a movement he felt the sting of his ridiculousness.

The child had been playing with a soft doll as he came down the street. He thought of his brother's little girl, Diana; probably about the same age - Diana was fairly big for two. Golden curls. "Aaa-ha!" The little girl was holding the doll by one arm and now, with a swinging movement, she threw the doll into the roadway. "Aaa-ha!" Instinctively, Adam moved off the pavement and recovered the doll. He hunched down beside the child, cradling his rifle against the inside of his leg; "Hello honey! Beating your dolly, then?" He raised the child's arm and cradled the doll against her breast, "Now, put nice dolly to sleep, eh?" The child stared at him and put one of her hands on the rifle. "Ga-ga. Doll-ee!" He put his arms around her shoulders, "What you call the ..?"

At that moment the young woman came out of the door. She was in her early twenties, medium height and well-formed; the cleavage of her generous breasts was revealed above her knitted blouse and her black skirt did nothing to hide the suppleness of her thighs. Adam looked up into her face. She had the child's wide-set eyes above an attractive retrousse nose and her blonde hair cascaded generously on to her shoulders.

Adam hid his pleasure: "Think your little girl's fallen out with her dolly." He smiled and stood up taking the child's hand and bringing her towards her mummy. The young woman didn't look at him; she bent forward and raised the child into her arms and, as she spun around, the doll fell from the child's fingers on to the pavement. "Hello!" Adam had again retrieved the doll and was offering it to the back of the woman. She spun around and stared at him, her eyes rising from his boots slowly; insolently her gaze lingered on his face then, their contempt aided by the hint of a curl in her lower lip, the eyes travelled down him again. She spat on the pavement, tightened her grip on the child then turned through the doorway of the house and slammed the door.

Adam stood with his rifle at the high-port, his left hand

extended holding the doll.

The billet had been an old linen mill that had been slow to make the changeover to synthetics after the war and had eventually been forced out by its more dynamic competitors. The extensive workrooms and offices had been cut up into separate lots and leased to a multiplicity of enterprises. The barefooted troglodytes of yesterday had given way to their high-heeled, mini-skirted counterparts of the Seventies.

The mill had stood sentinel over many a Belfast riot. Before the turn of the century and again in 1912, in 1921 and 1953, it had aborted its undernourished human complement into the mean streets of the Falls and Shankhill roads to watch them clash in vicious anger over the priorities of misery disguised by those who imposed that misery, in the mantle of religious belief. It had known the annual tensions of July when its slaves contested the erection of the emblems of their slavery and its walls bore the paint and whitewashed clarions of these earlier struggles. A man had died at the entrance to its general office when, during the hunger marches of the Outdoor Relief strike, in 1932, he had failed to outrun a police bullet, and a young woman had been martyred to the cause of religious intolerance in its main gateway some three years later. Yet it was the starlings and the black smoke who had left their evidence on the grim environs.

But in August 1969 even the indomitable mill fell victim to the riot. The petrol bomb succeeded where time, the starlings, the financial vicissitudes and the heaving bodies of its workpeople, locked in combat for their notions of the proper placings of some theological commas, had failed. The monument to misery went up in flames, not because it had been a monster that sucked life out of the many to over-nourish the few, but because the Catholics of the Falls were being burned - and were burning.

Now what was left of the mill was a military fastness. The gentlemen who controlled things were still of the mind of those who owned the mill in its year of building: discipline had to be maintained over those who work and live within the shadow of the mill and if it breaks down before men and guns, then more men and more guns are required to enforce it. Adam Charters, Corporal Buick, Sergeant Jackson and the rest, now billeted in the mill, were among the new enforcers.

Adam Charters had left school when he was fifteen. He could have left at ten for his agile intelligence was not bent in the direction of academic scholarship. His interest, his persevering and absorbing interest, was motor cars. When other kids in the vicinity of his North London home were poring over books, kicking a football in the slum streets or watching telly, Adam was in a back-street garage lending his improving abilities for the price of five Player's Weights.

When he was nearly sixteen he went to work as a vanboy with a supermarket chain but before he had completed six months he was caught joyriding in the firm's van which he had taken illegally from its garage. He was brought before the courts on the ten or twelve counts which the local police squeezed out of his enterprise and he was charged at the bar of his father's anger with "disgracing" him, "letting the family down" and, among other more serious charges, being "bloody useless anyway".

Adam did not get the "spell in the cooler" his father predicted. Instead, he was fined the sum of fifty pounds and put on probation for two years as well as being disqualified from holding a driving licence for a similar period. His mother and his older brother had attended the court proceedings and his mother had spoken on his behalf to the magistrates but Adam felt these august people were not impressed by his father's absence.

His mother had paid the fifty pounds. She got the money from a moneylender - they would live less well, to the tune of twenty-five bob a week for a year. Maybe Adam would get another job ... maybe tomorrow ... But the people who wanted muscle also wanted honesty and a clean record for the wages they paid; it appeared that, in the single act of taking a jaunt in his employer's van, Adam had robbed himself of the ability to load and unload all other vans, dig roads, move heavy burdens or perform any of the other menial functions for which he was educationally equipped.

It was inevitable that he should be thrown into the areas where illegal thieving lurks and predictable that he should be lured into its web. It was also inevitable that, at that level of crime, he should be caught.

His probation officer was genuinely concerned, especially since Adam's period of probation was almost up. The officer was eager to help but he knew that without "gainful employment", and with a previous conviction, Adam was unlikely to win the indulgence of the court. Finally he suggested that Adam should consider applying to join the army.

The probation officer spoke well for Adam; he drew the attention of the magistrates to the grimmer aspects of his working-class life and extolled his virtues: "He has been completely co-operative with the police and, even as Sergeant

Johns stated in his evidence, he made no effort to use violence to resist arrest; this is because he is essentially a gentle and non-violent person. What he lacks, gentlemen, is the acquisition of some skill or other that will equip him to earn a living and, in asking the sympathetic consideration of the court, I can say that young Charters has made an application to join the army and, dependent on the attitude you ..."

Adam had become a soldier in the Light Infantry.

On the fourth evening after his arrival in Belfast, Adam lay on his bunk in the mill. He had placed his kitbag against the wall at the head of his mattress and stood his pillow on end over this to provide a platform for his back; his shoes were removed and his knees were crossed over and raised. Nestling on his thighs was a folded copy of the BELFAST TELEGRAPH. On the front page of the paper was a photograph of a young girl, nineteen or so, pretty ... well, she had been, but the photograph that now shrieked out at him showed a ghastly cut down the right side of the girl's face right across her eye and extending to her chin. The caption read: "Terror Bomber's Victim."

Adam addressed no one in particular: "Jesus Christ! Have you seen this bird? Poor bloody girl's destroyed for life! Says here she may lose the sight of an eye." Corporal Buick moved over beside Adam and took a quick look at the picture then he said "The bastard't did that deserves his balls cut off!" Steen took a look and handed the paper to Carter. The latter viewed the front page and then turned the paper around to the back sports page saying as he manipulated the sheets "Bet whoever done it said his prayers afterwards - probably had his rosary beads in the same pocket as his gun, eh! ... Ha! See this? Bloody nig-nogs aren't 'alf doin' well in the bleedin' Test!"

Adam pulled the newspaper from Carter. "She was a nice kid that, too. Bet the bloke as done it feels pretty sick lookin' at that," he said. Buick looked at him, "You've a lot to learn, lad; these murderin' scum don't ave any consciences. How the hell any man could open up a girl's face like that ..."

"You hypocritical bastard, Buick!" Sergeant Jackson turned laughingly to the others, "Have you seen this boy wield a bloody baton? He loves it! Goes bloody berserk! I saw him one night up at Bloodymurphy - a young bird she was ... fifteen perhaps ... he opened her bloody skull and was still bashing away when I pushed him off!" Steen laughed. Carter said, "I 'ave a four-inch trophy on my bloody leg from that night and it was a fucking bitch that heaved the brick!" Sergeant Jackson said, "Well, Corporal ...?"

"That was different." Adam did not join in their laughter at the discomfited Buick. "I took a helluva lot that night from that little bitch. She bloody goaded me 'Go on! Belt me!'" He mimicked the Belfast accent. "So I bloody hit the little fenian whore, but you couldn't say that's the same as this bloody bombing. These bloody murderers ... do they know what innocent person's going to cop it?"

"What about the R.A.F. during the war?" Jackson had seated himself for the argument. "No I don't mean the fighter pilots, I mean the bastards who got into their big planes and hid in the stratosphere above the fighters and the ack-ack ... five hundred miles south-south east, course so-an-so, and drop your load within a two mile radius on top of the city that should be there. Bombs away - and Bob's your Uncle! Were they cowards and murderers, too, Corporal?"

"Jesus, Sergeant, you're not comparin' the R.A.F. with these bloody terrorists?" Buick was happy to find the talk leave his Ballymurphy escapade "I mean after all ..." Carter's voice was louder, "Bloody hell, Sergeant! It was a different thing. That was war."

Jackson was enjoying himself. "And what do you think the I.R.A. would call this?"

Carter said angrily, "Doesn't matter what THEY call it - its bloody terrorism!"Buick said. "Well aren't they trying to overthrow the bloody govermint? That's treason, ain't it?"

Jackson laughed, "Oh, aye ... treason. You know someone once said 'Treason doth never prosper; what's the reason? If it prosper none dare call it treason!'"

Adam had been listening interestedly to the discussion; now he shook his head, "Crikey, Sergeant, I don't know anything 'bout what's goin' on in this Gawd-awful hole but I do know that the people here look at you with their bloody eyes filled with hate .... oh hell! I just don't understand."

Jackson looked reflective: "You know, lad, I've been in this man's army over twenty years; I've seen that look before many times. I saw it first in Palestine, I saw it in Malaya, I saw it in Cyprus and then again in Aden. No, Charters, they only love us for a short time ... you know yourself, lad - you've done your training - we're not equipped for the business of bringing peace."

Buick was angry - the more so because he just KNEW he was right; knew that any Tom, Dick or Harry just can't be allowed to take up guns - they weren't even soldiers! Who gave them the right ...? The anger was laden on his voice when he spoke, "Sergeant Jackson, with respect, Sergeant, you're talkin' a lot o' codswallop. The I.R.A. is just a bloody gang. They have no right ..."

Jackson still smiling quietly, intervened without heat, "How big must a gang get before it gains the respectable status of an army? As for right ... well, tell me Buick, have you reasoned out the whys and wherefores of the problem here? Look, boy, talk to any of the people here about the problem; oh aye, you'll get different answers but they're all quite articulate on the subject ... they know something about it. You know damn all about it, you're like the rest of us, you do what you're told!"

"But planting bloody bombs, Sergeant ... Surely to Christ ..." Carter did not want to rile the Sergeant.

"I honestly can't understand, Sergeant, 'ow you could mention the R.A.F. and them bloody gangsters in the same breath" said Buick.

Jackson got to his feet, "All right, Buick, if the I.R.A. had bigger and better means of making war, if they could send their war planes over London, if they had our H-bomb, if they could pollute our rivers with poisonous bacteria and throw canisters of nerve gases at our women and kids from the sky, would that make them respectable enough for you, lad?"

"But they've no right to make war, Sergeant, that's the point, who are they to decide what to do?"

The merriment was deep now in Jackson's eyes. "Ah well ... we've made some progress now, haven't we? Now we've shifted our ground. Can we agreé that, after Belsen, Hiroshima, Churchill's policy of mass bombing of Germany, Vietnam, Biafra and all the other historical incidents of our civilisation, the Chamber of Horrors has been emptied? Can we now agree that there is nothing new in the world of violence and that the I.R.A.'s capacity for violence is, by comparison with some of the events mentioned, puny indeed? Now the argument hinges on the right to use violence. Tell me Buick, did you give three cheers for the Hungarians when, quite illegally of course, they tried to overthrow their government and fought the Russians? Did you know that your old man was probably supporting the illegal French and Italian I.R.A.'s in the early Forties?"

"That was a different bloody situation ... the bloody Germans and Russians were aggressors!" It was Buick again, angry.

"That's what the I.R.A. say we are, Buick."

"But, seriously, Sergeant, ye couldn't say that ... that" Carter was hesitant, "planting bombs in buildings ..."

45

"As opposed, Carter, to DROPPING them ON buildings" interjected Jackson.

"Ah now, let me finish! I didn't interrupt you. No ... planting bombs and throwing bloody nail bombs and that sort of thing. Coming up sleekitly and popping off at a man in a sentry post. Christ no, Sergeant! They're dirty bastards!"

"Well, you know, Carter," Sergeant Jackson was tiring of the argument "the nail bomb is not quite as effective as our own anti-personnel stuff. As for popping off at a bloke ... in military parlance the surprise attack is good strategy and the development of weapons from easy-to-hand materials is what we call good improvisation, man! Have you ever cheered in the pictures for one of our commandos creeping up on a Jerry sentry and getting a knife into his jugular vein before the poor bugger can gasp a prayer? It's all part of the game lad! You can't humanise brutality - and that's the business we're in. Let's do the bloody job, for Christ's sake, without being hypocrites! Leave the empty moralising to the civilians, as far as I'm concerned I.R.A. men are bastards because I'm here and they aim to blow my bloody head off - and I aim to get in first!

"I'm a professional soldier; rights and wrongs are none of my goddamn business; if I started thinking about rights and wrongs I might decide that, even if I was not completely wrong, I didn't have a monopoly of right - that way I become a less effective soldier! Let the C.O. be your conscience, boys. The brass will tell you when to love them and when to hate them and don't be bloody surprised if, one of these days, this I.R.A. gang become good enough at the violence game to make it too hot, or expensive, to continue the contest. Some of you may yet be on a guard-of-honour for some of them calling at No. 10."

Sergeant Jackson was a rare old bastard, Adam thought. Bloody good soldier, though. Now that Buick would be right vicious! He said, "Look Sergeant, I admit I know nothin' about this Irish thing - what's more, I don't want to know. I knew quite a lot of Paddies at home, though ... not bad fellas - a few Guinness, a bird ... just like the rest of us only they had this Irish brogue, like. But they didn't seem to worry about religion and they were bloody friendly but, Christ, you can't say they're friendly here!"

"You know, Charters" Jackson looked serious, "I was with the 1st battalion in nineteen sixty-nine - we were the first lot in here after the troubles of August of that year and, by God, we were welcome, lad! Falls Road, Shankhill Road, Catholic and Protestant, anywhere in Belfast, we were welcome. When you went out on patrol you came back with a bellyful and pissed their hospitality all night after. I got to know some people at Ardoyne really well and even spent a week-end leave with a family - they'd probably shoot me on sight now! An old fella in that house used to tell me about Belfast - about its past religious pogroms and all that but, as he saw it, our coming, and the circumstances of our coming, represented ... how's this he put it? Ah yes, 'an historical milestone' or, another of his quotes, 'the British Army represents a tremendous initiative for peace here.'

"He argued that, for the first time in his memory, there was a force that was being well received by both Protestants and Catholics in Belfast. At that time if anyone in Belfast had insulted one of our chaps the Catholics would have dealt with them. The I.R.A. was insignificant - they had no one behind them. Of course there were guns around - this bloody country's hiving with them - but our policy then seemed to be to eliminate the fear that creates the desire to use guns rather than disturb the balance by searching for them.

"Then, apparently, the politicians took a hand; there was a change of policy. We started to pull their bloody homes asunder looking for guns. Sometimes we found something, sometimes we didn't and often we were raping the very houses of those who had extended hospitality to us. The Catholics said we weren't searching for Protestant guns and ..."

"But the bloody Protestants weren't shootin' at us, Sergeant." Buick was growing tired of Jackson's discourse.

"As a matter of fact, any shooting incidents that had occurred up to that time were very isolated and they included a battle with Protestant gunmen - in October, I think it was, sixty-nine - indeed that was the most serious incident; a copper was shot dead on the Shankhill Road and two of our lads injured. Point I'm trying to make is, every time we made a raid, even if we got arms, we created a desire in a widening circle of Catholics for arms - we were recruiting for the bloody I.R.A.!"

Jackson took a step backwards, preparing to go, "That's the way I saw the situation, anyway, and I was here on the ground at the time, among the people. I blame the bloody politicians - the bastards always leave us their dirty washing and we get the kicks. But, as far as you lot are concerned, my advice is don't think about it. Don't personalise it. Just remember that those people out there hate your bloody guts and some of them want to do for you so distrust all the bastards equally - that way you'll live longer!"

Jackson smiled, he was going now. "But don't let this lad fool you," he ruffled Buick's hair playfully, "he's a good lad with a club." Buick grinned and the tension was eased.

After the Sergeant had gone Adam stared sightlessly at his newspaper. Why the hell did they want to fight? Jesus, he had no hatred for the Irish. Catholics and Protestants were only stupid words. Some of the birds were pretty, too! Hell! Jackson was right; just look out for yourself!

"Come on lads, at the double!" Adam grabbed his rifle with right hand and snatched up his riot-vizored helmet with the other. The dull thumping of rubber soled boots resounded in the corridor outside the old offices that served now as a billet. Adam hurried through the door and pressed into the runners. Outside in the courtyard of the old mill Major Hickson stamped about impatiently while Jackson deployed the men into the waiting vehicles.

Adam was in the last of the Land Rovers to move out. Steen was beside him, Buick and Carter on the bench opposite and, as the vehicle slowed through the gate-way, Sergeant Jackson ran forward, caught the roof of the fibre-glassed armour, and swung himself aboard. Carter started to sing:

"Oh the Falls! Oh the Falls! Oh the Falls!
It gives me a pain in the balls!
It's only a notion that you get promotion
So bugger the Pope and the Falls!"

"Pack it in, Carter!" Jackson was severe. The Land Rover sped down Albert Street and turned right into Durham Street. The men were quiet. Nervous. Carter fiddled with his rifle; Adam noticed that he was quite young - a rather delicate-looking boy. Sergeant Jackson was tight-lipped and hard.

"Right lads, out!" The Land Rover had come to a skidding halt in Leeson Street. Adam was out behind Jackson. From further up the street came the noise of riot, the shouting, the squealing of the women - it was worse than the breaking glass or the shattered sequel to a hurled brick. The yelling, shouting, screaming, all the miscellany of sheer bloody riot fury, increasing now in volume as more of the rioters became aware of menace at their backs.

"Corporal Buick, Charters, stay with this lot. Watch your rear! Come on Steen - wake up. Carter you're not dressing for a bloody dinner party. In behind!" The vehicles had all spilled their complement; the men were formed in rough lines behind the advancing Saracens. Jackson was moving through to the front, his riot baton in his right hand, all the time making short loosening-up flicks with his arm, Carter was the last man away and when he had taken a few paces forward he turned his head around and looked at Adam and the honesty of his gaze provoked a fleeting pity in him.

The Saracens halted some forty yards from the main body of rioters. As the first bang signalled the discharge of baton rounds Adam could see the men groping for their gas masks. The rioters were now retreating back towards the two vehicles they had originally been attacking and as these began to withdraw rapidly into the Falls Road the pace of the rioters retreat quickened.

Buick smiled over at Adam. "The bastards don't like the sniff of that! Man if old Jackson gets his hands on one of them he'll slay him!" Adam grinned, he was thinking of Carter. "Bet the boys in the two 'pigs' at the top there are glad to get to hell out - Corporal Buick ... Christ! They're behind us!" Seconds compressed into a moment of indecisive terror. The Land Rover nearest him was blazing, a stone ricocheted off the ground to his left and a puddle of flame accompanied the shattering of glass at his right. "Corporal Buick!" Adam was running! He heard Buick draw level with him and together they ran in the direction of the main body of troops now retreating to their defence.

They met at the intersection. Carter had led the retreat back and Adam's eyes grabbed thankfully at the young man's fear-ridden face. Buick had disappeared into the main body of troops, Carter was facing Adam, slightly removed from the others. Movement seemed suspended for a moment as the two met. Carter smiled at him, his face seeming ridiculously small beneath the huge helmet and vizor.

As the crack echoed away Carter looked puzzled but he fell without any protecting movement of the hands or arms. He lay still for a second and then he writhed; his knees came up to his stomach and he rolled into his side and shuddered and swung on to the other side, then was still. Blood oozed from the side of his mouth on to the concrete; his face momentarily convulsed and then his eyes opened in the terrible frankness of death.

"Get in here, you stupid bastard!" Sergeant Jackson pulled Adam behind the Saracen. He fell over the crouching figure of Buick and then he sat up, his back against the armour of the vehicle. The vomit had rolled down the front of his combat jacket and was now accumulating in his lap.

Major Hickson's arrival with the heavy armoured vehicles

at the Grosvenor Road end of Leeson Street had distracted the rioters and probably prevented them pressing home their advantage on the two military defensive positions in course of hurried preparation on either side of the street, where it intersected with McDonnell Street.

Hickson took stock of the position: at the Falls Road end of the street he had two armoured troop carriers; halfway up the street on his left a party of his men were impotently boxed-in behind two armoured cars and a Land Rover; facing them a small knot of men were confined in the narrow space between two Saracens forming a rough V on the pavement. This latter position was particularly vulnerable; if he moved against the huge mob they would filter into the adjoining streets and reform behind him and he had not the forces to circumvent his positions and deploy men at the other end of these streets. His immediate position was the centre of the mobs' attention at the moment - for the rioters had seen one of their number being pulled behind his vehicles - and, if they had not seen his men setting on this unfortunate, those closer had probably heard the captured man's cries.

He decided to make radio contact with his vehicles at the Falls Road end, instruct them to retreat up the Falls Road and come in behind him at Grosvenor Road. This would open the top of the street to allow the rioters to retreat before his slow pressure and give them the illusion of a victory at one end. It would be slow work; he daren't move quickly in case pressure from his end would crystallise the mobs' fury against his beleaguered outposts.

Adam was feeling slightly better now. At first the sight of Carter dying had robbed him of conscious fear but Jackson's harsh tones and vicious pulling of his arm had cut through the lather of repellence and brought him back to terror. In a peculiar way his mind had not recorded his being sick and he was startled now at the evidence in his mouth and on his clothing. He was still half sitting, half lying, on the ground with his back against the armour of the vehicle and now fear was shaking at his whole body. Around him the separate shouts, yells and squeals had again taken on the corporate constancy of riot but now the assault was mainly one of noise. The missiles were fewer; some stones and bottles were being bowled harmlessly under the vehicles but only an occasional stone was landing in their position from over the top of the Saracens. The mob had won a victory but, without leaders, it lacked the mass wit to press home its advantage.

Sergeant Jackson, Corporal Buick and the others were

pulling the backs of seats and whatever other portable equipment they could find out of the vehicles and piling them under, and in the spaces between, the armoured trucks. Jackson looked around at Adam. "Sit where you are lad. Hickson's down there with half a bloody battalion ... we'll be alright ... he'll soon clear this rabble. You'll see. Feelin' better now, eh!" It was not a question and Jackson immediately turned away. "How d'ya like being the meat in a bloody iron sandwich, lads?" None of the men laughed and Jackson started singing, loudly and badly.

For a moment Adam tried to think ahead to tomorrow when all this would be over and he wondered if the others would rib him for ... or worse ...

CHAPTER SIX

The Big Man

Johnny Cairns had left Nora's house and gone back to see Charlie Shields in one of the houses in Sorella Street. He confirmed Danno's report that the mob in Leeson Street were showing some signs of breaking up. He also recounted the disposition of the troops on the ground and suggested that the I.R.A. section should move in to attack the military as soon as they could get the rioters disengaged, and before the main body of troops could link up with the two improvised positions. Cairns emphasised that in these circumstances the diversionary attack from the Grosvenor Road by Hagan, Speers and Boyle should be of a more sustained nature in order to pin down the main body of troops while the greater part of the I.R.A. section was dealing with the less-formidable outposts.

Danno was dispatched to one of the neighbouring houses where the rest of the section was waiting. He was to give them details of where the attack would now take place and advise Hagan, Speers and Boyle of the place from which they would carry out their diversionary attack.

For some time after Danno had gone Charlie Shields talked quietly to Johnny. With them in the room was Charlie McGivern, the Battalion Intelligence Officer. McGivern was the owner of the house and he had sent his wife and two children up the stairs immediately after the arrival of the I.R.A. party. He was a man of medium height, very thin, with sharp features, narrow chin and peculiarly protruding eyes that gave him a rodent-like expression. Ironically, his voice, even lowered to the whispers of the occasions, had a rich fullness of tone and his pronunciation was tediously correct.

McGivern was talking: "We have received definite information from a number of reputable sources that at least three British agents are actively working in this area. On two of these we would appear to have quite definite intelligence. There is a Captain Rodgers whose family lives in County Louth - in the Republic. This fellow is a Catholic ... educated at the National University - speaks Irish, incidentally. I would think this one is unlikely to operate in the pubs and bookmakers' offices - indeed he would stick out like a sore thumb in such places. His most likely sphere of operations would be gaelic clubs - language, sport, dancing; he could be easily absorbed in that kind of environment. The Director of Intelligence feels we could neutralise this fellow with the mere mention of his name - and County Louth family connections - in the UNITED IRISHMAN. Personally, I would incline to the view that we should try and get a more definite bearing on this gentleman and see if we could not apply enough pressure to use him ourselves."

Shields had been waiting: "How come we've so much information on this fella and yet know nothing of where he's operating?"

"Oh, we can get all the background information we want on this boy. Our source is perfect but it lapses when it comes to his present activities, cover, etc. We have, however, as I say, enough to neutralise him, which would be the safest short-term method of dealing with him, but other little bits of information I have, too indefinite and delicate to mention now, would indicate that this fellow could be a big fish, worth waiting on. I would not be inclined to accept that his services are being used simply because he is a Catholic and able to speak Irish."

Johnny nodded; what little he knew of McGivern had built his respect for the man and, as always, he was impressed that McGivern's usual taciturnity was waived for him. It showed not only the man's trust in him but, also, the confidence of the entire Battalion Staff.

Shields had lost his earlier depression. It crossed his mind that he was always very much a victim of the immediate - fools depressed him, intelligence boosted his confidence. What he did not consider, because he didn't know it, was that, in his own book, he readily identified intelligence with accent, dress and formal education. McGivern's confidence was flattering - this was executive stuff! He said, "And the other two? Do we have much on them?"

McGivern smiled, "You mean the two others that we know about. We must not think that because we have information about three of them, they are limited to that number. We have some well-placed contacts ... our intelligence end has improved immensely ... better now than at any time since the early Thirties - which, in turn, is a good barometer of public reaction to our campaign and our chance of success - for remember that people who operate for us do so out of conviction and not - or very rarely - for rewards of a more tangible nature.

"It is, of course, much more difficult to get information about the army than it is about the police. The police used informers among our own people and these rarely co-operated fully with them, and, again - certainly in the case of those who co-operated willingly with the police, usually for the price of drink or the like - they were the type that rarely had the intelligence either to be in positions of prominence or to allay suspicion of their activities. The police worked on tit-bits of information gained from such sources and from loose talk among poorly trained, inactive and frustrated volunteers with all the time in the world for bickering and feuding. Very often their sources were known to us and could be used to advantage.

"It was always a matter of surprise to us just how much information we got about the police anonymously - probably the result of disgruntlement in their ranks and, doubtless, from Catholics whose fathers had forced them to become reluctant coppers.

"With the army, of course, it's different. Their agents are professionals - well trained, brutal bastards who are able to carry out their nefarious work without any legal constraints. Their cover is usually well thought out and seldom with strings leading back to an easily-available source of information. Still, we are having our successes and they are improving. Yes, it's a far cry from the old days when we were inactive and completely unsuccessful - then, their information came easily and they were always on top of us."

Shields said, with some heat, "The bloody movement was riddled with stool-pigeons."

"True." McGivern took the interruption in his stride. "Because the movement was demoralised and in decay. Our object then was to shoot the odd cop whom, legend had it, was a particularly bad villain. We're too busy now for that nonsense. The police are disgraced and discredited and emerge only rarely now and then, behind the skirts of the British Army - but what I was saying ..."

Shields was really bitter now. "The R.U.C. will never police the Catholic districts of Belfast again. Not ever! That's for sure! The only way they can come in now is behind a battalion of soldiers and if Britain wants to impose the Unionist Party's private army - which is all the R.U.C. ever were - on the people here, then she'll have to foot the bill for the maintenance of her bloody army here, AD INFINITUM!"

Johnny Cairns said quietly, "I think even the Government knows that now. They must be very keen to get new estates of working-class slums built so that they can break-up the Catholic ghettos. The irony of the situation is, though, that the Unionist Party that created the ghetto mentality must now end the ghettos if they are to get back any semblance of what they call law and order and now the attitudes of Unionism's own extremists, whom the Party daren't offend, is creating new ghettos every day!"

"Poor Faulkner! Who's next for Prime Minister?" Shields was being unusually flippant. "But ... you were saying, Charlie ..."

"Actually, the point I was going to make was that the British Army, while they have a central intelligence agency, usually, in such a situation as they now find themselves in here, second intelligence agents to local field commanders. These agents usually confine their activities to a restricted local area and report back to the local commander. Their central boys don't like this type of operation - nor do we, for often this type of one-off exercise succeeds where the more lugubrious and devious methods of the specialists fail. The thing to remember is that dress, accent, fervour, occupation and the like, are meaningless in themselves. All recruits have to be screened thoroughly - this is where the Provos are falling down - and again, volunteers should not be burdened with information superfluous to their immediate needs."

"Agreed," interpolated Shields, "but what about the other two agents you were speaking of? What do we know of their activities?"

"Well, my information on one of these characters is second-hand - from the Provos, actually - through the Brigade O.C. As you know members of the Brigade Staff have had a number of meetings with their opposite numbers in the Provisional movement in an effort to eliminate the type of incident between their members and our own volunteers that we all regret - incidents that have caused loss of life and left our most active supporters bemused and the British amused. While, obviously, our differences with the Provos are too deep and intractable to allow of sustained and long-term co-operation in the field, we should at least be able to avoid armed conflict with one another. Well, at any rate, when the detail of some of these recent incidents of conflict between ourselves and the Provos was examined, a common denominator emerged in them all. That common denominator is the activities of a certain member of the Provos called Pearse Doyle.

"This fellow hung about the fringe of their movement for a number of months. Lived in digs on the Antrim Road and joined in some of the stone-throwing and petrol-bomb attacks on the British Army in the New Lodge area. Finally, he became a member of the Provisional Alliance - an all-action and very popular member. Claims he was born in Birmingham of Irish parents who made him a rebel before he was ten. Claims he was sent to Ireland by an English firm of roofing contractors about a year before the troubles here began. Like so many who have come into both the Provos and our own movement, entry was gradual - indeed, apparently, this fellow had been in contact with and actively assisting the Provos for months before he was ASKED to join."

Shields said, "And he's a bloody spy all the time! The stupid bastards! Isn't it just too bloody typical?"

"Well ... no, Charlie." McGivern spoke slowly. "It is hardly fair to blame them here; we all know the circumstances: in the district ... fighting with the rest against the soldiers ... incurious ... almost assumes that, in fighting, he IS part of the movement ... wins confidence and popularity. No. It shouldn't happen, of course, but, in the circumstances, let's face it, it can happen."

Cairns asked, "Well is this just a suspicion resulting from this fellow, Doyle, being associated with all the incidents between ourselves and the Provos? What I mean is, if he is as active as you suggest he is, suspicion may arise from a conspiracy of circumstances. Or, if there any real evidence against him?"

"Oh yes, indeed!" McGivern said. "What you say was true in the beginning but additional facts have emerged. One: enquiries were set in foot in Birmingham; they reveal that Doyle - his name really is Doyle - PETER Doyle -left his home in Birmingham over seven years ago as the result of a dispute with his parents about some married woman he was then going around with AND his father and mother - both Catholics from Enniskillen - had met and married during the war WHILE THEY WERE BOTH MEMBERS OF THE BRITISH FORCES!"

"Ooh!" Shields was impressed. Cairns peered into the silence for a few moments, then, "Not the sort of thing a fellow's likely to talk about at any time in Republican circles in Ireland and, surely, in these times, he could be forgiven for gilding the lily a bit. Are these all the 'additional facts'?"

"No, Johnny, there's more. Apparently it has been established beyond all shadow of doubt that Doyle was not in Ireland in 1969; that, in fact, at the beginning of 1970 he was in an English prison, ostensibly doing time for burglary but, coincidentally, Seamus Burke and Alfie Gillingham, both Belfast Republicans doing seven years on arms charges, were in the same prison and Doyle was using his Irish bit to get on friendly terms with both men AND he was inexplicably transferred from prison after only two months of an alleged three-year sentence!"

"Jesus Christ!" Shields breathed out the expletive. Cairns was looking eagerly at McGivern, "Any more?"

"There is, indeed! Mr. Doyle, it transpires, has no employment permit - required, as you know, under the Unionist Party's 'Safeguarding of Employment Act'. Apparently he did work for an English firm of roofing contractors who were doing a contract here - but only for three weeks in August 1970. He worked as a labourer - you may well wonder why a firm should bring over a non-specialist worker to Belfast. He left the firm at the end of August, Seventy, and the Labour Exchange here has no record of him ever having taken out Insurance Cards. I would think that a reasonable cover was being prepared for Doyle by the army authorities but was abandoned when he was so readily and unquestioningly accepted into the Provos."

"It certainly seems pretty damning," said Cairns. "I take it the Provos are handling the matter themselves?"

McGivern laughed, "I understand that 'Killer' Quinn who was his O.C., is handling the matter and is greatly disturbed by the constitution of the court his Batt. Staff has nominated."

"The pot and the bloody kettle!" Shields shook his head as he spoke, "Quinn would try him alright - before he shoots him! Christ, the British don't need an agent provacateur when Paddy Quinn's about!"

Cairns laughed with McGivern and said "Well, that's two you've told us about; what about the third?"

"Ah! Number three ... the most immediately dangerous of the lot. An ex-member of the British Army's infamous 'Aden Gang'. He is a lieutenant Oliver Clements ... six feet two inches and built like a tank. A Larne man, originally ... his family went to Canada some years ago ... was a sergeant-instructor in the British marines ... got his commission in Aden as a reward for murder and, what is euphemistically referred to as, 'counter-espionage' work. Plenty of guts ... absolutely ruthless ... drinks moderately ... smokes heavily .." McGivern was speaking slowly, obviously satisfied with the impresion his detailed information was making.

"We have everything that's on his file but - and this is what makes detection difficult - he has a roving commission. He's his own boss. Goes where he likes; does what he wants and passes it on as he sees fit. Doubtless he uses a daily-changing

code to pass on whatever information he picks up to whatever
source he deems to be the most effective in dealing with it.
This man's job is to remove dangerous elements without the
necessity of involving complicated legal process and, in at
least one case, - the murder outside his home of Dick Stitt last
September - we are pretty certain he was responsible.
Clements can be anywhere; he is especially ..."

"The bastard's probably throwing stones at the British
Army in Leeson Street at the moment!" Charlie Shields broke
into the tenseness.

Before McGivern could reply a knock came to the door. It
was Danno back to report.

"I wudn't be surprised if the poor kid's dead. Jasus but they
gave him an awful doing! Y'should ha' seen the rifle butts goin'
in to work on his head! "T'hit that lad w'everything - boots,
rifles, batons. He cudn't have stuck it, y'know."

The big man was standing beneath the television in the bar
at the corner of Cupar Street. People were coming and going,
bringing reports from the Leeson Street riot front. On the
coloured screen Harvey Smith lined up his mount to beat a
four-fault thirty-eight point three seconds round but the
drama of the horse-trial arena found no response in the Falls
Road pub. Too much was being reported by the frequent
battlefront-to-pub correspondents for the big man to gain a
wider audience than the three poorly-dressed and elderly men
who had accepted his invitation to have a drink.

One of the men said "My sister lives down there, just where
them bloody armoured cars is. She's on her own wi' the three
wee wans - they tuk her husband three weeks ago an' interned
him in Long Kesh an', as God's m'judge, he was in nathin'. The
only thing he iver thought about was fixin' at that oul house
and his oul motor - and, d'you know ... Mr. ..."

"Tony Kane," the big man flashed a smile. "It's John, isn't
it?"

"Naw, he's John. I'm Sammy Hughes and that's Frankie
Polland - Frankie's from the Ardoyne."

The big man was blowing his nose in a dirty handkerchief.
He put it in his pocket and drew out a crumpled packet of ten
Number Six. "Jasus! That's a hot spot! Ah was up there one
night wi' ma brother-in-law ... Ah've only two fegs, lads ... he's
known there - a mate he used to work wi'." He offered the
packet; two of the men refused but John took one. He crushed
the packet in his hand and threw it at the foot of the bar

sniffing loudly up his nose as he put the corrugated cigarette - in his mouth. "Mindya a wudn't like to live up there - but they can bloody fight! The soldiers niver got beyond Flax Street, yonder. A fella wi' a tammy-gun - game as a bloody fightin' cock!"

"Well, as A'm tellin' you, the fuckin' soldiers wrecked m'sister's house."

While John was impatiently re-starting his story Polland had said "Are you from about here?"

Tony Kane turned on a big smile and took Polland's scarce-heard question with his hand raised to postpone John's story "Meta-foric-ly speaking, Frankie, I'm from about where the action is! Ah 'ony wish to Jasus ah hadn't this bad ticker or ah'd be wi' the boys over there. Mindya, ah wus a lapsed Catholic before all this - but it brings ya' to yer senses." The big man looked solemn. "Actually, a'm in digs on the Lisburn Road wi' the blackest oul Orange bastard outa hell. Sorry, John. You wur sayin' ..."

John thrust his head forward, "Aye, the bloody soldiers ripped open tha furniture, broke the flures and ceilin' and bate poor Tommy Murphy - that's the brother-in-law - fornenst his wife and wee childur. Quinn an' Sammy Mullin wur down to luk the place over afterwards and they said ..."

The big man looked interested.

CHAPTER SEVEN

The Trial

Some effort had obviously gone into making the attic clubroom resemble a courtroom. Most of the steel stacking chairs, along with tables and other furniture, had been piled against a back wall. Only a section of the room, comprising about a third of its entire area was being used and this area was illuminated by a single unshaded light that sent movement in grotesque projection far into the shadows. The dartboard had been removed from its double-door fitting and, draped over this, was a small tricoloured flag of orange, white and green.

A short distance out from the flag-adorned wall three men were seated at a long narrow table. Their backs were towards the wall and, to the left of them, about three feet out from the long table at which they sat, another small table had been placed to enable Volunteer Con. Williams to record the proceedings. Facing Williams, at the right of the long table, sat the accused while, further out in the shadows sat a group of seven other men. A young man wearing an olive-drab combat jacket and a black beret was seated beside the door of the room; a Thompson sub-machine gun nestled between his legs, the butt trapped between his shoes, while his fingers played between the barrel and the cooling fins of the gun.

Liam Dempsey, a solicitor's clerk and a staff captain in the Provisional I.R.A., was acting as President of the court. At forty-eight years of age he was easily the oldest man in the room and, despite his staff rank, he was a comparative newcomer to the movement - in fact he was a member of just over one year's standing.

A wild streak had taken Dempsey to London six months before he was due to sit his finals for L.L.B. at Queen's University and, after three years bumming about the lunatic left in London, he had returned to Belfast, married and got a clerical job with a local firm of solicitors. He had the education and intelligence to do better but, just as his earlier wildness had revolted against the prospect of a legal career, now, by a strange antithesis, he was struck with a mildness of character that militated against professional ambition.

He had remained a quiet family man living with his wife and two teenage children in a housing estate at Finaghy until

August 1969. Even then, he was only slightly less quiet. He was more conscious of being a Catholic, perhaps – in a broad political sense; he was angry at the authorities, not because Catholic homes had been burned out and people had died, but because the Government had allowed themselves to remain prisoners of their own political past and were proving this by trying to fob off the blame for the murder and arson on the very people who had been the victims of the murderers and the arsonists. His was one of the many voices that, at that time, suppressed their anger and counselled restraint. The Government really recognised its guilt, he reasoned; it wanted to bring about change... to dismantle the old 'Protestant Parliament for a Protestant People' image; but, so successful had their earlier inculcation of sectarian poison been that it would take time now to eradicate it and the Unionist government had to be given that time for, despite their criminal past, they were the only instrument for extirpating the poison that still affected the Northern community.

Dempsey's voice was not a lone one; in the spring of 1970 it represented, consciously and otherwise, a fairly wide concensus of 'informed' Catholic opinion – but, then the summer came...

A logical extension of Dempsey's philosophy was that a guilty Government would forgive those who, in the period of its probation, trespassed against it. Inevitably, not all the Catholics felt as Dempsey did; some, especially in those areas that had experienced the carnage of 1969, felt they could sleep better with a gun under their pillow and, indeed, among the Protestants, too, the notion was rife that the Catholics would seek retribution for the events of Sixty Nine. The desire for guns was not confined to any one section of the populace.

The British Labour Government had, after August 1969, forced the resignation of the then Inspector General of the Royal Ulster Constabulary and replaced him with an English policeman, Sir Arthur Young. Probably more than any of the would-be pundits, Young grasped the essentials of the situation. Like Dempsey, Young realised the inevitability of people looking for the security of a gun after the events just past and he realised, too, that where there exists the desire there also exists the means of satisfying it. Accordingly, he paid more attention to placating the warring sides, to building up confidence and a feeling of security in both communities, to eradicating the DESIRE for guns than he did to risking the uneasy peace in searching for firearms.

It was when Young was replaced by his local deputy, a traditional R.U.C. officer whose standing in the past did not endear him to the Catholic community, that Liam Dempsey became really angry and, later, when it became obvious that the immediate priority of the Government and the British Army was the capture of all guns in Catholic hands, that anger became tinged with real fear. Then, it appeared to Dempsey and all who thought like him, the ultra-Protestant Unionist Party were using the British Army, as well as their traditional instrument, the police, to divest the Catholics of what little measure of security they found in their scant armament.

Dempsey had previously felt only faint sympathy for the I.R.A. It was a sympathy that manifested itself not so much in satisfaction with the things they did as in sorrow for the individual I.R.A. man who was killed or sentenced to imprisonment. In fact his sympathy was not political but, rather, an understanding of the feelings and motives of those of his fellow-Catholics who choose the path of militant republicanism. Now, with the hardening of government attitudes and the unleashing of the British military machine against the Catholics, he felt he was left without option. He had to find some hope of security, some escape from inert fear in the insecurity and active fear of the I.R.A. Like most of his kind, he was not concerned with the programmatic niceties between the 'official' and 'provisional' I.R.A's. -the Provos were on the offensive and he found Napoleonic comfort and satisfaction in this means of defence.

His administrative qualities were quickly discerned in the I.R.A. and his promotion to the Battalion Staff followed rapidly. Unfortunately, from his point of view, his legal training and occupation was also recognised and more and more now he found himself in the distasteful position he now occupied at the long table in the back-street club off the Falls Road - presiding over a court-martial.

The figure at his right was Sean O'Sullivan, a crippled school teacher who had been interned by the Government from 1957 until 1961. Sullivan was fiercely patriotic and, from experience, Dempsey knew that the very fact that a man left himself in a position to be accused before an I.R.A. court was, in itself, grounds sufficient for Sullivan to convict him.

The third member of the court, on Dempsey's left, was a man named Curtis. Dempsey had met him only once before at a Staff meeting but beyond that, knew nothing about him.

Dempsey looked at the accused man and wondered how he felt. He had never seen this Peter Doyle before tonight so he could not compare his demeanour now with his normal manner. He felt that this was important; people change in circumstances - the change from one attitude to its diametrical opposite can take a lifetime or can be compressed, in the crucible of circumstance, within moments. What had happened to Doyle since he was first questioned? Had he recognised the monstrousness of his offence? Had it, perhaps, made him truly what he had pretended to be? Dempsey cogitated the question; that was the failure of justice, it stopped behaviour at a given point in time and it held inexorably to that moment, destroying, if need be, the good that is for the bad that was.

The man, Curtis, had read the charges and when Liam Dempsey had asked Doyle how he answered to them he had said; "I am not guilty of the charges as they read - that is to say, I admit that I was in the British Army and that I joined the I.R.A. for the purpose of carrying out counter-espionage work, but..."

Dempsey interrupted him, "You plead innocent of the charges. You must leave it there for now but you will, of course, get the opportunity to give account of these matters after the prosecuting officer has stated his case and presented his evidence." He was conscious of the lugubriousity of his language and with "Will you leave it there, now?" his voice trailed off meekly.

O'Brien, Paddy Quinn's Company Intelligence Officer, a young clerk from the Belfast fruit markets, seemed near the end of his recitation - a recitation frequently interrupted by the court President. Now, again, Dempsey was bending forward across the table, his clenched knuckles immediately above its surface, waiting for a convenient moment to break into O'Brien's monologue. "...if then, Doyle is telling the truth when he says that after he realised what we really stood for, that we were not criminals but patriots fighting to free our country from the criminal imperialism of successive British governments, why hasn't he been able to tell us more about his activities within that criminal conspiracy - the British Intelligence Service? Who did he report to? What was the method of contact? What was the precise date of his remarkable conversion? He 'doesn't remember'! He doesn't even..."

Dempsey rapped louder on the table; the rising anger of O'Brien's tones had brought the little noises of creaking chairs and movement of feet and bodies as those at the back took renewed interest. This time O'Brien heard Dempsey, and the sneer borne on his unfinished sentence stayed on his lips as he turned to face the court President.

"The prosecuting officer must not assume that because Volunteer Doyle has not availed of his prerogative to nominate an officer of Ogligh na Eireann to present his defence, that he is not entitled to make a defence. Remember, you must stick to the charges presented to the original court of enquiry; anything additional thereto may only be introduced at the discretion of this court. Evidence of the defendant not having done something is not proof of..."

"I have not departed from the original charges - these have, in fact, been confessed to by Doyle." O'Brien was being openly insolent, angry at 'bloody Lawyer Dempsey messing about'. "I have stated..."

"You have said that Doyle..." Before Dempsey could continue O'Sullivan said, audibly, "O for Christ's sake! While we play Perry Mason here with this bastard his bloody mates are butcherin' our people across the Falls there, in Leeson Street!"

Dempsey was furious; he fenced with his anger as he removed his spectacles and was surprised at the calm of his own voice: "In view of these remarks from a member of this court, I have no option but to order that the accused Volunteer be held pending instructions from the Brigade O. C. about a new trial." Now his voice was shaking with his anger, "How we can talk about justice..."

Curtis was standing, "Look, this is all bloody nonsense. The bastard has confessed that he joined the I.R.A. to spy for the British Army. That's what the charges said he did! What do you want to do? Give him three of the best with the cane, tell him to say three Hail Mary's for penance and to mend his ways and then send him back to bloody Palace Barracks!"

"The Volunteer..." Dempsey raised his voice to shout down the roar of protest; "Yes, he IS a Volunteer! He was accepted into the Irish Republican Army and until it is proven beyond all reasonable doubt that he..."

Everyone was standing now. The man at the door looked nonplussed and uncertain but he, too, had got to his feet and was now facing the others, holding the Thompson in the action position but with the muzzle pointed downwards.

Dempsey had gathered up his papers and was making for the door - warning O'Brien as he did so that he was responsible for the prisoner's safety. He passed behind the sub-machine gunner and had his hand extended to the door handle when the door burst open, striking him on the face and sending him onto his backside on the floor.

Paddy Quinn charged into the room, stopped momentarily and then elbowed his way brutally towards Doyle who was standing at the end of the long table with his head lowered and his fingers arched lightly on the table.

"You fucking bastard!" Quinn clutched at Doyle's throat with his left hand; his right arm rose and fell several times in quick succession but his anger defeated his purpose. The foresight of the pistol which he was using as a bludgeon scraped Doyle's cheek below the left eye but, otherwise, its strength was dissipated on the shoulder padding of the victim's coat. Doyle raised his hands in an effort to protect his face; he tried to move back out of range of the blows but he tripped over the chair which had recently seated him and careered backwards on to the floor.

As Quinn aimed the pistol O'Brien broke the spell; he jumped forward, thrust his right arm against Quinn's chest and forced down the gun-holding arm. The others were active now; they were around Quinn, between him and his victim. Quinn was in a blind fury; he cursed and swore. "The bloody bastard!" His foot made contact, through the legs of the others, with Doyle's leg. "Control yourself Paddy for Christ's sake!" "Jesus, man what's got into you?" "You'll shop the bloody lot of us!" Together they pushed Quinn to a chair and, still around him forced him to sit down.

Doyle was on his feet; he had rubbed the back of his hand across his bleeding cheek and now the left side of his face was covered with blood and the continuing trickle was running down his face in a rivulet onto his chin and falling in drops onto his tie. The guard stood a few feet from him in a ridiculous action posture with the tommy-gun raised and pointed at him.

Dempsey was holding his mouth but his eyes and ears had provided an antidote to his pain. He stood, dumbfounded, looking at the scene, his hand again extended to the door handle. He retched as he swallowed the blood in his mouth then, quietly he opened the door and stepped silently onto the stairs.

Someone had moved sufficiently to give Quinn sight of Doyle. "Ask that bastard what he did with the jelly he took from Morgan's. Ask him! Ask him! The fucking bastard – go on, ask him! Go on, you bastard, tell them! You lousy spying cunt! Tell them!" Incredulity edged anger aside. "Y'know what he did?" Quinn's voice had taken on a quieter but more piercing tone. "Y'know what this cow did for his British paymasters? In order to antagonise the people of Ballymurphy and the Whiterock against us... go on - tell them, you bastard!... tell them who makes war on women and children for thirty pieces of silver. And he gave wee Sammy Morgan six quid for helping him and warned him not to mention it to us in case we would be angry at them doing an unofficial job. Jesus Christ! The bastard!"

"For God's sake, Paddy, stop the swearing man and tell us. Make your point!" Curtis was shaking Quinn as he voiced the impatience of the others. Doyle's face had gone ashen and his eyes burned with fear. Dazedly he stepped backwards and fell into the chair which someone had put upright. The machine-gunner moved in closer.

"The bastard blew the water pumping station on the Whiterock in order to alienate our support among the people and cause trouble between us and the... the 'officials' -and he used our stuff to do it!"

All eyes turned away from Quinn and fixed on Doyle. Hatred, puzzlement, anger and contempt lashed out at him in their gaze. He had his hands by his sides now, falling below the seat of the chair; his legs, nearly straight, applying pressure on the floor, forcing his body hard against the chair-back. The muscles of his face munched nervously and the blood flowed quicker now - but it was the wildness in his eyes, the sheer abandonment of hope, that was frightening.

Suddenly he rose to his feet like a man in a fever. No one moved; even the guard did not seem to read new danger. They just stood off and stared. Doyle's mouth opened and closed several times and he steadied his shaking form instinctively with his left hand on the table then he completed the slight movement of his legs that allowed him to place his right hand with firmness on the back of the chair. Saliva issued from his lips and mingled with the droplets of blood on his chin. He was a man in agony, an agony compounded of stark fear at the prospect of an impending terror of torture and death, and the terrible impediment to the disclosure of his motives - motives which had been, at best, only half-felt and now seemed so totally irrelevant to his plight.

His eyes were on the ground now and his body convulsed. He was whipped, defeated, desperate. Inevitably he must meet his fate from those who, like himself, knew pain, fear and desperation - but it was not their turn and they would not understand. The need to tell them, to make them understand, was more important now than anything else; it was not only that he wanted to beg for his life but because, too, he had an irrational fear of ignominy after death. He must accept their punishment for it was their way to hate, even more than treachery, the sycophancy of public cowardice. Now the fear was receding; he could straighten his shoulders, meet their gaze in the search for understanding.

He was confronting them! His eyes were now asking no mercy but yet without arrogance. Fear was still in his voice when he spoke but his words were neither fearful nor offensive.

"I will not deny the things you accuse me of. They are true - all true. But I must deny shame and the accusation of cowardice. You know that, if what I have done, I had done for the I.R.A. you would see only virtue and bravery in my action. Would the I.R.A. repudiate the services of a member who was prepared to gamble with his life by associating with the British Army to get valuable information? Would you call such action shameful or cowardly? I am not pleading for leniency from you but I would ask you why you are seeking more in the way of retribution from me than..."

They were standing about him, quiet, listening. Quinn, forgotten now by the others, had risen to his feet. His eyes still blazed their anger and his irritation with his comrades was revealed in his sidelong glances. His brain was a chafing mass of confusion as blind emotion, untempered by considerations of a moment in time beyond the present, poured hot anger through him.

"... The support of those who favour the I.R.A. is a legitimate target for those who fight the I.R.A. It was this support that I aimed to break when I planted the bomb at Whiterock Road. Of course, women and children suffered - they always..."

Quinn bulled his way through the human barrier that stood between him and Doyle. He stood for a moment, legs akimbo, before the man. Even the short movement, vicious in its determination, had left him breathless and he gulped air through a mouth contorted in an agony of blind, ruthless hatred. Then he raised the gun.

The echo of the two shots chased their cause and, for a full second, the room reverberated with a single, terrible, noise.

Part of Doyle's features had disappeared in the area between his nose and left eye and a pumping spring of blood oozed from his neck. For an endless second the still-erect form of the man belched its horror at its audience, then the knees collapsed quickly and the bloody form toppled in a heap.

They stood around in a collective, conscious, faint - only O'Brien falling to the mercy of unconsciousness. Quinn did not stare at his victim; he had turned and was already bounding down the stairs.

CHAPTER EIGHT

"What's it all about?"

Johnny Cairns had left Danno with Shields at McGivern's house and gone back in the direction of Quinn's place. As he moved through the mean streets he could hear the din of the fighting in Leeson Street. Obviously more people were being attracted to the riot. His comrades would have a difficult task getting the co-operation of the people - especially so if the Provisional I.R.A. was encouraging them to remain and become involved.

Johnny decided to turn back and take a look for himself. He walked at a steady pace down Clonard Street and re-crossed the Falls Road on to the Leeson Street side. The Luger in the waistband of his trousers was rubbing against his flesh; he stopped, took out his cigarettes, placed one in his mouth and moved into a doorway to shade the light from the wind. Before he turned again he had unbuttoned his jacket, moved the gun into the area of his navel and buttoned up his coat again.

· At the top of Leeson Street a crowd of several hundred people were assembled, their excitement silhouetted against the flames of a burning 'bus that lashed into the night further down Falls Road. The people at the top of the street were the elderly and the middle-aged. None were strangers to each other, for riot, like all fearful social phenomena, breaks down reserve and inhibition. They were a great mass of people in continual movement through one another, delaying to talk to one another or to one of the ever-changing groups that converged, listened, discoursed, broke up and reformed in a new pattern of characters each with its story, its rumour, its fear.

These were the fathers and mothers, the grandfathers and grandmothers who knew that somewhere down that ribbon of riot and rebellion were their kin, or who feared they might be. They were here in anxiety trying to dissipate their fear in anger or defiance or simply seeking the solace of others in like plight - others of the ghetto who had gone through it all before and who would understand.

Johnny elbowed his way into the seething mass of human movement in the street. The houses on either side now funnelled and amplified the din of falling stones and bottles and the more raucous battle cries of the front line of the rioters, punctuated every now and then by the dull crack of baton-round dischargers. Ironically every door down the corridor of hatred was open and groups of people stood around these little oases of fixed conversation.

Johnny was forced against a small knot of people at a doorway. He moved in towards the wall and stood still waiting for the ripple of people to pass by. The little group at the door resisted the movement of the crowd and, when the strength of the movement had waned, shifted back into the semi-circle around the doorway in which stood a thin woman who was obviously the resident of the house. As the noise eased the theme music of Panorama came to Johnny's ears from the partially-opened living room door. The conversation of the group had been maintained; the thin woman was saying "not at all Nellie! They were married down in St. Peter's, for I mind it well."

Johnny chuckled grimly in his mind; these people had absorbed riot and struggle into their daily lives; had learnt to live with it and adopt the pattern of their mundane lives... births... marriages... deaths... sleeping... sickness... loving... joy... sorrow to the whim of violence. Could they ever again adapt to peace when social madness created barriers which, if they rose superior to them, physically and mentally equipped them to absorb the grief and pain, the bitterness and hatred of continual strife into a normal background of living?

As he passed further down the street the activity of riot became more evident. A production-line of flagstone breakers, carriers and throwers had been established and, at one place, a small group of young men supervised the distribution of bottles of an oily liquid with rag wicks tied at their necks from steel-wire milk crates, but only to some of the hands that eagerly solicited them.

The petrol bombing was not, however, on the grand scale; only occasionally did the small candle of light course its path over the heads of those at the front of the riot. Sometimes the flicker of light was extinguished in the wind of its own course and the bottle shattered on the roadway spilling its lethal contents; sometimes the delicate flame held, capturing the vision and the voice of the mob before it burst its wild carpet of fire in the no-man's land between the soldiers and the rioters.

But the pace of riot was slow; all the brutality of language was present but Johnny could see that the rioters had found neither spirit nor purpose in leadership. Those keenest to on the battle were the young people - to whom it was just another nightly happening - and, now, contention within their own ranks dampened their effectiveness.

Johnny took in the situation quickly. The position of the troops had obviously not changed since Danno had reported to him and Shields earlier. The army commander at the Grosvenor Road side had two alternatives: he could attack the mob but he obviously had not the forces to deploy men through the maze of streets and would, therefore, find his front and his superiority of weaponry restricted by the width of the roadway, and the mob was so dense throughout the entire length of the street that its compression might endanger the two precariously-disposed outposts at the corners of McDonnell Street. The alternative was to play a waiting game; the vastness of the mob was a real danger but its potential was not being exploited by leadership. It could flare up in a bitter frenzy of general rioting or it could break up. The military commander appeared to have reasoned that the best way to cool the situation was by taking only such action as would minimise the danger to his men. Such action was now confined to the occasional use of rubber bullets directed at those straying too close to the barricade of vehicles or those identified in the act of throwing petrol bombs.

Johnny came further up the street and passed between the two military outposts at the corner of McDonnell Street. Young people milled around the vehicles on both sides of the street but, amazingly, despite the odd stone and bottle being thrown at the vehicles, some of those immediately around the military were engaged in not wholly unfriendly banter! Johnny could see the sergeant, on his right, between the two Saracens, actually smiling at a group of young people. He moved closer.

"You bloody think WE enjoy this?" It was Sergeant Jackson. "Look, lads, if we'd any bloody sense we'd all be home in bed. Right?"

One of the youths thus addressed by Jackson moved in closer and actually leaned on the mud-wing of the Saracen, his head not more than a yard from the soldier. "Ah, but we have a right here - this is our country. You shouldn't be here at all!"

"Go' blimey, lad, you know where I come from there's more bleeding Paddies than there's in the whole of the Falls - maybe in the whole of Belfast! - and I don't throw bloody stones and bottles at them."

A growing group was now around the space from which Jackson spoke. Somebody said "Do the bastard!" but the group

showed more approval for the one who said "No - let him talk!"
A teenage girl said, "Ah, but our people in England don't go
over wi' tanks and guns to make the English people do what we
want them to do!" and a young man followed with "Maybe if
England minded its own business and allowed us freedom to run
our own affairs there'd be no need for the Irish to emigrate to
England to do your donkey work."

Jackson looked serious; "You could well be right, boy. I
just don't know - I'm only a poor bloody soldier doin' as he's
told."

The replies were a variation of what was obviously a stock
rebuttal: "That's what the German war criminals said at
Nuremberg"... "You do what you're told - kill whoever the
officers tell you?"... "Holy Jasus! You're a hired gunman..."
"Not allowed to think for yourself, eh?"... "How d'ye know yer
bin told right?"

Jackson smiled, "Alright, so maybe I am a stupid bugger
but you must admit, we stopped the Protestants burning your
homes and shooting' you - now that couldn't be bad, could it?"

"They're still at it an' you're protectin' them!"... "Aye,
you've tuk their place now - you're murderin' us instead!"...
"Sure youse are comin' in an' wreckin' our homes, now!"...
"'Twas England bred that hatred between Catholics and Protestants!"

Two other soldiers were now visible, one on each side of
the sergeant. Johnny stared at them. The one on the right
was a corporal, alert and unfriendly; the other was a fresh-
faced, nice-looking lad and Johnny could see that he was sick
with fright. They would speak with a different accent to the
people around here but they probably came from pretty much
the same environment themselves with basically similar
prejudices about the Irish, the Jews, the black peoples or the
Russians, or some other mindless notion that could carry the
blame for their material miseries.

Jackson was now looking with due seriousness at the group
that confronted him across the bonnet of the Saracen. He
shook his head, "Look, honestly, as far as I'm concerned, I don't
want to kill or hurt anybody and I don't want to see others
doin' it either - an', of course, y'couldn't really blame me for
not wantin' to get it myself! There's a young kid dead over
there... I knew him... he was... well, he was a nice lad. He was
just like any of you lads... a nice lad. His name was Carter.
He's dead - so... has it helped anybody? How d'you think his
old lady will feel when she hears that he's copped it? Seriously, why d'we want t'go killin' each other for? What's it all

72

about? Look, this is Buick; this boy here, he's Charters. What's the difference between us an' you lot? Now you look a sensible lad." Jackson was addressing himself to the most voluble member of the group, an aggressive looking teenager with a mop of black tousled hair. "I'd honestly like to know what it's all about; maybe you could tell..."

"He's a clever bastard, that sergeant!" Johnny turned to the voice at his left shoulder. The big man was not looking at him but across at Jackson and his audience. "I'll bet if he had a few more men with him and they'd not been cut off without their gas masks - that's why that lot down there have not been tossing gas - he wouldn't be asking them to improve his knowledge of Irish history. They didn't want reasons when they were kickin' the balls off that poor kid at the bottom of the street a short time ago or when they dragged poor oul Tommy Murphy away from his wife and kids for Long Kesh!"

The big man continued to stare in the direction of the soldiers. His eyes seemed bitter and the muscles around his mouth were taut over his teeth. Suddenly he looked around at Johnny, the look of bitterness dropped from his face and he appeared embarrassed - as though he had only now become aware of the other's closeness. "Makes you bloody mad, doesn't it?" The words were tossed off without heat.

Johnny smiled thinly at the big man. "Well, he's in a pretty difficult predicament. I suppose any of us would..." but the big man snapped back at him before he could finish "Y'think those bastards would talk if the shoe was on the other foot? Look, Mac, I've seen them in action! I seen them drive over a kid of five an' they didn't want to get out an' talk!" Again the big man's features changed, "Sorry for snappin' at you but I just can't stand them bastards - look, let's get this crowd organised an' we can really fix them!"

"No!" Johnny was angry. "That's exactly what we must not do. There's no kudos for the people in this kind of nonsense. If you want to help, I would suggest that you should try to get them off the street."

"Ya! we should lie down an' let them walk over the Cathlik people! Christ... we've lain down for years an' where'd it get us?"

"Nowhere. The same as this will get us! And, inciden- tally..." The big man was looking impatiently at the almost stagnant riot. Johnny's voice trailed off - the other was not interested, he concluded. Just another poor sod wanting to wash away the centuries in a street punch-up.

"If a few of the Provos come along they'll fix them

bastards! Jasus but I wish I didn't have this wonky ticker!" The big man placed his right palm over his chest. "Ah, there's dam' all going to happen here tonight - fancy a drink, Mac?"

"Not just now, thanks. As a matter of fact..." the crash of breaking glass and the rush and press of bodies interrupted the conversation. Some joker, bored by the mere shuffle of riot, had cast his own dangerous diversion by throwing a lighted petrol bomb into the air. If it was aimed at the military it was a particularly bad shot for its trajectory had taken it over the heads of the crowd, where its flickering light had mercifully signalled a warning and allowed those beneath to clear a base for its landing. Miraculously, the compulsion of self-preservation cleared a rough circle in which the shattering glass and instant splash of flame found no victims other than those who cursed their protest in the wild compression of the mob adjoining the area where the bomb had fallen.

Fingers of flame were extending outward from the inferno; they lapped voraciously at the viscous liquid, consuming it in its course and leaving little maps of discarded whiteness on the roadway. Only the centre burned steadily and furiously, climbing above the heads of the mob and sendng its eerie projections of forms, large and grotesque, high up on the walls and windows of the surrounding houses. Immediately around the blaze, enquiry and protest vied with each other in oaths and curses while those further to the rear pressed inward in new fear or anticipation - throwing their verbal release into the general cacophony of deafening incoherence.

It was the first time Johnny Cairns had really seen the mob in all its terrible unpredictability. This was the puss of the body social; a horrible Frankenstein compounded of ignorance, fear, kicks, insults; here was the degradation of kennel-like homes, kow-towing to authority, of knowing only the place at the bottom, frustration; here was the price society had to pay for newspaper--and-fish-and-chips in a caviare world; here was the mere poverty of employment and the dire poverty of the dole. Each part was a pliable "yes sirring" being; obsequious - broken under myriad decades of hereditary poverty and yielding, always yielding, to the big voice of a ubiquitous authority and answering only humbly and in accents contrasting with those of "better" people of greater state.

Here are the parts come together in a terrible whole! Here the small tongues shout together in deafening defiance - if without harmony. Here is a frightening power beating its arms, kicking its feet, scraping its hands in the ground for the weaponry of resistance. Here is ugliness of tongue, of language, of behaviour, all contorting destructively - ready to destroy streets, houses, buses, cars and all the other furniture of order. Here is beauty; the terrible, beautiful ugliness of the craven spirit awakening to a partial appreciation of its misery. Here is divine discontent! Here is purification - spluttering, swearing, struggling, in blind desperation to cleanse away the law that enshrines its misery and the order that is its subjection! Here are all the vices, the foulnesses, the loathsomeness, marshalled together, unknowingly, in the service of virtue - the virtue of human progress... of history!

But that virtue, that progress, needs articulation. This force needs controlling... needs its political genie to use it in the service of freedom and history. We must become its tongue - its directors, its..its... Somewhere in Johnny's mind Nora Quinn's voice said, "Its masters! Its new masters that will use it to sweep away the old regime of ugliness and impose on it the freedom to do what it is told!" Johnny's thoughts stumbled; hell! Nora's utopian! Her ideas are fine but she's utterly unrealistic - imagine talking REASON to THESE people! Nora's mocking voice repeated in his mind "these people! these people! THESE PEOPLE?" and he told himself that HE knew what he meant.

Nora was sweet... nice... a lovely girl. Yes, intelligent, kind, feeling... but - oh hell! She was a calculating, intense, incisive... conscience! Somewhere reason had to bow before the superiority of emotion. It was simply... Christ! You can't FEEL reason and people act on feelings! He must take that one up with her. But her reasoning was elusive - it always seemed to be a jump ahead with a neat, obvious little answer, ready to devour argument. But the telling argument - real reason - had to be forged from the materials at hand - from this! His eyes had wandered to the soldiers still illuminated behind their trucks by the dying glow of the petrol bomb and he only half heard Nora say "If it's chicken soup you want you'll not make it from wood shavings" and the message of his vision probed out his puzzlement.

He stared at the young soldier's face. Charters was more relaxed now and the play of light and shadow on his face highlighted his youth and the beauty of his frail humanity. For some reason Johnny's eyes were intent on the throat of the young soldier, the slender column that linked the senses to the powerhouse. Himself, Shields, Boyle, Hagan and the others, they would soon be around and about, closing like the fingers of fate on that throat. Their object - my object! - is to drive the movement of feeling... of hating... loving... laughing...

from that unknown face that was tied with a hundred strings to the hearts of others. Why had he to die and open the floodgates of sorrow in a hundred breasts? Maybe there is no one to care and he'll die unmourned. The thought hurt. Maudlin nonsense! He is a soldier, a mercenary of death - a mere order. He and his comrades stand between us and liberty and they must move over or die!

Again Nora cleared her throat in his mind but before he could grasp the fullness of her stricture his eye was taken with the big man who had been talking to him immediately before the petrol bomb was thrown. In the ensuing crush they had been separated and now the big man stood across from him and immediately beside the bonnet of the Saracen over which Jackson, Buick and Charters peered. Jackson's late audience had mixed in the excitement of the flames and the soldiers were free, for the moment, of the attention of the mob. Johnny's eyes picked out the big man; he was conversing with Jackson. He stood with his back to the Saracen and it was the slightness of his lip movement that impinged dramatically on Johnny's mind and the thought was confirmed when his eyes met those of the big man and the response to his look was a strange, panicked, friendliness.

Johnny Cairns stepped back into the enveloping crowd.

CHAPTER NINE

Pennies for the Bogside

It had started to rain; a mild cooling drizzle falling sparsely on the dusty streets and leaving the pavements with a fine film that made walking treacherous. Cairns walked close to the wall past the doors and windows of the narrow houses. He had met Danno as he left Leeson Street and had sent him back to relay his suspicions about the big man to Shields and advise him that no action should be taken at the scene of the riot until he reported back. He knew Shields would pass the word to the others and keep them appraised of the situation. He had also sent word to Shields that he was trying to make contact with the Provos to acquaint them with the suspected activities and location of the big man.

Perhaps the best way to make contact with the Provos would have been to go back to Sorrella Street and get some of the local men, all of whom probably knew someone connected with the Provisional I.R.A. The only Provo he knew was Paddy Quinn. He laughed inwardly as his motive revealed itself; he wanted to see Nora. Perhaps - he shivered at the thought - it was a premonition.

What would his mother... no! ... more especially, his FATHER, say if...? The thought had often occurred to him but always in the safe surroundings of his workshop where definite judgement, borne dramatically on the mind's eye could be deferred by the more immediate claims of a faulty diesel pump or worn out pressure plate. But here walking along the wet street, with the thought of Nora in the context of a premonition... a premonition! Nora would laugh at that!

The wind carried the clamour of events in Leeson Street; a medley of dull sounds bound by distance in a constancy of noise - unidentifiable in its variations with people but rather with some odd remorseless engine throbbing its purposelessness for eternity... What would his father say? He saw the copy of the NEWSLETTER on the living-room table; he saw his own face stare up at him. He tried for the caption but it was beyond his composition. Christ! That would give the NEWSLETTER a headache! A rabidly Unionist newspaper explaining away a "terrorist" who was not a Catholic!

In the picture on the screen of his mind his mother was sitting on the edge of one of the big rust easy chairs; she was a small woman with a long body and she looked tall when she was sitting. As Johnny saw her now in his mind's eye her eyes were red - yes, she would cry; she would cry quietly, bitterly - not the tears that would wash sorrow away but deep tears from within, tears that would last even afterwards, when she had disciplined them to the moments of her seclusion. She would never know why he had died but her love would sanctify his purpose and, to her, there would have to be good in what he died for.

His father, grey and heavy, would be seated on one of the dining-room chairs, on his face a look of blank stupefaction. His face always went blank when he had a problem, he had never learnt the trick of hiding the fact that he was thinking and he would be thinking, thinking as he had never thought before - for the death of his son in such circumstances would represent - Johnny's mind baulked at the thought... no, it was true... it would represent only the biggest problem that James Henry Cairns had ever encountered. He would not feel the loneliness... the terrible irrevocability; he would have no pictures of yesterday and no pounding on the mind that never again....no feeling of physical pain as his heart pushed on his lungs... no loss of direction... of purpose. Just a problem.

What would they say in the street? In the shipyard where he was a foreman boilermaker - a wholly Protestant trade in the Belfast yards? He who had been twice Worshipful Master of the local Orange Lodge ... in the Black Preceptory - where Catholics were regarded like 'white niggers' - alright, if they kept their place! And the Masons, too! What would he say? How would he be able to explain that his son was the dead I.R.A. man on the front of the NEWSLETTER? John held on to the picture of his father; he even closed his eyes so that it would not elude him. He saw him sitting there, bolt upright, inert, inwardly devoured by panic as the thought of one terror brushed another aside and, as his thoughts marshalled and crystallised into a single pity. It would be for himself and not the dead architect of his misery.

Johnny lifted his face to the rain; he'd had enough of such thoughts. They had brought no moment of truth -he'd always known that his father would have loved him only if he had moulded him - but it was a sort of coming together of many truths that had ventured across his mind since that Sunday, twelve years ago, after the Apprentice Boys' Parade.

He was sixteen at the time and he had just returned from the city of Derry after having partaken in the annual Apprentice Boy's Commemoration of the closing of the City's gates before the forces of King James the Second in 1689. There had been no trouble during the commemoration ceremony and, afterwards, Johnny had gone with a few friends to explore the City. At a place some distance along the roadway that was the top of the ancient walls they had come across a number of elderly Apprentice boys in the company of a group of teenagers belonging to Johnny's Lodge.

One of the older men was leaning out over the parapet; beneath him was a wide debris-scattered rectangle of vacant gound adjoining two rows of back-to-back slums. This was part of The Bogside, one of the Catholic ghetto areas of the City. A number of ill-clad children were gathered in the square gazing up at the elderly man and his companions. The man on the walls had a number of pennies in his left hand.

"Hi, Mister; Mister - throw!"

"No mister! Over here - they got two!"

"Mister please! Throw me one!"

The voices of the children mingled with the laughter of some of those standing on the wall. The man threw another penny far out to his left and immediately there was a wild charge of young feet churning up the dust that enveloped the scramble of bodies shoving, pushing and writhing on the ground for the prize. As the children, dirty and dishevelled, emerged from the scrum revealing a grimy urchin holding aloft the penny the man shouted "Hi...ii!" while his right arm extended quickly in the motion of throwing a coin to his right. Immediately the children charged in that direction but the man had foxed them and now, with a movement under his left arm, he pitched the coin in the opposite direction. The children, too late, grasped the deception and turned about; some were knocked over in the quick about-face, others grasped at clothing in an effort to delay competition and one front-runner kicked another who was about to pass him and brought him to the ground.

The coin thrower was joined in his laughter by most of the older men but a few of the younger men were not amused and Johnny shared their embarrassment. Young Jim Cathcart, who was in Johnny's Lodge, said, "For fuck's sake knock it off! If yer gonna give the kids somethin' give it. Don't make cunts of them!"

The older man turned slowly to the youths; "Who was that?" His heavy face was stern beneath its uniform bowler. He stared at them, lashing them with his gaze. "Nice langweg, indeed, for an Apprentice Boy! The fenians there," he indicated the area below the walls where the children were again assembling and shouting for more pennies, "will have somethin' to tawk about, won't they? Yer here for a religis service an' youse use that sort of tawk. Man, them papish childer won't larn much about the true faith frum your example, will tha'?"

Cathcart had looked sheepish but the other's reference to example re-armed him. "Am bloody shure your example 'll get no converts, Trimble. Your a bloody oul hip-o-crate! If y'want to give the childer somethin'..." Cathcart shouldered his way past Trimble to the wall. "A coupla bloody coppers and he wants the bloody kids to grovel in the shit! Here kids!" He had pulled a handful of silver and copper, all the money he had, out of his trousers pocket, "Here! Divide that roun'. Buy sweets or somethin'!"

Most of the younger Apprentice Boys showed their agreement with Cathcart by going to the edge of the parapet and handing down exceptional largesse much to the delight of the children.

Trimble was indignant. "Ah wonder wud ya be so genrous ta yer own sort!" Then, turning to Cathcart, "Of course there's some doubt about who yer sort is - isn't there?"

Johnny and some of the others pulled Cathcart back and Johnny did not fully understand what he meant when he looked straight at Trimble and said "Am not ashamed at what ah done. Maybe there's a lessin in it for you."

Later, on the train going back to Belfast, Cathcart sat with Johnny and they discussed the incident at the Walls. "The bloody joke is that Trimble hisself lives in a stinkin' wee slum no better nor those down thar in the Bogside where he wus throwin' his pennies!" said Cathcart. Johnny urged his friend to forget the matter but Cathcart continued to fume.

It was then that Johnny learned that Trimble had reported Cathcart to the Lodge committee for attending a Catholic service. "Wus the fella tha' works wi' me's father, Johnny. I used to'go down ta ma mate's house all the time when his oul fella was alive. He wus a dacent oul spud - many a night he giv' Danny an' me the price of a smoke and nither him nor his wife iver wanted to know whither I wus a Taig or a Prod. He died wi' a heart attack and Danny an' the oul woman ast me if Ah wanted to go to the funeral an' Ah did wanna go an' pay ma respects. He wus buried from the chapel - Ah donno how tha' oul cunt, Trimble, knew Ah was there - tell yi the truth, Johnny, Ah didn't know we weren' allowed to go ta a Cathlik funeral - but Ah'd a bloody went anyway. But oul fuckpot heerd about it an' Ah'm carpetit befoer the bloody Lodge."

His mother had given him a second plate of soup. As usual, she would fuss over him until she was satisfied that he had had his fill. His father was sitting at the fire reading the BELFAST TELEGRAPH with its report and pictures of the day's Apprentice Boys Rally at Derry. He had read out some bits to Johnny and had come over to the table on one occasion to show him a half-page photograph of a Government Minister addressing the Rally. Johnny rested his spoon on the side of his plate; he was thinking of Trimble... of Cathcart. "Father. Do you think it's wrong for an Orangeman to go to a Roman Catholic funeral?"

His father continued for a time to hold the newspaper at chest level but Johnny knew that he had stopped reading. His face had gone blank - when he was thinking, and he was thinking now, Johnny always had an impulse to snap his fingers in front of his father's eyes. The paper came down slowly on to his knees and he shifted himself in his seat, cleared his throat and said, "Eh - what's that?" -just the same as when Johnny had asked him years ago if some men really 'went' with other men.

Johnny told him about his friend Cathcart being in trouble with his Lodge for going to his workmate's father's funeral.

"Ah! but that's not for goin' to a Roman Catholic funeral; that's for attending a papist service."

Johnny could not appreciate the distinction. "Surely, father, the 'service' bit is only part of the funeral in this case and, at any rate..."

He was surprised by his father's vehemence. Masses were a blasphemy... the Roman Church was anti-Christ... papist priests were servants of the devil ... Catholics were cunning ... the thin edge of the wedge ... get us caught up in this unholy innocence! Spain, Portugal and the Ulster Constitution became interwoven with his father's theology and 'fenians', the I.R.A. and Satan were mentioned as members of the same conspiracy.

Johnny was shocked. He knew his father was not an unkind man and that, in normal circumstances, he would not be anxious to learn the religious or political beliefs of the recipients of his generosity. He knew his father was a member of all the Orange and Loyalist organisations but he thought that this was like his own membership of the Junior Orange Order and the Apprentice Boys - a sort of traditional social-cum-religious outlet, happily without the need to pursue the purposes of their grim, bitter and, to some extent, historically indistinct, past.

"But, surely father, you can't really believe all THAT?

81

What you are saying is that not only is the Roman Church a false religious doctrine but that adherence to that Church makes people cunning, deceitful - you even said, 'dirty'! You are saying that Catholics are, in fact, completely different to other people. I'm sorry, father, but I think that's a contemptible doctrine; it's like... you know, father, one of the teachers was telling us about one of the Nazi leaders during the last war. What as his name...? Julius Str..Streitcher, Stricher, I'm not sure - something like that. Anyhow, this particularly offensive character had the job of indoctrinating the German people against the Jews and he said all the things against the Jews that you've just said about Catholics. Seems to me that whatever the apologetics of Orangeism, the implications of its philosophy add up to an evil social doctrine that's no better than..."

"I don't hate Catholics." Cairns senior said huffily, obviously concerned that his son should have 'turned his tongue' on him. "An' the Orange Institution stands for freedom and religious liberty and teaches us to love our enemies."

The heat in his own voice surprised Johnny and even as he was speaking he realised that the Cathcart episode was not the beginning of this; a whole series of little doubts, irks and questions had been coalescing in his mind over a period; these had loaded the gun and the incident in Derry had merely squeezed the trigger.

"Love your 'enemies', father! How bloody noble! Love them but don't mix with them! Love them but be vigilant for they are our enemies! That, in a nutshell, is our loyal Orange philosophy! Oh yes, we can quote the legalistic formula of brotherly love, religious liberty and all the other patronising bits but let's leave the 'fenians' in no doubt about who is boss; let's march up and down the bloody roads in our thousands with our flags and banners boasting our victories and our martial music reminding the 'fenians' that we beat them before and can still do it! Rub their noses in it! You know well, father - you all know, and THAT'S what's so bloody disturbing - that, despite all the lofty theories, the protective propaganda of brotherly love and all that, there is the PRACTICE - the loathing of our fellow human beings because of a dispute over some silly theological commas. Yes, father, Trimble is fairly typical; march with our banners to divine service with our flutes and drums reminding the "fenians" we beat the shit out of them at Derry, Aughrim and the Boyne!"

The full strength of James Cairns was in the blow but it was struck with the open palm. It took Johnny across the left cheek and seared its anger in fingers of red welts across his face. His father said something about using foul language 'in this house' but even this change of approach he was not prepared to defend as he stormed out of the room.

The Cairns home had crumbled after that. Johnny had left school and taken work in a local garage. He lapsed in his membership of the Orange Order and the Apprentice Boys and acquired no new interests though he had more time to read now and broadened the scope of his reading to include those subjects which had wrought such a dramatic change in relations between him and his father.

After a time his mother gave up her attempts to reconcile her husband and son. Johnny had tried to build a new, man-to-man, relationship with his father in which each would accept the virtues of common ground and avoid the differences that had arisen between them. If the younger man was acquiring a new outlook he kept it to himself; but not so his father. To James Cairns there was goodness and evil and his concept of goodness was the centre of his moral universe. He could not be quelled; every subject, every activity, was reason for firm assertion of his views - not as an invitation to argument but, rather, as a stance that defied argument. Inevitably, Johnny adopted his habits to the avoidance of his father.

He was concerned for his mother. Even though she attempted to multiply her kindnesses to both her husband and son in their separation her resolution not to take issue with his son was construed by her husband as an act of betrayal. She was a woman torn in her affections, walking a domestic tightrope and enduring silently the quiet abuse and innuendo of her husband. Less than a year after the estrangement, she was ten years older. Johnny felt his pity for her as she became quieter and more surreptitious in her normal attentions and he knew that these were the result of the encroaching frictions with his father.

When he was seventeen he joined the British Army.

Johnny Cairns had spent the last two years of his military service in Aden. As a motor mechanic in the big R.E.M.E. depot he was sheltered from the actual fighting with the Arabs though, as a British soldier, he had to endure the confinement and other hardships that resulted from the guerrilla campaign.

He was not insensitive to the brutality of his comrades and he was all the more shocked because he knew them. He knew Sergeant Erikson who had smashed the pelvis of a twelve year-old Arab boy as he stood at a street corner selling newspapers. "I put the full toe of my bloody boot right into his stinking rectum - the little wog bastard!" Erikson had explained to the Major that the boy had given him a "dirty" look and spat at him.

Jenkins was the best driver in the depot; a hearty, generous fellow who could always be relied on to help a comrade. He had shot the old Arab shopkeeper dead because he had come to the front door of his shop with a sweeping brush in his hand. "I thought the old bastard was going to have a pot-shot at me!"

Hoare, Cleaver and Herne had kicked the sixteen year-old Arab youth to death but the youth was on the Security Force's 'wanted' list.

Major Hynds - the lads called him Hans Anderson - was the public relations officer. He was a big man with an honest face who often prefaced his press comments with a sentence including the word "distressing".

The viciousness of the searches, the torture of prisoners and suspects, the indiscriminate shootings, the wanton destruction of property - they all knew about these things and, indeed, most of them, at some time or another, partook in one or more of these activities; and yet most of them were sincerely shocked at charges of murder or brutality. There was an unreasoned, unspoken, process of rationalisation; the enemy was cunning, deceitful, rebellious, murderous; he didn't come out in the open but hid behind civilian anonymity; he was everywhere with mouth closed, ears open and gun cocked. Whatever was done was done on the enemy. Killing and brutality, degradation and destruction, was not the way they would have chosen; it was the only way left open by the nature of the conflict.

When Johnny had returned to Belfast after his demobilisation from the army he had joined the Labour Party. For a time he immersed himself in political work in the solidly Unionist Shankhill district. But various influences were at play in him. The unimaginative and pettifogging reformism of local labour politics frustrated him; his experiences in Aden had crushed any feeling of loyalty that had lingered towards Britain and had opened the way for an increasing inclination towards the thesis that, economically, the country, north and south, was being stultified by the Border and the partition politics it had given rise to.

Johnny had been one of a minority of Protestants who had seen promise in the beginnings of the Northern Ireland Civil Rights Association. Here, he thought, was an opportunity to marshal the working people behind a non-sectarian banner for elementary democratic rights; to get them working together for an achievable political end. The Government, too, thought this a possibility and saw the danger in this attack on its sectarian foundations; so the Government resorted to force in an attempt to stop Civil Rights demonstrations and, to justify its actions, mounted a massive campaign to convince the Protestant working class that the Civil Rights agitation was a Republican plot.

It was the success of this propaganda that had created the conditions for sectarian rioting, brought down two Prime Ministers, rent the Government party asunder with dissension and bickering and set in train the events which prompted the growth and credibility of the militant Republican movement which, inevitably and inexorably, drew on the anxieties and emotions of the ghetto Catholics.

Among the Republicans whom he met in the Civil Rights movement, Johnny Cairns' Protestantism was symbolic; it demonstrated that Protestants and Catholics could unite in the struggle to achieve an independent Ireland providing that independence was given class orientation. Inevitably, the trust and friendship of the Republicans was reciprocated by Johnny in a sympathy with Republican ends and, later, when the British Government placed the British Army at the disposal of the local Unionists to use against the Catholics and Republicans, conditions became such that Cairns, and many thousands of like mind, became reconciled to Republican means.

He had met Nora Quinn in the house of a Republican a short time after joining the official I.R.A. Their friendship had been born in political argument and their love had matured in proportion to their mutual appreciation of each other's essential honesty of purpose. Nora was uncompromising in her opposition to both wings of the I.R.A. but she was not insensitive either to the material circumstances that begat the movement or to the plight of those involved - no more than was she unappreciative of the different conditioning and circumstances of the British soldiers and members of the local police.

Her criticism of the Republicans, her bitter opposition to violence as a political weapon and her theoretical refusal to differentiate between what she regarded as the political ignorance and immaturity of the active participants on all sides should have earned her the hatred of the Republican elements. In practice, however, she did discriminate between "the purposeful violence of Authority and the inevitable violent reaction of the oppressed." Again, she was utterly trustworthy and, while she refused to help the I.R.A. in its

85

military exploits, she could be relied upon to give succour to the wounded or the fugitive - though she would have argued that she would give the same help to their enemies.

If she had been plain her intellectuality would probably have been more readily accepted - and resented; but Nora Quinn was not plain. She was a tall girl with a strong, almost boyish, face in which vigour was feminised by the delicacy of her mouth and wide-set dark eyes. Her face was framed in the thick ebony brown of her hair that cascaded loosely on to her shoulders. Usually, her dress showed her protest to the pretty, frilly, female; she had kept the natural adornments of her femininity but, neither by dress nor cosmetics, did she add embellishment. She was neither the liberated anti-woman antithesis of the dolly-bird nor, even, her intellectual half-sister.

Nora had spent the latter years of her secondary school life in dedicated study, rising superior to both the poverty of her orphan-home life and the limitations of her Catholic voluntary school. But poverty had imposed its denials and her medical ambitions finally had to be restricted to a nursing career. She had started that career in the nursing school of Belfast's Royal Victoria Hospital where she was now employed as a staff nurse.

As Johnny turned the corner from Waterford Street he was thinking of her. To the others, Nora was ... well, Charlie Shields had said, "Christ, Johnny, she's a beautiful girl!" She dominated them and yet they did not resent it. He remembered now her baiting Shields: "Yes, Charlie, that's fine for you - you've got the material means of the good life ... though ... " she laughed and, unwittingly, thrust her parenthesis into Charlie's private thoughts, "I sometimes think that it takes a materialist to appreciate that man does not live by bread alone. But about this so-called Socialist Workers' Republic you speak about, won't you still have to work to produce things for sale and profit? Won't the overwhelming majority of people still be obliged to sell their only possession - their mental or physical ability to work - for wages, Charlie, just as now? And won't the economic laws that determine the value of wages in any society, whether the employers are private companies or the State, continue to exist?"

Charlie said, "At least we'll be free, Nora. We'll not have bloody British soldiers knocking down our doors in the middle of the ... "

Nora interpolated: "Irish soldiers, then? And who'll be

free, Charlie? The only freedom the working class will ever have as long as wealth is produced to satisfy the market and not human needs, is the freedom to spend their lives working for wages that keep them in mere poverty - with spells of dire poverty on the dole, when the market is satiated."

Charlie had laughed, stretched forward and tossed her hair. "God, Nora, you're smart as well as lovely - I wish I was twenty-one!"

The rain was heavier now. It would help - many of those in Leeson Street would risk a baton, a lungful of tear gas or even a bullet, but the rain would send them home.

The front window of Quinn's house was lighted. Good. Nora would surely be home. Johnny hoped her brother would not be there - but it was him he had come to see!

As he stopped at Quinn's door the big man turned the corner, close in against the wall. He stopped and flattened himself against the first doorway as Johnny disappeared into the short hallway.

CHAPTER TEN

Murder in Aden

Oliver Clements hated rain.

It wasn't just a matter of disliking rain as something that restricted one, that made one all wet and sent its sticky fingers down one's neck. It wasn't the normal dislike of those who say "terrible day, isn't it?" With Clements it was hate. He hated rain. The necessity of the stuff, its absolute essentiality, was lost on him; he didn't think of it that way. As far as he was concerned, it was uncomfortable and unpleasant- - an unpleasantness that was not within his will to control and, therefore, he hated it.

He didn't make a thing of it, of course. When it wasn't raining he never thought about it; just as he never thought about the motorist holding the crown of the road at thirty or the plane that was delayed or the newsvendor who was sold out of his newspaper or the waitress who delayed his meal. It was only when these things happened that his hatred was fanned into a flame, sometimes a wild, uncontrollable fury as though he was the target of some unseen conspiracy, some personal plot thought out in a vicious consciousness against him. It had always been so; it was a weakness that had combined with his great physical capacities to give him an impatience and volatility that was seen as strength.

He had never thought about it; that was not his way. As far as Oliver Clements was concerned, life was an island. You were fondled and fed through babyhood, educated in the way of usage for other bloody people so that you were an appendage of theirs ... an instrument ... device ... a loving little syrupy decoration adjusted and screwed into the right degree of pleasantness and service. "Do what you're told, Oliver!" "Oliver, Daddy WILL be furious!" "We don't want boys in our class with dirty nails - do we boys?" "The examiner will want to know ... " "Right, Clements, you go now!" "You will be EXPECTED to ... " They got you all screwed up! Love them, Clements! Do what you're told, Clements! You will have to ... Clements!

Jump in a stinking muddy puddle ... I bit your fucking arm, mammy dear! Shit on Pythagoras, dear teacher! Yes, look - it's my naked thing! Bugger you, Mr. Jones, Mrs. Jones and you, too, God Jones! Ballox the Major!

You're bloody shit, Alice dear!   Bloody, abominable, craven, demanding SHIT, darling.   Bloated with ignorance, sweetheart.   Oliver's little boy, Oliver ... sweet, hateful, spoiled little bastard!

I'm bloody Clements!   Remember me?   What about me? CLEMENTS ... Oliver - under "C": male ... education ... height ... weight ... religion ... state ... distinguishing marks or feature ... I.Q. assessment.   Right turn!   Forward!   About Face!   Fall down!   Jump up!   Lie on your fucking back Clements!   Adjust, man! adjust;   You must take this bloody woman, man!   He's your little boy, Oliver.   Of course I love your fashionable face, dear!   You're my little man - you pimple-faced, vicious, little fuckpot!

Oliver Clements ... R.I.P.   A good son ... intelligent pupil ... loving husband ... good father ... intelligent courageous soldier.   Pity the fucking battery ran out or he could perform for ever.

The good life.   Bloody rain!

Clements took out a packet and shielded his lighter with his hands as he lit a cigarette.   He delayed the flame in his palms, drawing heat until its burden killed it.

That bastard's up to no good!   I knew bloody well he was up to no good when I saw him in Leeson Street and he suspects ME!   We saw our guilt in each others eyes.   Clements squeezed further back into the doorway.   Still ... why did he oppose me when I suggested stirring it up?   This was Quinn's street; he had gone into Quinn's house.   Quinn was the local Provo bigwig .. hm .. if that bastard's a Provo why did he not want me to help to stir it up?

Clements mulled over the infinity of alternatives; it was mere coincidence that this fellow had gone to Quinn's house; they were having a meeting; he was going for... oh, Christ! he could be going for any number of reasons -but, for sure, he's on to me.   He knows!   That's why he had walked through the rain - had left the riot scene hurriedly.   He was passing on the glad tidings!   This theme now dominated his thinking.

Clements chuckled. It was his situation.   He had caused it, would play it through and would end it.   It was his own world in which he was God.   Nobody had written a book setting out the rules for a man standing in a bloody doorway with a point thirty-two Harrington and Richardson automatic tucked in the pocket of the dirty jacket below the old mac watching a house into which he knew someone had gone to tell somebody else that he was a bloody agent.   Fig. bloody one or one hundred and bloody one would show you nothing helpful in this situation and dirty tramps in old raincoats, lurking in wet streets, were never plotted on sand tables.

Lieutenant Clements! These are your orders. Be a good boy, Oliver. Remember what I said about biting your nails, Clements! Oliver, for the boy's sake, you must...! Should I knock the door and tell them I'm a good boy, Momma? Would it help if I told them I don't fornicate with strange women FOR THE BOY'S SAKE, Alice? Should I take two bloody great paces forward, Major Hartley, Sir?

Oliver will do what Oliver decides. It'll be my victory or my cock-up. No one will be told and my obituary will appear only in a fucking I.R.A. broadsheet. Hartley - no... more likely Hickson - will turn his old Etonian deadpan to the camera, gulp his bloody marbles and say, "Oh indeed, yes. The chap was in the army SOME TIME AGO but, as I understand it... an incident, you know - one doesn't want, of course, to say anything that might reflect on the dead. Presumably was involved with the terrorists in some way... Irish, you know... distressing... mysterious..."

They couldn't have made him a Wog if it'd happened in Aden. Interesting... What would they have said? Jesus! If it had happened when they had done Ben Rashi!

Rashi supported British Government policy in Aden but he was a politician with an eye on the future and he had, with astute measurements of speech and silence, gained the acclaim of Flossy, one of the Arab nationalist terrorist movements. As his stock improved with Flossy, so did it decline with the N.L.F. - Flossy's left orientated competitor in terror whose broadsheets normally referred to Mohammad Ben Rashi as a "tool of the imperialists", etc.

It was Captain Blake, who had served with Clements in the Paras before they were both seconded to Unit Two-Two of the Special Air Services, who had given birth to the idea. Normally, ideas, however outrageous, were encouraged but they had to be funnelled through Centre and, if repercussions were likely, Colonel Cole would have the final say, if necessary, after consultation with the department Head.

But off-the-cuff operations were common with the members of the Unit; the occasional unofficial killing - usually in anger or chagrin, rarely for gain. The regime dictated it; it was the inevitable by-product of an efficient, all-purpose, anti-terrorist terrorism.

The personnel of the Unit were not always big men, but, if they were not superbly fit, they had some other uncommon contribution to make to the top-secret corps whose function it was to use any means to combat the enemy.

It was during the Korean War that the British war lords had first come up against the use by an enemy of systematic torture and brainwashing as a technique for extracting information from the enemy. The Chinese and Koreans had developed the methods to an art form; it was no longer simply a process of kicking a man into useless senselessness. Beating itself, often brought its own will to resist and, in the ultimate, offered the prisoner the shield of unconsciousness or death.

The methods employed by the Chinese and Koreans were less clumsy and offered no escape. The prisoner's capacity to absorb punishment was measured and then his will to resist his interrogators was honed away by such methods as were thought requisite for his particular case. Sometimes the methods were the boot and the fist or a bamboo cane applied unsparingly to the genital organs; sometimes hallucinatory drugs were required or a process of mental disorientation induced by solitude and noise; sometimes it was electric shocks or the threat of on-the-spot execution, given point with the use of blank cartridges in a grim game of Russian roulette.

Whatever the means, it was a new weapon in the war game - a new machine gun, a new gas, a new H-bomb that would have to be met, equalled and surpassed. Patriotism, freedom, morality, human dignity and all the other laudables of our civilisation demanded it; it became a military preoccupation of the Great Powers - advanced by the exchange of ideas and techniques between the members of the two Power Clubs. Of course it was distasteful - an unpleasantness from which the public must be protected by the heroic and responsible. The great British public were protected from their Government's involvement through the use of "D" Notices and the counterparts of such notices were employed in other areas of democracy.

It was after the Korean War that the British Army began to develop its own techniques for the interrogation of prisoners and specialisation in brutality and torture devolved, largely, on men whose personality and behaviour in other branches of the Services showed aptitude for the trade. Such men were seconded from their normal duties and elevated to the S.A.S. where the entire curricula of explored brutality was imparted to them.

Patriotism was not the appeal; invariably the volunteers were 'loners', men who didn't fit in with the normal accommodation of civilian or even service life. They were a queer collection, a veritable psychiatrist's paradise of repressions and complexes that, normally, might have been the stuff of expert cracksmen, murderers, gangsters, rapists and all the other headline catching categories. They were held together in a web spun by a devious authority out of their own collective and very stupendous nefariousness.

Time, and the exchange of ideas, had widened their horizons of brutality and terror. What had been forged initially as a defensive counter, developed grim offensive overtones and brought specialisation in methods of counter-espionage that no Government minister would have cared to defend before Parliament.

Clements placed the end of his cigarette between the nail of his index finger and the inside end of his thumb and cannoned it across the pavement to sizzle out in the gutter. His mind reacted censorially. Shit! - this bloody situation didn't need all that caution. He was a bloody great pro playing the game against a lot of silly Irish amateurs who thought warfare had something to do with courage and resolution and honour and bloody baloney. Christ! they drove up in a stolen car and planted a bloody bomb and scarpered! The sum aggregate of their bangs wouldn't equal the devastation of one blockbuster! Courage and idealism, multiplied by patriotism and resolution, minus naivete over cunning plus a bloody great gun and the slags of the army would be mopping-up the fourth decimal point residue!

Bloody cunning! The unexpected!

Captain Blake had nudged him, drawing his attention to the black Ford Classic. "Know that bastard?" The driver was a light-skinned Arab in western dress; a slightly-built man, middle-aged, sitting close to the steering wheel, his eager eyes welding his attention on the road.

Oliver Clements stared into the slow-moving car; his puckered brows answered Blake. "That's Fuckface Ben Rashi - political ball thrower for Granny Florence. Flossy must be looking after the cunt. They say he has a charmed life, Clem."

"Think we could increase his weight, Skipper? By about two ounces - judiciously placed, of course!"

"Jacey! That would set the cat among the pigeons. Apart from ridding the place of the poxy little shit a whole lot of things could happen! You know he's always shoutin' about being threatened by the N.L.F.? Who'd they blame? Who'd they say knocked him off, Clem?"

Clements looked meaningfully at him, his broad face erupting into mischievousness. "They'd probably say ..."

92

"They'd say fuck all, Clem! They'd shoot the shit out of one another - that's what they'd do! The Flossy gunks would blame the N.L.F. and they'd shoot it out. The mass of the Wogs would blame the same quarter. The bloody wog politicians would be terrified and co-operative. It's a bloody wow, man! Think we should put it up to old Smartballs?"

"Put it up, shit! Let Smartballs get his own fun - this is an opportunity for a bit of private enterprise, Skipper!"

"You're a bloodthirsty Irish bastard! O.K. Clem. I'm with you but we would need to ..."

Clements tightened his mackintosh around his neck and nestled further into the doorway. The rain had eased to a steady drizzle - dense, feathery, blown out of its trajectory by a light wind. There was nothing on the streets except the fixed shadows of urban impediment dancing with a little movement in the light of a hiccuping gas lamp.

Most of the windows were still lighted but blinds were drawn and many of the usually-open front doors in the ribbon of mid-nineteenth century houses were closed. In the background could be heard the vying television channels - Clements, self-addressing, thought: the shit seek out their bloody lives in the imagination of their lunatic's lanterns; the risen people, Jesus! - they'd hardly rise off their arses from watching themselves on "Coronation Street" to go for their fish and chips! Christ - "each in his narrow cell forever laid" - and they're not even dead yet! Stupid-fucking-dangerous-bloody-industrial zombies... couldn't run a bloody "knocking shop"!

He had made up his mind when the door of a house further up the street opened, emitting a shaft of light across the narrow street; in the background, the raucous strains of a record player.

"Goodnight, Seedie. Now watch yerself, luv, going' over there. Ah wonder if it's stopped yet?"

"Cheerio, Josie. Goodnight, Jim. Goodnight, all! A'm sure it's all over now, Josie. Are ye leavin' me out, Cathleen?"

It was only three houses up from where Clements was sheltering. He could see the dim silhouette of the two women in the corridor of light that stretched across the street from the glass of the vestibule door while, across the street, their shadowy forms were magnified grotesquely on the dirty brick-work, doors and windows of the houses. They were talking but their voices were drowned by the music of the record player which had obviously been increased in volume when the guest had left. For a moment there was silence through which the voices of the women could be heard, indistinctly. Then, louder still, came the music - a poignant, slow moving melody, played, as a background to a heavily-brogued voice, on violin, flute and banjo.

Many years have gone by since the Irish rebellion,
When the guns of Britannia they loudly did speak;
When the bold I.R.A. battled shoulder-to-shoulder
While the blood from their...........

Shut your bloody mouth, you bitch. He gritted his teeth angrily as the voice of one of the women denied him the end of the stanza.

He went to his.............
....firing party he bravely did face
Then the order rang out, present arms and....
James Connolly fell in to a ready-made grave.

Clements was attracted to the tune; involuntarily he shut out the noises of the wind and the spluttering of the gas lamp, and struggled with the distraction of the womens' voices, straining to hear the words of the song - annoyed that they did not come through to him in such sequence as would allow comprehension.

The black flag they hoisted the cruel deed was over, Gone was a man who loved Ireland so well;
................in Dublin that.......
When they murdered James Con.............

The women in the doorway laughed and Clements felt the rush of uncontrollable anger that he felt for rain and slow-moving traffic. He loathed their unseen faces, their stupid laughter; the whisper of his own anger cut across his concentration: "Stuff your fucking stupid mouths, you...!" His mouth actually said the words and his ear flashed its caution - but the laughter petered into silence and he wondered if the volume of the record player had been further increased:

God's curse on you England, you cruel-hearted monster,
Your deeds they would shame all the devils in hell.
There are no flowers blowing, but the shamrock's still growing
On the grave of James Connolly, the Irish Rebel.

Clements grinned to himself as the music ran out. Poor silly bastards! Naive, stupid cows! give them "justice" on their side, their bloody martyrs and the naked bosom of poor, suffering, Mother Ireland; wrap it all up in a plaintive air and let them go to war! When would they learn that "justice", like God, was on the side of the big battalions? "Their deeds they would shame all the devils in hell."

Jesus Christ..... DEEDS!

They had gone around the back of the old house deep within Aden's Crater district. Both he and Blake were wearing the white overalls that said they were painters, bakers, mechanics, ambulance men or anything other than soldiers - though Blake was obviously giving point to the overalls with the old Hoover spinner in the back of the rickety old Ford Popular which he had procured before calling at Cusson's for Clements.

It was here that Mohammed Ben Rashi held court, so to speak; here where the ward-healing Arab toadies brought their favours and their requests. Ben Rashi did not live here, of course; his home was a modest villa outside the town, but here, in the basement, were his offices.

Rashi's old Ford Classic was parked on the grassless garden at the side of the house. Directly overhead, the sun, unsheltered by cloud, sent its burning shafts to the hard, cracked, earth where they folded back in low-lying concentrations of dead heat. Only the flies moved with a noisy consciousness of men's hibernation. Rashi would have no visitors.

Clements noiselessly lifted aside the white linen screen that, on its long wooden slats, covered the doorway. The door itself was held against the wall with an ancient wedge of wood secured from somewhere behind with a thick, threading, twine.

Inside the office was an ex-W.D. desk-type table at one end of which were two rough bundles of assorted sheets of paper held down by two almost-identical rust speckled stones. Behind the table, back to the wall, was a white-painted bentwood chair with a piece of foam rubber secured to the seat. Under the window was another table with an ancient-looking Hermes typewriter on it and yet another bentwood chair. The rest of the furniture consisted of brown cardboard boxes; they were everywhere - piled one on top of the other, some labelled, some open, showing their contents of newspapers, while others were slid into a roughly-made wooden fixture to form a make-shift filing cabinet.

There was no one in the room but, across from where they had entered, was another door, partially opened.

"Some bloody office, Skipper." Clements had not

whispered but had spoken low.

"Does a nice line in cardboard boxes, eh?"

Blake was going through the papers on the desk and Clements was moving towards the other door but had stopped to examine the contents of the top box in a pile. He was near the door when Rashi appeared but his head was lowered to the box and he was lightly startled when the Arab spoke.

"Ah gentlemen! You are carrying out some little research without my help. I can, perhaps, help?" The little Arab was standing smiling in the doorway. He was in sock-soles and was wearing only a shirt and linen trousers.

"Funny fucking fellow!" Clements left hand shot out and caught the little man's open shirt-front. He stepped to the left of Rashi and tugged viciously and, as his victim shot past his right shoulder, he rammed his fist, hard, below the Arab's ribcage." "Laugh on that - you parcel of Wog shit!"

The little man fell face-downward on the floor but immediately scrambled around on to his back and raised his body. He sat on his backside, his legs bent, his arms stretched out behind his body supported by his open palms on the floor. He was shaking his head like a dog just out of water but with less movement. His eyes were wide, staring wildly, not with anger but with appeal. His chin fell and attempted to rise but it could not make the effort and then he started to shiver. He was trying to speak but fear dominated his faculties and his voice was crowded out.

Blake was behind him. He moved a little closer, raised himself on the ball of his left foot and set up a measuring, pendulum-like, motion of his right leg. He looked over at Clements, intimating his movement with his eyes and then he brought his foot crashing forward. The blow took Rashi just above the nape of the neck, at the back of the skull; there was a cracking sound and then the man's head shot forward until it was almost at his knees. As though in controlled motion, the little Arab's body moved slowly to an erect position and he fell, sideways, on the floor.

"Long live the Provisional Government!" Blake said as he bent forward to inspect his victim.

"Nicest bloody goal-kick, Skip..." Clements voice trailed off; Blake was rising but his eyes were on the space behind Clements' back. He jumped quickly to his right, skipped once and spun around - his hand pulling at the thirty-eight under his overalls. Blake had not moved.

The girl in the doorway was European - blonde, beautiful, pale-skinned, European. She was in bare feet and was wearing a long, white, silken dress that was open all the way down at the front and pulled tight around her like a dressing gown. Her hair was long, golden blonde, its ends at one side covered by the neck of her gown. Her great blue eyes, set in the hallowed paleness of her white skin, were rounded in terror.

Silence. Nothing stirred in the room. The two men stood in the exact positions they had been in when each had seen the girl - this pale, beautiful creature who now stood, like a marble statue, firmly fixed for all time in the doorway.

They all moved together. Clements and Blake made for the door in which the girl was standing and the girl moved backwards and grabbed the door, pushing it forward. But Clements got to it before she had it closed. Blake had tripped on Rashi's feet but regained himself and was now behind Clements even as the latter applied testing pressure on the door. Both men pushed; it yielded slightly but the girl had the wall that angled off from the door on the inside to give her leverage while the continuance of the same wall, on the other side, restricted the joint effort of the men.

Now she began to squeal - a long, piercing, hysterical squeal. Her lungs emptied, the men heard her gulping for air, then "Nein! Nein! Ne..in!" the voice rose in terror again.

"Wait, Clem!" Blake had released his presure and stood back. Clements looked around enquiringly and then moved to the left of the door - but still with his hand against the upper panel keeping the girl from closing it. Blake was fumbling in his overalls. "Can't have that bitch wakening the bloody neighbourhood."

He raised the snub-nosed Webley and Clements eased his pressure on the door which immediately shot into its frame. They both stood off, listening to the gulping sobs of the terrified girl. The shots splintered the wood - one at stomach level, one at chest level.

They heard her slumping behind the door. Blake rushed forward and turned the handle and both men pushed at the door. The weight yielded easily and Blake jumped into the room. The two shots rang out and he turned about and collided face-to-face with Clements in the door frame.

"Right, Clem, that takes care of the homework - you look after the pupil, boy!"

Blake was looking out the back door when Clements fired the two thirty-eight slugs into the dead body of Mohammed Ben Rashi.

"Well - goodnight, Cathleen. See ya on Friday, then."

97

"Alright, Seedie. Ah think ye'd better go by Governor Road. Goodnight. God Bless."

Sadie turned from the door and walked up the street, away from Clements, in the direction of Springfield Road. His thoughts followed her, angrily, but he was glad she didn't have to pass him - even though he was confident that "Tony Kane" could have explained away any difficulties that might have arisen.

The rain had eased. Clements let down the collar of his mackintosh, shook the front of it and eased its wetness away from his neck. He stepped out from his shelter, then, and moved further up the street in the direction of the house into which Johnny Cairns had disappeared, less than fifteen minutes before.

CHAPTER ELEVEN

"The General's Goin' to Sing"

Charlie Shields stood with McGivern on the Falls Road, looking down Leeson Street.

The rain had thinned out the crowd but it was the audience that had, mostly, gone leaving elbow room for the more determined who were now engaged in a vicious stone-throwing exercise against the military at the Grosvenor Road side.

The two men walked further down the street and McGivern nudged Shields. "That's Dessie Hurley down there - no, across the street there, talking to that group of lads. He's the I.Q. of the local Provo Company. Dessie is up to something, you can be sure - he doesn't normally get involved in this sort of thing without a purpose."

"Could you talk to him - I mean do you know him well enough, Charlie, for him to let you in on it?"

"God, yes! Dessie's an I.R.A. Ecumenist, Charlie. Mind you, whatever it is, he may not be able to call it off but he will give me enough information to keep your lot advised on the best course of action."

The group of young men across the street had broken up and were running quickly in different directions into the crowd. Charlie Shields and Charlie McGivern moved closer to the wall trying to follow some of the runners.

A minute passed and then, suddenly, the stone throwers commenced a backward movement attended by a new outburst of noise. Back they came, exposing, for the first time to Shields and McGivern the two military outposts at McDonnell Street.

A great flash lit up the bottom of the street, a great, blinding, blue light that illuminated the darkness and exposed the military position at the Grosvenor Road end of the street in stark detail for a fraction of a second. The explosion rocked the street, reverberating massively off the concrete, shaking the houses and dying away in the lesser noises of shattering glass.

"Nail bomb!" said McGivern.

Shields had the palm of his left hand over his ear and was shaking his head vigorously. It was the closest he'd been to an exploding nail bomb in a narrow street and he was shaken by the power of its detonation. He bent closer to McGivern and was surprised at the fright in his voice when he spoke. "Christ! That was a big one, Charlie! - couple of pounds, I'd say."

"No, not really. Probably half a pound - four sticks of jelly. It's the concrete and the confined space. I think it went in under one of the trucks; you'd think there would be casualties."

Hickson was ashen faced and he knew that if he had been drinking a cup of tea his hand would have trembled. He made no apologies to himself for his fear. He'd been in the Korean fighting - he'd got the Military Medal there - and had served in Kenya during the Mau-Mau uprising and in Cyprus against E.O.K.A. but he'd never experienced anything like the Northern Irish troubles.

The I.R.A. was a shrewd enemy and some of their impro- vised armaments - like their imitation Claymore anti-person- nel bombs - were too bloody good for comfort! They had adapted better than his field-trained, modernly-armed troops to the artifices of urban warfare and their indigenous support in the Catholic areas gave them quick civilian cover and an urgent line of retreat. Hickson was also conscious that his men were becoming demoralised by the pimpernel tactics of their enemy.

He was personally opposed to the way the military authori- ties were conducting the campaign. Quite soon after coming to Northern Ireland, in August 1970, he saw the way things were going and he reckoned the consequences of the army's activities would serve the I.R.A. In the first place, the G.O.C. was allowing senior officers on the ground to over react to even trivial incidents. Massive concentrations of troops were being poured into the mean streets in search-and-purpose operations - often hours after incidents - when common sense showed the futility of such initiatives. Inevitably, the soldiers worked off their frustrations on the civilian populace and, just as inevitably, the civilians reacted, not only by physically opposing the troops, but by increasing their opposition to, and hatred of, the political forces behind the military.

The I.R.A. were the beneficiaries; it was almost as though they had spun a web to ensnare the soldiers and the military commanders were strengthening that web daily by their attempts to cut its strands. When Hickson had arrived in the Province, the Provisional I.R.A. was a mere nebulous out- growth of the 1969 sectarian pogrom; its writ was enforced with deterring harshness in many of the Catholic ghettolands.

100

Now the Provisional I.R.A. were the heroes of those same districts, carrying their mandate and overwhelming support without need to resort to pressures or harshness. Hickson was convinced that this situation had been brought about by the acceptance of inept and politically biased policies by the army's top brass in N. Ireland.

Now a situation had been achieved where the discipline of the troops was breaking down. The situation was really grim and there was no light at the end of the political tunnel. The civilian population in the Catholic areas hated the troops with a desperate hate; it was a hatred that showed in the sullen stare of the men, the open contempt of the women and the bitter derision of the children. It was the interchange of these three in the group reaction that triggered off and sustained the rioting.

The soldiers, for their part, reciprocated the hatred of the civilian populace in the Catholic areas; they showed their hatred in the viciousness and humiliation of their searches of the person, the brutality and destruction with which they carried out the mini-curfews and raids on peoples' homes and, more sinister still as far as Hickson was concerned, the easy assumption with which they took life after one of their number had fallen victim to an I.R.A. bullet.

It was naked hate facing naked hate with the politically unconnected bearing the terrible brunt of the tactics being pursued by both the I.R.A. and the British Army. The military bullied their way into the back streets as though the I.R.A. was in complete occupation and every man, woman and child they met was a member of the I.R.A.; a civilian reacted in word or deed to some real or imagined action of the soldiers and the street joined in followed by the adjoining streets - followed by the I.R.A. Using the cover of the confrontation the I.R.A. would attack with deadly swiftness; sometimes it was a single shot, sometimes a concentration of fire, some-times a nail bomb, or bombs. A soldier would be killed or wounded and, again under cover of the mob, the I.R.A. would disappear.

Most often the rioting would continue, sometimes for hours, sometimes even for days. The bewildered, tired, frightened soldiers would shoot a rioter or an innocent by-stander and the flames were fanned to new viciousness. When it was all over, the I.R.A. had disappeared and growing bitterness among the people of the area had matured to deep hatred and prepared the ground for new enlistments in the I.R.A.

Hickson was not alone among the senior officers who were critical of army strategy and who felt that the military were more and more succumbing to the pressures of the very politicians who had made it all happen in the first place. He was not a politician; he didn't pretend to understand the question or to know the answer but, more and more, he was becoming convinced that the strategy in which he was caught up was compounding the crimes of hatred and division and making a solution more difficult - if only by increasing the strength and support of a relentless and fanatical enemy that could not compromise.

He was a professional officer whose Sandhurst theory had been augmented by bloody service against a ruthless and well-armed enemy in Korea. There he had been afraid many times but only in the terrible candour of the fighting. One could get away from it: the machine could organise respite; engagements had beginnings, middles and ends and the duration of the conflict was measurable in terms, at least, of territorial conquest.

Here nothing was predictable; battles commenced with a spit on the face or with a bottle thrown by the hand of a ten year-old child, or with the scream of a woman's voice. Of course the army had the fire-power to end it all in hillocks of dead bodies but that was a fire-power that would, in the modern world, give victory to the enemy and which, in its terribleness, would have transcended the hatred of most of the officers and other ranks.

To Hickson, the professional soldier, the whole thing was degrading. They were being used. He had seen his troops humiliated and outfought, not by the I.R.A. but by groups of men, women, and even children. The soldiers were battle-trained, highly mechanised and superbly armed but their training and equipment were irrelevant against the remorseless, untiring, hate-incensed rioters. The brick and the bottle were the most effective weapons in such a struggle and the rioters were extremely proficient in their use. Hickson could not forget easily the sight of a detachment of his men, tired men, who had been engaged in a night-long battle - their superb weaponry laid aside - exchanging bricks and bottles in the dawn light with a group of teenage rioters.

It had been in the New Lodge Road area of the city. The riot had been sparked off when a child was killed by an army Ferret scout car. Immediately, the great majority of the people of the district were on the streets. Mild-mannered barmen, middle-aged dockers, ex-army pensioners, overworked housewives, young men and women tired from a day's work in the mills and factories, men and women whose imposed source of income was the dole; they were all here - the meek and the mild, the reasonable and the fearful gathered with the daring, the politically-dedicated, the hooligan and the fool. They were all here, coalesced into a fearsomeness of revenge.

Whether the child had run on to the road or been neglected by a parent, whether the army driver had shown recklessness or exercised care, whether he was uncaring or racked with remorse - these things were unimportant. The single fact was that the army had killed another child; the same army that had shot a youth at the top of the street a few days earlier - a youth whom, the people believed, was not a petrol bomber; the same army that spat on wee Sally Brown's face at the corner of Lepper Street; the same army that pulled down the ceiling of Granny Murphy's bedroom; the same army that broke Paddy Hughes' jaw.

Children were frequently knocked down and killed in the narrow streets; John Smyth from the top of the road had slapped Sally Brown across the face; two of the local lads were in the reformatory for breaking open Granny Murphy's gas meter and Paddy Hughes was a despicable bully who had the neighbourhood terrorised.

But the army had no Paddy, Tom, Jack or Joe; it had anonymous soldiers - all part of the great machine of oppression.

The mob had seized buses, cars and lorries and set them on fire. At the junction of New Lodge Road and North Queen Street, two buses, a large van and a lorry laden with timber were on fire. Tongues of bright orange flame leapt fifty feet into the air and thick black smoke billowed upwards into the evening sky and wafted away in low, heavy clouds over the city centre to tell the rush-hour crowds, coming home from work, that it was all happening yet again.

On the New Lodge Road itself, worse than the awesome fingers of flame and the black choking smoke, worse than the clamour of the gathering mobs, was the fear. It was everywhere, like the smoke, to be gulped down in great lungfuls of sheer dread that took the place of anger in the collective consciousness as time revealed the monstrousness of that which had been done. The terrible protest had been made in tremendous destruction - the magnitude of which the poor judged in terms of money. But they had lived their lives with their backs bent before the lash of Authority and, to the faint-

hearted who had engaged in the deed or acclaimed its per-
petrators, that Authority had the power of God-Omnipotent;
onmipresent, watching them from the roof tops, allowing them
their moment of sin before it would react - surely and
crushingly.

The faint-hearted, along with the brave who had pressing
matters to attend to, were going back to the doubtful security
of their homes, delaying only long enough to impose such
authority as they could on their young. Authority had not yet
struck back; it was mustering off - collecting its armoured
vehicles, its guns, its shields and riot vizors and those who
waited on the streets knew that, already, Authority held the
perimeter of the district in a ring of steel and was preparing
its pistons to pulverise the opposition on the streets. In the
shouting camaraderie of fear they broke up the pavements for
ammunition and barricades.

Hickson had arrived in a Scout Car on the Antrim Road
from where he surveyed the scene down the long stretch of the
New Lodge Road. Groups, composed mainly of teenage boys
and girls, threw some missiles in the direction of the soldiers
that surrounded him and the other officers but they were well
out of range and only the cat-calls and abuse reached the
military. Hickson told his officers to deploy their forces at
the ends of the various streets leading into the district and
ensure that the rioters made no movement outward. As long
as fire-arms were not used or a concerted attempt made by
the rioters to fire further property, troops were not to be sent
in.

As he turned back towards the Scout Car, he stopped and
then retraced his steps to Captain Wilson who was instructing
his junior officers. "Oh, and look, Wilson, for heaven's sake
ensure that anyone leaving the area, people going about their
peaceful pursuits, are allowed to leave without undue bother.
Be more careful, of course, with people coming in, but for
Christ's sake, no incidents! And watch that new lot up there
on Halliday's Road - they're new and probably shit-scared with
all this and we don't want some clod opening up!"

Hickson had been summoned by radio telephone to Brigade
H.O. at Girdwood Park, a short distance down the road. The
Commander of Land Forces in the Province was visiting the
Brigade and wanted the Major's first-hand report on the New
Lodge situation.

The Lieutenant-General was emphatic in his concept of
how the situation should be handled - even if dogmatism was
precluded by his liberal use of "we". "Wouldn't we feel, Major,

104

that if they are allowed to hold the streets they would grow bolder, and might we not think there was a danger that growing bolder could be reflected in notions of territorial gain? Are we not, perhaps, merely putting off the evil hour?"

Hickson argued with all the vigour that his position permitted.

The seizure and burning of vehicles was a unanimous reaction in panic but, already, the great majority of those who had partaken in the action had returned to their homes and the minority that remained were building barricades - "not, surely, Sir, for the purpose of breaking OUT!" If the army attacked this minority, those who had returned to their homes would be back on the streets and, then, unless the troops went in, in sufficient numbers to take over the streets AND the people's homes, they could not win "without shooting people." Give them time and the crowd on the streets will thin out and tomorrow, when most of them are out at work, the engineers could go in with bulldozers and clear away the barricades.

"With respect, Sir, I would suggest that if we can possibly avoid a street confrontation with civilians, we should do so. In the first place, there is nothing to be gained by our physical occupation of the area; again, we cannot guarantee that we can successfully occupy the area - since the situation imposes its choice of weapons - and I would further suggest that, either way, it is humiliating and demoralising to the men to involve them in this type of operation, unnecessarily ... "

"Really, Major!" The Lieutenant-General accompanied his interpolation with a sidelong, eyebrows-lifted glance that showed his growing impatience with Hickson's commentary. Hickson took the warning; it added hardness to his voice. "Yes Sir - indeed, I am convinced that street battles between troops and civilians serve only the I.R.A."

The troops had moved in at nineteen-twenty hours. They had met only token resistance until they came to the main barricade, about one hundred yards down the New Lodge Road; then, the neighbourhood was out! Bottles, pieces of concrete square-setts and iron gratings were tossed at the soldiers; most of the troops still had to carry their S.L. rifles lest some I.R.A. man opened up on them, but they had no menace for the rioters - who knew the army dare not use them in such a situation - and the rifles, along with the clumsy riot-protection gear, only acted to the disadvantage of the troops in the rapid movement of riot determined by the rioters.

The troops used rubber bullets and tear gas but, in the main, the rioters had learned to counter these weapons. Their front line was the braver, fitter, teenage element experienced in the strategy of street warfare. Experience had made them expert in avoiding the rubber bullets; not only could they often see the individual soldier aiming the discharger and anticipate the bullet's line of travel, but they could take advantage of gateways, doorways and street corners for cover. Their movements were rapid; they would spring from behind a corner, heave a missile at the massed soldiery, and disappear into new cover.

Most of this element used improvised gas masks of cloths soaked in vinegar but the real tactic against gas was to break before its heavier concentrations, retreating down the side streets on either side of the road. The soldiers would then advance but their main body had to hold intact before the more-rapidly retreating mass of women and older men who had positioned themselves behind the front line of rioters. Now the troops were exposed on both flanks to the renewed attacks of those who had sought refuge in the side streets. So the battle went around in circles; the break-and-retreat, the attack on the flanks, the occasionally-successful move to encircle the troops by passing through the side streets and regrouping at the rear of the main body of soldiers.

At three-hundred hours, groups of Protestants from the adjoining 'Tiger's Bay' district, cut through some of the side-streets and attempted to attack the flank of the Catholics. Most of the men on the ground, and even some of Hickson's officers, saw this as Wellington saw the Prussians but Hickson was horrified. He radioed for reinforcements but even when they arrived, it was necessary to augment them with half of one of his own companies to drive back the Protestants and keep them confined to their own quarters.

At eight-hundred hours the fighting still continued - the main battle then in progress at the junction of New Lodge Road and Lepper Street. Hickson's men had suffered many casualties, from slight cuts to severe lacerations - one soldier had sustained a broken ankle and another was in danger of losing an eye - and the men were dog-tired. He ordered the troops not to advance on the rioters and not to use any more rubber bullets or gas and he effected partial cover for the men by bringing up lorries and interposing them between the rioters and his men.

For a time the missiles continued to fly but the rioters soon sensed the change in the military's tactics and the missile-throwing largely subsided and gave way to the war chants of the area. Hickson came through to the front of his men with a loud-hailer. He was noticed by the front line of rioters and the message of his intentions was carried back in the crowd, diffusing a measure of quiet and interest.

A young fellow in the front row of the mob raised his arms and shouted: "Oh Fuck! The general's goin' to sing!"

The shouted comment brought a peal of laughter from those in the front of the crowd who heard it and the laughter went through to the rear and brought its relief.

Hickson let them see him laughing, too. He stepped out to the front and raised the loud-hailer. He couldn't call them "ladies and gentlemen" - that would get derisions! "Folk"? Jesus, no! "People"? - that would need a pre-fix and you can't call people you've been fighting all night "Good"! What the hell ...

"Hello! Now listen to me please. I want you all to return to your homes peacefully. If you do that my men will be withdrawn to the top of the road and we can start the day in peace. I have deliberately avoided using water cannons and dye, but now I must warn you, if you do not return to your homes I will be ..."

The man had advanced to the front of the mob. Twenty ... dark ... bulky; denim jacket and jeans - an activist. His voice carried. "You want us back in our homes so that you can raid them and attack us separately. What proof ..."

"I promise you there will be no raiding ... no reprisals. We will withdraw to the main roads. My men are tired - they have been fighting for over twelve hours now and ... "

"For Jesus sake, General, we've bin fightin' for over FIFTY YEARS an' we're fresh as a daisy!"

It was the denim-jacketed youth and, again, his voice carried. The crowd cheered his speech and shouted their own additions but good humour had taken the place of fear and anger.

Within half-an-hour the soldiers were withdrawn and the peace of the area was being broken only by the hurrying footsteps of people going to work.

Hickson had many similar experiences in Belfast. No - he was not afraid of the I.R.A. Soldiering had nothing to do with bravery. Soldiering, in the sense of winning battles, was a question of armament and training and he knew that in both departments his men were superior to the I.R.A. - as they were, also, in numbers. In a straight fight between his men and the Republicans, with both sides equally balanced, it would be a question of terrain; in open battle conditions his men would win but not in these sewer-like streets where every house was a potential refuge for the enemy - a refuge against which mortars, rockets or grenades could not be used.

The key to the whole matter was the civilians; it wasn't necessary to win them but, simply, to neutralise them and stop THEM from starting battles which the army could not win.

Riot situations did terrify him. He felt humiliated and degraded opposing teenagers armed with bottles and brickbats and women armed with tongues against which there was no defence. When it came to rioting, these people were the crack troops, a panzer elite, who were without equal. They were terrifying.

He had played his old and usual strategy throughout the evening here in Leeson Street; the strategy of containment. He did not know that one of his men had been shot before his arrival and now lay dead among the group of terrified soldiers battened down behind their vehicles at the corners of McDonnell Street. He did know that the nail bomb that had exploded under one of his own trucks had injured a trooper's hand and torn away the left hip of Sergeant Hawkes and he was sick at the death of the youth who had fallen beneath the blows of his own men when he had careered through their line of defence a short time ago.

Obviously it was no longer just a riot; the nail bomb indicated the presence of the I.R.A. Containment was now useless but there were still those two beleagured army outposts in the street surrounded by several hundred rioters.

And Major Hickson knew that he must advance.

CHAPTER TWELVE

Dermot

Johnny Cairns had found the outer door of the Quinn home ajar. He pushed his way into the telephone-kiosk hallway, illuminated by the light from the living room shining through the glass panels of the inner door, and knocked.

The door was opened by a dark-haired, lanky youth who surveyed Johnny with some suspicion.

"Hello. Is Paddy - Mr. Quinn - in?" Johnny leaned inward; Nora was coming out of the kitchen with a tray in her hands. She looked towards the door, her eyes dancing with their message. "Johnny! Come in Johnny! It's alright, Dermot. Oh, Johnny, I'm glad to see you... I didn't expect... Look, sit down here near the fire. You'll have some tea? We're having some."

Nora's face was flushed. She and Johnny had agreed that, because of her brother's antagonism towards him, Johnny should not visit the house. That he should do so, unarranged and at a late hour, indicated a seriousness to his mission and now, as she busied herself with cups and teapot, her mind had created an infinity of terrifying reasons for his visit.

Johnny, too, had thought about this and he sensed the girl's concern. Nora had gone into the kitchen to fetch another cup. John Hegarty was seated in an easy chair in the corner across from the television smiling broadly at Johnny and indicating the T.V. screen. The sound of the television had been turned off but the changing pictures zoomed from a general view of some panel game or quiz to the stark close-ups of the participants and Hegarty's hands and face mimed its disconcerting, lunatic reaction. The other man, Dermot, had resumed his seat with some uncertainty.

"I just wanted to have a word with Paddy, Nora." Johnny thought the "just" might allay her concern. "I take it he's not in? Do you expect him back anyway soon?"

"So it's Paddy you're interested in now, is it?" She was laughing lightly now, her movements more composed - she had grasped the significance of his remark and Johnny's interest in seeing Paddy, peculiar though it was, was less grave than the least of her imagined concerns. "Dermot's been waiting on him, Johnny, for the past half-hour - he's been trying to convert me - haven't you, Dermot?"

Dermot looked uncomfortable; he laughed awkwardly and looked down into his cup.

"This, by the way, Dermot, is Johnny Cairns, my fiance - who comes around at all hours of the night with strange, dark messages for my brother." Johnny felt the question in her banter. "And this is Dermot Quinn - no relation, Johnny - one of Paddy's friends."

Both men raised themselves in their seats and shook hands. Johnny knew that Nora's "one of Paddy's friends" was her way of telling him that Dermot was a Provisional I.R.A. man.

Hegarty's moment of excitement had passed. He had turned his body around towards the T.V., his attention wrapped in whatever his mind made of the changing pictures. The slice of toast in his left hand went occasionally to his mouth, but it was an instinctive movement that added to the debris of broken bread and crumbs that nestled in the folds of his trouser front and on the carpet about him. Even with his mouth full he spoke, giving his madman's reactions and opinions, but the sound came only in low chortles, the changing cadence of which told his emotions.

Nora followed Johnny's eyes. "Poor John. You know Johnny, that television is his life. He knows, when I am on day duty, the time I get home at - he's often sitting on the window sill when I arrive - and as soon as I come in he must have the T.V. on. If I go out for the evening, he'll sit there - he's quite safe - until I get home, or if I'm late, until the programmes are all over, then he goes home. Paddy says he's Ulster's greatest loyalist - sits right through "The Queen" every night!"

"Poor lad." Johnny said and he felt the constriction in his throat.

"Best of it is, Paddy's better to him than I am; he buys him sweets and model cars - he plays on the floor with them, like a five year-old child - and yet Paddy daren't go near him. He sobs like a baby if Paddy lays a hand on him - I saw him once run into the kitchen and try to hide behind the gas stove because Paddy tried to put a pullover up against him to see if it would fit."

Dermot's face showed its genuine pity. "Was it the Prods that did it, Miss Quinn?"

Nora looked at Johnny, her look apologising for Dermot. "Dermot, it was neither a Catholic nor a Protestant that did that. Frankly, I don't believe in either religion but I'd never accuse them of that. John Hegarty is a victim of the notion that the world can be changed - or Ireland, anyway - by killing or maiming people. It is a notion which heroes and cowards, wise men and fools, sincere men and charlatans have always nourished - in Ireland and elsewhere. John Hegarty, that poor, mindless youth, is THEIR victim. It's what we were talking about before Johnny came in ..."

She turned to Johnny "Dermot and I were freeing Ireland before you came in, Johnny. He favours the romantic approach but your coming interrupted his justifications. Right, Dermot. You were going to tell me about a free Ireland and how it can be accomplished."

Dermot looked at Nora then, quickly, at Johnny.

"Don't worry about Johnny, Dermot. He's alright. I think you'll find that even if he says he doesn't go all the way with you, there's really not much difference in your philosophies. Now, quite seriously, if its worth fighting and dying for, Dermot, you must surely have studied it; you must understand your position fully and be able to justify it..."

"Now, Nora, you're not being quite fair to the lad, are you? After all, he's only ... well, I mean, you and I are older, more politically mature, more ..."

"Johnny," Nora's voice had lost its softness, "Some of those kids in the British Army are not very mature either, are they? We'd both agree that the system exploits their ignorance to do its dirty work but ... but the I.R.A. - both varieties - shoot them! Don't they? Isn't it just possible that the ignorance is common to both sides and that, whatever side gets the victory, the manipulators, the men of property, will get the fruit?"

"We're against capitalism, Miss Quinn. We stand by the Proclamation of the Irish Republic. But we say that Ireland must be free first and then the whole country can choose the type of system it wants. Democratically."

"How do you feel enslaved now, Dermot? I think Johnny and you would part company on the implications of that question and it's the lynch-pin of my argument, too. Tell us why you feel you're not free NOW Dermot and how the victory of your brand of Republicanism will make you free."

Dermot sensed the danger in the question; he looked at them for a moment, laughed nervously and said, "Well, you must know what I mean ... I mean Ireland has not got control over her own destiny. It's England that controls us and ..."

"And what about the south of Ireland, Dermot? Have they freedom? They have their own government - do they control their own destinies?"

Dermot was still ill at ease; his puzzlement made him cautious and the effort of his thinking showed on his face. "Well ... you see, Miss Quinn ..."

111

"Nora!" said Nora.

Dermot reddened. He had never met a girl like this before; she was beaut ... well, a real smasher! Elegant as hell and well-spoken, too - but not la-di-da. She wasn't taking the mickey out of him, he knew that; she was serious - even her informality was in earnest - but she ... somehow she overawed him, left him feeling self-conscious and tongue-tied. He looked over at Johnny; Nora had said he was "alright" - and, of course, he would be, in the O.C.'s house.

"Look. I'm not much good at explaining things; I'm just a volunteer - I leave the political side of things to the people who understand politics."

"But surely, Dermot ..." Johnny began but Nora's voice cut across him and he conceded to her.

"Dermot! So you are prepared to take the most precious thing you possess, your own life, and place it in the trust of those who, you think, understand. So the Republican volunteer is just like the British soldier. You just do what you're told because you are told it's for Mother Ireland! So you get self-government for all Ireland, Dermot, like they got it in India, or Pakistan, or even the south of Ireland, and as far as the great majority of people, the working class, are concerned, Mother Ireland is simply Mother Hubbard!"

"What Nora means, Dermot," said Johnny, "is that simply changing the government does not, in itself, bring freedom to the great majority who live out their lives in poverty and insecurity. The freedom we want is freedom from want and it's necessary to have a SOCIAL revolution to achieve that - not just to change the government but to abolish capitalism and institute a Socialist system of government."

"And that, Dermot, is where Johnny and I would part company. He says abolish the government of capitalism and establish the government of Socialism. He would say we must establish a "socialist workers' republic"; I say both these propositions are contradictory in terms. I would say that Socialism is a classLESS society - so, obviously, a "workers' republic", whatever else it may be, is not Socialism. I would say that the State is an administrative device of class society and that Socialism will not require government of people but simply administration of things. What Johnny and the so-called "official" I.R.A. want to establish in Ireland is ..."

Dermot, obviously taken aback, looked at Johnny and asked bluntly, "You in the officials? The N.L.F.? That's Communist!"

Johnny and Nora both laughed at Dermot's discomfiture

112

and Johnny said, "It depends what you mean by Communist, Dermot ..."

Dermot was in before Johnny could continue. "I mean that the official I.R.A. abandoned the struggle for a Republic based on the principles of Pearse and Tone and want to establish a Communist State based on the ideas of Marx and Lenin."

"Whatever you OR Johnny may think, Dermot, I am bound to say that Lenin was about as representative of the ideas of Marx as Paisley is of the ideas of Jesus Christ. But you are right, as far as your information goes - no, Johnny ... let me finish; the official I.R.A. want to establish in Ireland the same sort of State-capitalist society that exists in the so-called Communist countries ..."

"You know that's not true, Nora. There are important distinctions; we don't want to impose our attitudes from above, we ..."

"Why the gun then, Johnny? Oh I know, capitalism maintains its grip on the mind of the working class. Break that grip first and, then, let the workers choose democratically! Can they? Can they decide that the State bosses, whose control of the means of production gives them the same power and privilege as ownership gave the old capitalist bosses, should be moved aside in the interests of the community?"

At that moment they were distracted by Hegarty. He was jumping up and down on the easy chair, making a sound through his pursed lips like a child imitating a racing car and he was clapping his hands with delight, his eyes intent on the T.V. screen. The programme had changed to an animated cartoon film of Tom and Jerry; the cat was involved in one of those long spectacular chases that brought him under carpets, up chimneys and through walls after the mouse and the animator's skill had found a response somewhere in the dim buried past of Hegarty's mind.

His face worked grotesquely, the movement of his mouth stretching his jaw from side to side, and his eyes moved madly in their sockets. He stopped clapping his hands and instead, gesticulated desperately - indicating his anger, or questions, or advice, or whatever incomprehensible emotion his understanding of the pictures evoked. Saliva was flowing freely from his mouth on to the stained pullover that carried the tally of Hegarty's excitements.

Suddenly the chase ended, the screen blacked out for a moment and then the credits appeared. Hegarty's movements ceased and his head craned forward in the direction of the television set. His jaw had dropped and his face showed a wild caricature of disappointment and annoyance from which he was rescued by a "Blue Band" margarine advertisement.

Johnny looked away and his eyes caught Dermot who was still staring at the sad metamorphosis of Hegarty's face. The youth's mouth was drawn tight and his contracted jaw muscles gave him a gaunt look. Johnny saw the edge of the tear that the pressure was resisting. They would all weep - and yet, the Luger in his pocket had eight John Hegartys packed in its magazine.

Nora broke the spell by getting up; a box of Kleenex was lying on the wooden arm of the couch and she pulled several of the tissues out and wiped Hegarty's face. He looked up at her and laughed his open-mouthed laugh and she chided him, this martyr man-child; she put her bent hand under his chin and shook his face gently from side to side and she smiled her loveliness to him.

She threw the used tissues in the fire and returned to her seat sensing the embarrassment and constraint of her visitors, fighting back the nausea that fourteen months of Hegarty's madness had not yet subdued.

"More tea - anybody?" They would not want tea but ...

Neither man accepted her offer and neither helped her off the subject. Dermot still sat awkwardly upright in his seat and Johnny was making visible his efforts to say something.

"No, Johnny, as I was saying," Nora was resuming their topic with effort, "When the new political clique came to power, whatever their intentions, they would still be obliged to organise production for the market - the world market - unless, that is, you aim at a spuds-and buttermilk Republic nestling in the deep furrows of its economic Celtic twilight. It is the market that would determine wages, unemployment levels, etc. etc. The capitalist WORLD market. You would be in the same position as the so-called Communist countries -your leaders would not be running the system, that is contrary to its nature; rather would the system be running your leaders, determining everything they could do, destroying their plans, their hopes, their ideals and their promises.

"But even worse, Johnny, all the old frustrations and miseries would still exist among the working class of your Republic - the frustrations and miseries that, in avowedly capitalist countries, find a safety-valve in illusionary change. You know what I mean, Dermot - from Labour to Tory, to Tweedledee from Tweedledum; but in your Republic, as in all the countries where politicians have tried to make a capitalist market economy work through the medium of State involvement, you would be forced to block the politics that give the illusion of change. You would have to resist the attempts of the disillusioned and unconvinced to throw "the Party" out of office - even if it means, as it always does, constructing an authoritarian regime that closes the avenue to genuine democratic change.

"You spoke of Marxist-Leninism, Dermot, and I know that it's the fashion of the Commies and the Lefties - and Johnny's Republicanism is just a hash of Gaelic romanticism stirred in a thick coating of debunked Leninism - to couple their names. But if these people, and their critics, would take the trouble to acquaint themselves with the works of Marx and his co-worker, Engels, they would find the same criticisms there that I am making now of their nonsense - the nonsense that Socialism can be established either in one country or by minority violence. They would also learn from the same source that State control is a phase of capitalism - but they prefer their Marx from the pen and the speeches of Lenin - the dictator who prostituted Marx to justify the actions that conditions in Russia in 1917 imposed on his Party!"

"You see what it is to get her going, Dermot?" said Johnny, "A veritable little soap-box utopian who hasn't even learnt that politics is the art of the possible."

"The correct formula for standing still, Johnny - preferably in the Government Party," she laughed.

"But, Mis ... I mean .. a .. Nora, what do you think is the answer? What I mean to say is, the answer in Northern Ireland, now? The Catholic people have to resist. We've suffered for years and then, in 1969, they burned us out of our homes and shot us because we were no longer prepared to be second-class citizens. And, after sixty-nine, what happened? We accepted the British Army as a peace-keeping force but because we were not prepared to allow the police, that shot us and helped the Protestant mobs to burn us out, back into Catholic areas, the peace-keepers of the British Army were turned on us. You know what happened last year around here - the Government that bashed us about for years were allowed to set the British Army on us, to break up our homes, shoot us, beat us up and do whatever the hell they liked. It was only after that that we started to fight back. What else could we do?"

Dermot's voice had risen as he spoke and his last sentence was almost a shout. Nora looked at him. What could they do? Dermot's was the plaintive, insecure cry of the Provisional

I.R.A.! What could we do? It was the justification for murder, arson, intimidation and all the other ingredients of terror; the apparently unanswerable postulation that history always uses to justify its crimes.

"Poor Dermot!" Nora's voice was filled with compassion. "What could we do? I sometimes think that the system's greatest crime is not that it cheats us of our material needs but that it cheats us of knowledge - deliberately waylays us into the path of frustration and ignorant assumptions.

"You said the Catholics were second-class citizens discriminated against for fifty years by the Protestants. So the Protestants, the discriminators, Dermot, they must be the first-class citizens. Now please. Think about it. A couple of hundred yards away from here, across the Shankhill Road, the Protestant ghetto, are these your first-class citizens? Are these the beneficiaries of discrimination against the Catholics? And what about the Catholic capitalists and businessmen who live at peace with their neighbours in the 'stock-broker' belts? Are these Catholics discriminated against?"

"But the Protestants get most of the jobs that're going; they certainly get all the good jobs. They get an unfair share of local authority housing, too." Dermot looked to Johnny for support but he had lost this argument before and, anyhow, he was preoccupied with events in Leeson Street.

He was thinking that Shields would be getting impatient. Maybe things were cooling down enough to allow the Section to move into action. He could leave a note for Quinn - Nora always refused to work for the I.R.A. even to taking messages ... Wish to Christ this lad hadn't been here ... wish he'd go away!

"Dermot, I don't want to go back into history; suffice to say that the propertied class in Ireland, at the turn of the century, the established capitalists in the North and their fledgling class-brethren in the South, were politically divided. In the South, they wanted control over their own political affairs in order to legislate conditions in which they could nourish their developing capitalist economy - they needed to restrict competition with tariff walls and import quotas. In the North, on the other hand, capitalism was well established, developed against the British home market. So the Northern capitalists needed to maintain the link with Britain to sell their wares and the Southern capitalists needed protection from British capitalism.

"The workers, North and South, because they mistakenly

associated their interests with the fortunes of their masters, were lined up behind the capitalists in their respective areas. The Southern capitalists rallied the people there behind them by appeals to patriotism and the notion that if they had their own government they would be free. The Northern gentlemen achieved their end by exploiting historical fictions and blatantly promoting religious bigotry - in fact, they nourished the prejudices which you, Dermot, have just enunciated. Naturally, the Unionist Party did not come out and say it discriminated in favour of Protestants - though it nearly did. No, Dermot, it publicly repudiated the suggestion but privately, it promoted the idea that it did among Protestant workers and it distributed some little rewards, in the way of jobs and houses, among its working class supporters to give credence to the idea. But if you think about it, you will see that the nature of the rewards showed the poverty of the recipients."

Before Dermot could reply the noise of a loud explosion rent the district and the loose frames of the windows shook. They remained silent, listening, then Johnny said "That was pretty close ... loud. Could have been a big one in town."

"No, it was a nail bomb; they make a big bang. Probably in Leeson Street." Johnny wondered if Dermot's confidence was based on knowledge or experience.

Dermot rose to his feet. "I'm sorry ... Nora, but I'll have to push off now. The talk was very interesting - I'd like to hear more sometime - but I still think we've got to fight if we are going to get anywhere."

Nora tried desperately for effect. "But, Dermot, don't you see that the friction between the Catholics and the Protestants was a squabble over things like houses, jobs and all the other poverty problems of capitalism. We'll get nowhere killing one another over the crumbs that fall from our masters' tables and, whether we have a Republic or not, our problems will remain - they are an essential part of capitalism everywhere. We've got to stop the killing! We can only find a solution to our real problems by getting together with those we have been led to believe are our enemies. It's not British soldiers or Ulster Protestants we want to kill - it's our own ignorance."

She was unconscious of Johnny's presence. Dermot was the urgent unit of her problem. Oh God! There were so many Dermots too busy rushing to the romance of destruction, eager for a place in the lists of Ireland's dead ... the felon's cap ... the martyr's crown. There was no MASCULINITY in Reason ...

117

no poetry ... no romance. The jungle and its values had built its walls ... time and persistence - but Time had Persistence at war!

They were still talking as they opened the vestibule door and they delayed just long enough for the big man to move away into the darkness of the street.

CHAPTER THIRTEEN

Preparation

Quinn had been to Leeson Street. His big frame had moved about the crowd acknowledging the nods of those who knew him and who would nudge those who didn't and speak his fame or notoriety. He had spoken to Dessie Hurley and, after the nail bomb had gone off, he knew that it would be said that Quinn got things going.

He'd seen McGivern and Shields. That bloody muck wouldn't speak to him - not that HE would answer the bastards. What were they friggin' about after? Some of the bloody glory, suppose. Bloody nail bomb had shook the soldiers! Christ! He'd arrived on the scene earlier and got things moving and a bloody soldier had got it; now, he was only back and several of the cows had probably got it with the nail bomb!

At the front of the rioters the situation had lapsed again into desultory stone-throwing and cat-calling though several rounds of rubber bullets had been fired at the crowd by the troops to keep possible nail bombers out of range.

Quinn had passed through the crowd.

"Hello Paddy! Got the bastards well fixed tonight, eh!"

"Three, maybe four, to nil, Paddy! The yella bastards don't know what to do!"

"Hi' Pat! You'll be taken up, man, for frightnin' the poor sodgers!"

"Good lad, Jim!" "Harry, boy!" "Enjoyin' the fun, James?" Quinn greeted them all; they all knew Quinn! He had lengthened his step and avoided the backward movement of a tall man by skipping briskly around him. "Hello, there!" All eyes would be on him - indeed a few young fellows had gathered around him and were keeping pace with him as he walked forward towards the Grosvenor Road end of the street. "Sarah - you oul rascal! What are you doin' round here?" Quinn spoke to them whatever the pressures! The young fellows had forced out a path for him through the crowd. People resisted the pressure but looked around, recognised him, and crushed to the side. "Quinn must be looking at the damage." Ah, there was the enemy! "Hello John - fraternisin' with Her Majesty's forces, are yi?" "Hello Tommy!" He had gone to the front of the crowd; several people had shouted over to him. They'd know something would be happening after this - they'd expect it!

He had surveyed the row of army vehicles, taking up different positions at the front, viewing the army defences from different angles, then, abruptly, he had turned around and still with the coterie of youths about him, had retraced his steps up to the corner of McDonnell Street where he had stood on the roadway between the two army positions and laughed aloud. "Jesus Christ!" Again he had cut his way through the crowd, moving back towards the Falls Road side. McGivern and Shields were still standing on the pavement where he had seen them earlier and he had turned to the group of young people around him and said, "Look lads, don't stand around; I don't want to be conspicuous. O.K.?"

He had walked with his head down when he passed Shields and McGivern, taking short, inconsequential steps. They did not look his way but he knew they had seen him and he spat on the roadway.

Ten minutes later, Quinn was on the other side of the Falls making for his home. Maybe that stupid little bastard, Dermot, had gone there and not to the bar.

Private Charters was cold. He looked at his watch; it was more than four hours since he had eaten - must be two hours already lying behind these bloody 'cans'. The fear had gone now; the vacant feeling in his stomach was hunger.

Carter's body had been placed in one of the Saracens. Poor Carter! But Carter was dead - it was meaningless to say "Poor Carter". It was poor Charters, poor Jackson, poor LIVING! Adam did not know if Carter's parents were living or not - he'd not really known him all that well - but they probably were. Maybe his Mum and Dad were having a row at this very moment, or having a drink, or watching telly or doing some of the other LIVING things. They would not know that their freckle-faced, fair-haired son was dead. They did not know yet that they were among the "poor"! They did not know that someone who did not know them, who could not gauge their loss, had squeezed a trigger - half-an-inch of finger movement! That because some anonymous being, who would open a door for them, or move aside to let them past, or make them a cup of tea, or do any of the myriad things that people do in the unconscious rationale of living, had felt wronged, some equally anonymous Carter had to die and, in dying, stir up a whirlpool of sorrow that would send its cold, sad fingers into the hearts of some and its bitterness into others.

Adam was surprised that he felt no real bitterness. The

face of Carter's mother that he had conjured up in his mind had increased his remorse but it had also soothed away his hatred. His dead comrade was too near, perhaps. No. It was the enforced inactivity of his present position; he was not simply FEELING; in concretising his feeling in the simple mind-pictures of those who would die a little with Carter, he was THINKING and he was transcending bitterness - knowing its futility, understanding that Carter's death was a Shylockian revenge on the whole of humanity.

Why? Why? Why had the short thread of Carter's life to run out before all the sciences had been tried in an attempt to arrest the atrophication of time on his ageing body? What purpose had his end served? Some politics or other! Politics - the grey areas beyond the physical act of being. Or was it about things? What little did a man want? Food, clothes, a place to live - to live ... to LIVE! To live in the sheer enjoyment of living! Not in the British way-of-life or in the Irish way-of-life but in the LIVING way-of-life! Jesus! - the thought made Adam look down at his rifle - What a bloody wonderful thing it is. Eighty quids worth of S.L.R. - a million tons of human thought - a billion-billion tons of human experience and ingenuity! All to do the job our savage forbears did with a stone! Surely there must come a time when its function would be to lie on green baize, beneath glass, embarrassing a learned curator's explanation to incredulous children.

Charter's reverie was broken by the explosion. He did not see where the nail bomb had landed but the flash and the panicked movement of the crowd back towards his position indicated that it had ben thrown at the troops at the Grosvenor Road side.

"Bloody hell!" It was Steen. He and the private who had been driving their Land Rover had scrambled into a low kneeling position close to the wall. Some of the men who had availed themselves of the security of the inside of the Saracens were looking out and asking those on the ground where the bomb had gone off.

Buick said "I'll bet it's bloody Hickson up there! Jesus, the bastard'll have us slaughtered to save his nice peaceful fucking rioters out there! Why the bloody hell doesn't he move or give us the word to move? We could shift that shower of shit in less than two bloody minutes!"

Sergeant Jackson was sitting on a riot shield, his back propped against the side of one of the armoured vehicles. He was smoking. Now he turned to Adam, indicated Buick with his cigarette-holding hand and said, "Field-Marshal Sir Ballox-Buick, you see. He had a plan!" Then he said, aloud to Buick, "Corporal, it's this arse-hole resting ole sergeant you should direct your criticisms at - not Major Hickson. He might be a silly old shit in ways but he's done more bloody fightin' than you've done shitin'. Maybe I haven't the benefit of your Sandhurst training but the little knowledge I have leads me to believe you must act on the balance of probabilities. Maybe these bastards will have their fun and go home; maybe it'll get worse. I see it as evens. But I bloody well know that, if we use the only means open to us to get out of here, neither them nor us will be goin' home for a while and, probably, some of us - I mean US, Buick - never."

"Oh bloody hell, Sergeant, we're bloody soldiers, our job is ..."

"Our job is to try and get some peace going, Buick. Sure we could turn a machine gun on the bastards and those who weren't dead would scarper like frightened rabbits, but remember lad, our Government says this is part of the United Kingdom and that makes that bloody lot out there disorderly citizens of the United Kingdom.

"Look, Buick," Jackson had raised himself and was speaking with new earnestness, "Hickson, as I say, may have his faults - he's certainly not the dazzling bloody major - but it wasn't the Hicksons that got us the kick in Cyprus or Aden or any of the other places where we were once the top of the bloody walk. Maybe if Hickson was running the whole bloody show here we wouldn't be in this position tonight. But be sure about one thing, be bloody sure about it, Hickson's no windbag; whatever he does, right or wrong, he'll do it in your best interest."

Jackson slumped back into his original position, raised his cigarette to his mouth with great affectation of fatigue and drew heavily.

"I'd still make a bloody example of those fenian bastards. Just give this little tool here the chance", he indicated his rifle, "and those fucking bead-rattlers would be running a shuttle service to the cemetery!" Buick's face said he meant it.

"Shootin's too good for the shit!" It was Steen, quiet-voiced and earnest.

Jackson looked at Adam as though he was taking a tally. Adam said, "Poor Carter."

The Sergeant's mouth was set in its cynical twist as he quoted: "'Peace is indivisable, they say; yet here, for peace, we tantalise each other's life with death'."

Hickson was consulting with his junior officers. He had allowed time to pass since he had taken the decision earlier to sweep the rioters up the street and he knew that he was wavering now in that decision - still hoping that the mob would thin out. It was a hope that was nurtured by the fact that, following the throwing of the nail bomb, no further indication had been given of I.R.A. presence.

Apart from the throwing of the nail bomb and his one serious casualty (at this time, he still did not know about the death of Private Carter) the affair was really more noisy than serious. There remained the comparatively small group of persistent stone and bottle-throwers, but apart from these, the composition of the crowd seemed to be changing. The street had been thick with people earlier; then the crowd had thinned out somewhat, and after that its numbers varied from time to time but generally appeared to be getting smaller. He guessed this was the only action in the area tonight and that the comings and goings of people represented mere spectators induced to the scene by noise and rumour.

No. As Belfast riots went, and particularly riots on the Falls, it was not really serious. Precipitate action could make it so, could bring them in from miles around and not just to watch, either. But he had to make contingency plans.

Now he was briefing Captain Clark and Lieutenant Mairs. Each would take a detail of twenty men and circumnavigate the block on either side endeavouring to take up positions in the narrow streets that would flank the advance of the main body of troops. This would allow them to give cover to the men who were cut off at the bottom of these streets and to protect the flanks of the main party when they were moving forward. It would also mean that the rioters could not use these streets as avenues of retreat but would be forced back along the main street. It would have, too, the practical and psychological value of forcing the most active participants in the riot - those at the front - to retreat rapidly to avoid encirclement. The flanking parties, after they had taken up their positions in the adjoining streets, would move first, in response to a double whistle blast, in order to be on hand to protect the two outposts as soon as the main party started advancing.

Unless there was an active I.R.A. presence among the rioters, Hickson expected them to yield easily. Batons and rubber bullets could, of course, be used but if the crowd yielded easily before their advance, then they should not be used needlessly. Their purpose was to clear the rioters off the streets; taking prisoners was not a priority if they were achieving this end – "We don't want to give the silly bastards any totem poles." If petrol bombs, explosives or firearms were brought into use against them then the men could fire for effect – in accordance with the conditions of their "yellow cards".

Clark and Mairs set off to detail their sections and Hickson descended from the armoured vehicle and went up to the barricade of vehicles across the mouth of the street. He stepped up behind two of his junior officers; "Well, the stones seem to have eased – are the pavements all used up? What's happening?"

"Definite thinning out, Sir, I'd say. Seem to be breaking up," said the Second-lieutenant.

"Good! Good! Let's have a look." Hickson went into the narrow corridor between two of the vehicles and peered out, then he extended his hand backwards and took the night glasses from the lieutenant. He held the binoculars to his eyes for a full minute then lowered them, backed out from his position and turned around to the two officers. He looked thoughtful.

"Hm ... well, we've got what we were waiting for. Yes, indeed.. They're breaking up, alright; moving off. I don't like it! Oh, I don't mean the moving off. No. I think they're moving 'way because they've been told to ... far too quickly! Smacks of organisation. Look. Look, Lieutenant, here, you have a look; watch carefully for groups moving away – see if they are being told by someone to move off. Oh, aye, of course, the glasses!"

The senior lieutenant took the glasses from his chief and turned towards the vehicles. Captain Maithison was coming over from the corner.

"Sir!"

"Yes, Maithison? Our friends are going away, I see. Did you notice anything peculiar at all?"

"Well, sir, just that there's a group of determined chaps lingering on before our position – but they are losing their support very quickly, Sir. The crowd in the back are moving away in groups – God, yes! I see what you mean, Major Hickson. It could mean that ..."

"I would say "does mean", Maithison. 'Fraid so. Didn't read that way earlier, mind you, but there was always the chance they would cash in. Set it about, Maithison, like a good chap. Nothing on Sergeant ..." He stopped; the lieutenant was at his side, "Well?"

"Definitely, Sir. Saw some chaps moving among them and then they moved off. Notice also, Sir, that the composition of the group in front of us here has changed. No youngsters. Would you think, a holding party, Major?"

"I would indeed! Yes. Well now - look, see to the men. No one between the vehicles. All flaps down! See that those chaps on the far side are alerted."

Just then there were two dull bangs from a hand-gun somewhere in the street to the right; then silence. A minute passed and then, again, a single shot from the hand-gun followed by the sharp crack of three rounds fired in quick succession from a high-velocity rifle.

It had started.

CHAPTER FOURTEEN

Death in the Living Room

When Nora came back from letting Dermot out Johnny was standing with his backside to the fire. He was anxious to get away; he was, he knew, leaving things a bit thin and Shields and the others would be getting concerned. But he had to see Nora alone, if only for a few minutes. Hegarty was there, of course, sitting sideways on his easy chair with his legs drawn up, his eyes riveted on the television screen, his face, hands and eyes still conveying the drama of his mad comprehension. Hegarty did not matter; events in the room were beyond his concern.

Nora left the front door partially open when she returned but closed the vestibule door behind her and immediately turned to Johnny. They were both embarrassed; Johnny lowered his head slightly and a trace of colour touched the girl's cheeks. It was the house, of course - the private arena of her constant friction with the brother with whom she lived and whom she detested. Johnny knew how much she would have liked him to be a regular visitor in her home and how her concern for the actions of her bullying, unpredictable, brother militated against her desires. And now, here they were together in the tiny living room.

"I'm sorry, Johnny. Dermot's so young ... such a nice lad. God ... you feel so ... so responsible for them. Oh, Johnny, I'm glad you came!"

Johnny said "Nora!" She had put forward her hand but he had not yet taken it. Her eyes were wide, her cheeks flushed; the wide nostrils were quivering. Their eyes were fixed on each other now; cutting away all background, inducing the pure form, each of the other into the wild vortex of their minds. "Nora!"

"Johnny!"

It seemed as though their tension had given a volatility to the atmosphere around them and the message of their names ignited it and their bodies fused. One of Johnny's arms was around the responding softness of her waist and the palm of his other hand was on the back of her head pressing her lips against his mouth.

She held him close to her with a fierceness he had not known in her. He freed a nostril for breath but she denied

126

him, struggling to maintain the pressure of her mouth on his. All the time her head was moving from side to side forcing him to yield. She lifted her head to breathe and, with a mouthful of air, said, "Johnny! Oh, Johnny!" and again her mouth was on his.

Suddenly she thrust him from her and, still holding lightly on his arms, said, "Johnny, why do you want to see Paddy?"

The urgency of her question struck him; she was constantly argumentative about his I.R.A. association, but never questioning - indeed she often rebutted his efforts to cross the line of political argument with minutiae of I.R.A. activity. Now her tone left him in no doubt that she wanted a definite answer and the thought occurred to him that her attitude was being dictated by her complete distrust of her brother and the fear of their association.

Johnny told her about his recent experience in Leeson Street and about his prior information on the British agent. He explained that he had nothing to go on beyond the fact that the big man he had met fitted the description given him earlier and the look on his face when Johnny observed him in contact with the troops. As he told her about the latter incident he realised that, away from the moment of its happening, it was, indeed, brittle evidence. He had difficulty himself now recalling the condemning detail of that moment; the evidence of a "guilty LOOK!" - it almost sounded foolish to himself now to have based his mission on his perception of a man's mouth movement and the look in his eyes and cast of his head - the almost imperceptible detail of a face in night shadow! He felt guilty about the defensiveness of his emphasis; "I'm convinced, Nora, he was the character we have heard about; his whole attitude, quite apart from his physical similarity, showed it. At any rate, I think it's important that your brother should pass on to the others my - if you like - suspicions."

They sat down together on the couch, their knees touching, her right hand in his. He put his left arm around her and tried to draw her head towards him but she resisted. Her face was drawn and the dark pits of her eyes reflected the troubled imponderables of their tomorrow and showed their pain. Physically, now, she was with him, in the warmth of his presence; but her mind disdained the pleasure of the moment - probing the sadness of life away from him. Again his arm tightened on her neck and he brought pressure to the threshold of pain, turning his body towards her and speaking her name in a whisper that rasped in the thickness of his throat; but she only tightened her grip on his hand and put strength into her resistance.

"We must talk, Johnny; we must talk seriously." Her eyes were in front of him and her voice was soft even if the inflexion showed her urgency.

His mind said: not now, Nora! Can't you understand that I'm guilty already of dereliction of what I must do ... the men are waiting ... the scene is set ... life and death are stamping their feet in the wetness of the streets awaiting MY signal ... history is being held in suspension ... men are stealing minutes more of life than fate decrees while I press for the softness of your body and the soothing warmth of your kiss. Shields, Danno, the brothers Gallagher, Hagan, Boyle, Speers and the others - men who have mortgaged their security and comfort, their love and loved ones in underwriting the cause of a new freedom - what would they say, these earnest instruments of history, if they saw me here, now, in this warm room craving a kiss?

Aloud, he said, "Please, Nora ... please ... not now. Again - later. I can't stay any longer; there are some people waiting for me and, really, I shouldn't have come here. Please understand! I promise you, later ..."

"Later ... later! Johnny, can you be sure there will be a 'later' for us? I don't want to be whispering into your grave, Johnny! I don't want the memory of a brave man to soothe away the sorrow of my widowhood. I love YOU, Johnny - you, JOHNNY CAIRNS, as you are now; not brave, bold, proud, dedicated Johnny Cairns, who died for Ireland!"

Johnny had taken away his arm and relinquished his grip on her hand; he was sitting upright now, breathing heavily and trying to shrug off the anger that was welling within him. Nora would have more to say: it was not her form simply to throw off the top layer of her thoughts without delving deeper into the substance of her argument. The sentiment was real enough but it was a dramatic, almost despairing, counter to his urgency - and he had no time, now. Still it was a challenge to his love and the honesty of his actions.

"I didn't expect that from you, Nora. The doctrine of the comfortable; the gospel of doing nothing to improve our condition that will disturb the limited comfort of that condition. So we should sit back while others make the sacrifices? We should wait until the grand day of Socialist Reason arrives when we will press an electoral switch and, hi presto! The millennium! The wageless, moneyless, world society of peace and harmony! For God's sake, Nora, we're living in the present! Sure, I accept that your object is the final answer - but what's to be done NOW?"

Nora had hope in her eyes. She was not competent to deal with unreasoned idealism - with the notion that if you opposed that which was patently wrong, simply because it was wrong, cruelly, pressingly wrong, then you had right on your side. Even the words, the emotional vocabulary of their idealism, "right", "wrong", "justice", was the measure of their misunderstanding - a confusion of the relative conditions of slavery with the urgent, feasible, reality of freedom.

"Johnny, people are always making sacrifices for all manner of things. We can't simply dedicate ourselves to the cause of sacrifice and, because there IS an easy way to a full and happy life for all - a way made difficult by the confusion promoted by those with an economic interest in the present scheme of things and, unconsciously, maintained by people like you - does not mean that we should disdain it simply because there is no sacrifice in blood or suffering involved. We can't, Johnny, for ironically, the easy way, the way without blood and death and hatred and violence, the way through the avenue of reason and understanding, is THE ONLY WAY to freedom!

"We can't IMPOSE freedom. We can't tell the working class that they can have strawberries and cream and if they don't want them, force them down their throats. Oh, I know you say 'mere words', a dream of reason, but in the last analysis, we can only gain freedom in concert and that requires words ... words and, if you like, dreams. Less heroic, perhaps, less romantic than guns and sacrifice - but the mountains of sacrifice, the millions of dead, Johnny, have brought people no nearer freedom. What about the last time? What about nineteen-sixteen? Nineteen-twenty? Was there not enough suffering then to appease the gods of sacrifice? Not enough dead? Not enough ..."

"Ah!" Johnny was eager. "There I would agree with you - but the dead ... the sacrifice, was not, then, invested in real freedom. It was lost in the limited vision of ridding Ireland of the British. That's why the I.R.A. now - the official I.R.A., I mean - is primarily concerned with what is to follow our victory over British imperialism. God, Nora, you know I'm not a complete simpleton, a gun-crazy romantic! None of us are. This time, I assure you, it will be different!

"But, honestly, love - look, I'm not running away from the argument but I must go. It's really pressing - I must go!"

She allowed him to raise her to her feet. He put his arms around her waist and kissed her but the emotion was gone - lost in his urgency, and he did not even appear to notice the restraint in her response.

Then, suddenly, she grasped him fiercely, her arms beneath his, about his waist pressing with all her strength. "Don't go, Johnny! Please don't go! I'll never ask again - I promise you! Just this time - this once. Please!"

"Nora! Look, darling, tomorrow we'll ..."

She had released herself, stepped back and was staring wildly into his face. Her hand shot forward to the front of his coat. "You have a gun, Johnny!"

He tightened his overcoat about him and was grasping for the buttons, stepping back further from her. "Look, don't worry, Nora. I promise you ..."

The noise outside the front door stopped them, he in the act of buttoning his overcoat, she with her arms slightly raised, her eyes fixed on him and holding her fear. Each heard the noise of their breathing, the queer purr of the electric clock on the mantlepiece and the thunder of Hegarty's movements in his seat.

Silence.

There was a mighty crash as the vestibule door flew open striking the wall that right-angled away from its hinges. The door struck the framed portrait of Nora's late parents and it scraped its way down the wall and shattered on the floor accompanied by the crashing of the big man on the floor of the living room.

"What the fucking hell are you spying about?" Paddy Quinn's great form filled the doorframe. Mad anger lit his drink-infused face; his lips were back from his clenching teeth, his cheeks straining above his jutting jaw, his eyes, half closed and cruel, burning their message of hatred at the great bulk of man slowly recovering across the living room floor.

The man raised himself to his knees and slowly clambered to his feet - his head touching an arm of the ornamental light fitting in the centre of the ceiling. Quinn was inside the door now, his left hand pushing it forward then, his back against it, pushing it closed. He was not as tall as the other but if anything, he was even more massively built - a massiveness that was emphasised in his mood, whereas the other man had adopted a deliberately cowering position. Johnny had put a protecting hand to Nora and, with a sweeping gesture of his arm, had put her behind him towards the doorway of the kitchen. Only for a moment had he taken his eyes off the stranger.

Quinn raised the back of his hand and brushed away the

drop from his nose. "Caught this cur in the bloody hall when I came to the door - earrywiggin'!" He jumped forward, his hand, rising from low down his side, travelled in a wide circular movement and, with his full vigour behind it, his open hand struck the big man, flat and noisily full, upon the left cheek. "Well ... who the fuck are you?"

The man buried his head deeper into his shoulders, the red welt of the blow showing on his face. He took on a craven, obsequious look - shoulders stooped, head bowed, looking at Quinn's feet. "Jesus ... man! Let me ex ... explain! I wasn't doin' any harm - I was only ..."

"You're a fuckin' copper, aren't ya?" Quinn had taken the lapels of the big man's mackintosh and was shaking him vigorously.

"Honest to God, I'm not!"

"What's your name?"

"Reilly - Tony Reilly."

"From?"

The big man raised his head slowly, now; his eyes, lightly searching the room, passed Johnny's face and flicked back, momentarily. He grinned crookedly, with deliberate uncertainty, and again his eyes caught Johnny, fleetingly. "A'll tell ya - honest. Maybe A'm up to no good - sure, A'd lift sumthin if Ah got the chance - but A'm no bloody copper! A'm certainly no bloody copper!"

Johnny's brain was racing fiercely; he was trying vainly to shut out the scene, to get back in his mind to Charlie McGivern's house ... Charlie McGivern's voice. He remembered the name "Clements", easily; the rank, description -even the history that McGivern had given him - he could remember. But his forename ...? He needed it for effect and it was in his mind, eluding his concentration, playing hide-and-seek with his thoughts. It was ... was ... what the hell! No, that was one of the others. It was ... yes! That was it! It was Oliver! Lieutenant Oliver Clements!

Quinn had taken his hands from the big man's lapels but the bellicose expression remained on his face and the set of his body was still threatening.

"Ya wudn't shop me to the coppers, wud ya? If they get me A've had it - that's why A'm hangin' aroun' this district an' A've helped the people roun' here too, when they've bin fightin' the bloody soldiers."

Johnny said, "Yes. He's right. I saw him in Leeson Street earlier - didn't I? You were trying to rustle up support for a go at the military."

"Ah, God Almighty! Sure you're the fella Ah was talkin' to - that's right. You were there when the petrol bomb wus thrown - Ah know your face now." The big man turned a wide grin on Quinn. "Ah told ya Ah done ma bit, didn't Ah?"

"Lieutenant Oliver Clements, isn't it?" Johnny kept his eyes on him, watching it sink in. "From Larne, originally. Folks in Canada. Served with the S.A.S. in Aden ..." Johnny's gaze passed momentarily to Quinn and was held for a second by the latter's expression of puzzled bemusement.

When he looked back at Clements the big man was already drawing the gun from under the breast of his mac. The craven look was gone; his great height and bulk now dominated the room - a mighty man with a look of haughtiness and arrogance that made the old clothes he was wearing seem incongruous.

"Yes, gentlemen!" He clicked his heels mockingly and bowed stiffly from the waist, "and of course, madam." The gun was pointed at Quinn's midriff. "Our interesting friend here would appear to have a little knowledge - and you know what they say about a 'little knowledge'."

The man had lost his peculiar northern Irish accent. Now his speech was deliberate and his previous accent hardly discernable in his polished, but nondescript, enunciation.

"Well ... you fat pig! Our less-violent friend here would seem to have confirmed my suspicions."

The movement was fast; the muzzle of the gun had struck Quinn on the ear and left temple and Clements had stepped back again. It was a hard but glancing blow and now the blood was oozing down the slivers of opened skin and flowing in rivulets down Quinn's cheek.

"That's for starters, you might say, you fat pig! You are a fat pig - a fat pig - a fat Irish pig! Aren't you?" Clements was gnashing his teeth and grinning viciously, then he broke into a high-pitched laugh, "He-he-he-he-he. Fat Irish fucking pig!"

"He's a madman!" Nora's voice was a whisper and Johnny's hand went quickly on her arm. The big man's eyes swung violently on to her and then, turning his head slightly, but still holding the gun on Quinn, he focused on Johnny, probing deeply with his eyes.

"I want you, my clever friend! The boy with the know-ledge, eh? I think ..."

Everything seemed to happen at once. Clements had turned his body towards Johnny without changing the position of his gun arm and the gun was now pointed in the middle distance between Nora and her brother. At the same time, two things happened; Nora jumped protectingly in front of

Johnny, and Quinn, his big body upright, charged at Clements.

The two men collided; Quinn fell backwards off his victim, lost his balance and fell heavily at the feet of Nora and Johnny. Clements had fallen back, too, before the weight of Quinn's charge; he had tried to regain his balance but his backward movement brought his heel in collision with the raised hearth and he fell backwards heavily, landing on his backside on the hearth, scattering the brass companion-set and ending up with his head against the low mantle shelf and his back covering the full aperture of the fire.

For a second there was near-silence in the room, then Clements issued a shrill cry as the hot coals burned into his back. He bent his body forward trying to scramble off the hearth. Quinn was turned now on his hands and knees muttering savagely and incoherently in his heavy gulps for breath. Johnny had moved to the right and Nora was standing transfixed behind the heaving bulk of her brother - now placing himself to spring on Clements.

The seconds were suspended; Clements had raised the gun in his extended arm pointing it directly at Quinn's middle. His face was a hideous mask of hate, his mouth was contorting viciously and the knuckles of his hand were white around the gun butt. "Fucking Irish pig!"

Quinn made his move and Clements' index finger squeezed on the trigger. No one had seen Hegarty raise himself to a standing position on the cushion of the easy chair, his alarmed eyes staring fixedly at the gun. Now he sprang through the space between Johnny and Nora. His heavy weight had fallen across Quinn's shoulders, impelled towards the gunman. A mad, incoherent, eerie, inhuman, roaring weight of humanity that now slumped between the two men, its legs against Quinn's stomach and its head and shoulders in the lap of the killer.

Hegarty, the congenial madman, was dead.

Clements bullied his way out from under his victim and was now crouching on one knee in the middle of the floor raising his gun arm at Quinn. The two shots blended into a single roar. The big man's eyes rolled in their wide sockets and he toppled over on his right side and fell groaning on the floor. His fall vibrated the ornaments in the china cabinet. The thick red blood gurgled from a gaping hole in Clements' neck.

Johnny had lowered the Luger to his side. His face was white and his body convulsed. The acrid smell of cordite filled the room as the little swirls of grey smoke eddied upwards. Johnny turned around and was sick in the corner.

Nora was on her knees beside the dead Hegarty.

Immediately after the shooting they had carried the bodies of Hegarty and Clements to a vacant lot at the bottom of the next street. They would just be two more mystery killings for the armchair sleuths of the newspapers to conjecture on.

A few neighbours who had been attracted by the noise had come about, and it was several men from among these who had carried out the task of disposing of the bodies. Paddy Quinn had left them to it but Johnny had ensured that Nora was taken to a neighbour's house before he made his departure.

The rain had cleared as he crossed the narrow streets towards the Falls Road, his mind now filled with Nora's white shocked face. She had not spoken to him before she had been taken away. They had put a man's jacket across her shoulders and were gently pressing her towards the door and she had stopped in the frame and turned her head around to where they were preparing Hegarty's body on the sheet for its short transport. The first tears had come suddenly, flowing freely down her cheeks and her lips had moved in silent expression of her grief.

CHAPTER FIFTEEN

The Battle Continues

Charlie Shields   ᵤ been furious. The section was now billeted in two adjoining houses in Sorella Street with the exception of Hagan, the sub-machine gunner, and Boyle and Speers, who were in a house in one of the streets on the other side of the Grosvenor Road awaiting the time to attack the rear of the main British army position.

Johnny had taken Shields' tongue until the latter had exhausted his anger. Then. he told him about his mission to Quinn's house and about the shootings. Shields seemed more upset at having tongue-lashed Johnny without hearing his explanation than he was at the intelligence. "Jesus Christ! What a bloody terrifying experience! God, Johnny, I'm sorry for the narking - I didn't know. I confess, I thought the worst of you."

Johnny said nothing; he was embarrassedly conscious of the fact that the drama of his explanation left no explaining his delay with Nora before the incident.

"I think you should sit this one out tonight, Johnny. You must be shaken, man. Look. Leave now and make your way home - no one around there is likely to know you so there's not even a remote chance of you having unwelcome visitors tonight. You can be on the other side of the Falls and well away before this thing starts. Give me the rod - just in case..." Shields was really concerned.

He fought the desire to go - though Nora allied herself with Shields, in his mind, to force him. It would be capitulation. It would be a surrender to his doubts; an acknowledgement that nothing could be done. Nora's dream vision could not be the answer to the problems they now faced; it was not reasonable. People would require scores of years of education - my God! The proposition was totally inhibitive! Nora's sad, pale, face argued back at him: could a Republic, even if it could be achieved by force of arms, even if its fabricators could, through some form of political alchemy, make a million opponents docile to the splendour of the new freedom, could it solve any of the basic problems? Poverty, unemployment, bad housing, insecurity - no republic anywhere in the world had achieved an answer to these problems. "Before you raise your gun, Johnny, before you kill another human being, you must,

YOURSELF, know HOW your new Republic will solve these problems for if it can't, the struggle, the deaths, the miseries and the bitterness are all in vain."

His mind evaded the question. Nora, your solution is inhibitive; we can do nothing for people now if we accept your view. Her response would not be shut out: "We can give more people the answer; we can free them from the restrictive thinking that is YOURS, Johnny. We can arm them with a political H-bomb, with knowledge, and, as more and more demand the orchards of living, so even more will get the apples!"

Shields was looking at him. "I'm sorry Johnny but we'll have to push off now. Will you take my advice and go home?"

"No, Charlie," he said and got to his feet feeling for the two spare magazines and loose ammo for the Luger.

They had sent a runner over to Hagan and the other two men. They were to take up their positions immediately and open the attack at eleven-twenty, by which time Shields would have the others in position. The original plan of attack was to be scrapped. Now the section was to divide into two units, one under the command of Shields and the other under Cairns. Cairns' unit was to proceed down the Falls Road to Panton Street from which they could reach the city side of McDonnell Street. Shields' unit would open their attack from a frontal position in Leeson Street, trying first to knock out the two army positions at the Leeson Street, McDonnell Street junction in the initial stages of the battle, when, it was hoped, the main military party would be occupied by Hagan and his comrades enfilading their position from the Grosvenor Road.

A number of small packs, each containing four two-ounce sticks of gelignite taped together around a core of six-inch nails, was distributed and Cairns ensured that those who received them had the means of lighting the short lengths of safety fuse that protruded from one of the sticks of each bomb.

Johnny and his squad of four men reached McDonnell Street safely and had separated on to opposite sides -the two young Gallagher brothers staying with him on the right, approach, side. They were close enough now to see Sergeant Jackson's position at the corner of the street and remarkably, the military had taken no precautions to protect themselves from attack on this side but were obviously depending on the main body of troops, at the Grosvenor Road end, to sight and rebuff any attempt to approach them from the lower end of McDonnell Street.

Johnny stepped into an open doorway and looked at his watch. It was almost eleven-fifteen - more than five minutes to go. He would tell the others not to proceed further up the street until he gave them the signal, immediately before Hagan would commence firing at eleven-twenty.

He stepped out on the pavement again and noted with satisfaction that the others had remained close against the walls on either side. Suddenly Liam Gallagher broke from his cover in a doorway and came racing towards him but before he could deliver his message, Johnny saw the party of soldiers deploying on both sides of the street from the same direction, and the same manner, as his own smaller force had done a few minutes earlier.

The British party showed no inclination to advance quickly and the lead soldiers had only come up the street far enough to allow the entire party, in close order, to take up stationary positions against the walls on either side. Cairns guessed that their object was to sweep the street and link up on the flanks of the main army group which was obviously intending to relieve the two outposts in Leeson Street.

Johnny thought quickly; the best counter was to have his men "disappear" off the street into houses on either side - allowing the flanking party an unimpeded approach when the military indicated commencement of their closure movement. After they had passed the I.R.A. party could re-emerge with a clear target in front of them and an open line of retreat at the rear.

He pushed Liam Gallagher into the hallway from which he had just emerged after checking his watch. The two volunteers on the other side were together now and he watched them disappear through an open front door and saw the door closing. He craned his head forward; Phillip Gallagher was not in sight; he, too, had obviously sought refuge in one of the houses. He found himself laughing inwardly; the telepathy of fear? Or was it good training? Neither praise nor blame could be levelled in a situation denying alternatives. He moved quietly back into the hallway beside Gallagher and closed the front door.

There were nine members of "C" Company, 1st. Battalion, Belfast Brigade of the Provisional I.R.A. in the small room of the house in Leeson Street. Their ages ranged from 'Skip' Donnelly's sixteen years to 'Chuck' Duffy's thirty-five. They had all been engaged in actions of one sort or another over the previous months and, though the intelligence would have surprised them, if danger and destruction were the measurements of experience, they were all veterans by comparison with their O.C., Paddy Quinn, for whom they were now waiting.

Tousle-haired Skip, whose nickname had been earned in some forgotten boyhood escapade, was a bomb artist. Normally he worked with Glover, who was also present in the room. Glover usually 'borrowed' the Cortina - the praises of which both youths sang louder than Fords - and carried the gun. Sometimes, if security at the target was very strict, Glover would accompany Skip into the chosen premises, the latter bearing the box or the duffle-bag containing the bomb. Skip would usually approach the security man, most often a British Legion commissionaire or a uniformed guard from one of the security firms, with a broad grin on his face. "'Scuse me, mister, but I was asked to deliver this here and to advise you that you have three minutes to clear the building - that's right, mister, it's a bomb!" Glover would then draw the colt automatic to ensure their uninhibited retreat while the terrified security officer would set about giving the alarm.

Sometimes Skip worked alone. He'd left a television set in a down-town repairers once; after he left the premises he 'phoned the repairers from a nearby kiosk to tell them they had two minutes to leave the building. Five minutes later three shops and an office block above them, all part of a new complex that had cost over one hundred-thousand pounds to put up, were blasted so severely that they had to be demolished subsequently.

Bespectacled Adrian Rice, who now sat beside Glover in the Leeson Street room, was the company Engineer. Rice was a house-repairer and general handyman of modest abilities who should not have known anything about bomb-making - but he did! He'd learnt about explosives from Chuck Duffy; straightforward stuff, like making the I.R.A.'s own specialities 'Lummite' and 'Paxo' on the kitchen stove, handling gelignite and gun-cotton, priming a stick of 'gelly' to detonate a bomb, constructing 'observation' and 'contact' mines as well as making timing devices with a contraceptive condom, bees'-wax and sulphuric acid or an alarm clock. He was an intense, interested student whose application and ingenuity had soon put him ahead of his teacher.

He was always on the look-out for new materials, new devices of destruction. Not long after he used the automatic switch of an electric blanket he had members of the Company scaling the short lamp standards in the back streets of the Falls to retrieve the timing clocks and once, after it was reported that one of his bombs had been pushed out of a building with the jet of a fire hose and had failed to explode on the street, he had spent an evening devising a bomb in which the explosives and detonator were water-proofed with polythene sheeting. The firing mechanism, which was not water-proofed, consisted of a Mills-bomb striker and coil spring held back by a piece of heavy cardboard which would break down after soaking in water. This would allow the spring to send the striker forward, piercing the polythene and exploding a point two-two cartridge into which the priming fuse had been fitted.

The bomb had gone to the place where the fire hose had been used previously but this time, it had been defused by an army bomb disposal captain who had wondered how it was intended it should go off!

Rice was the unknown terror of the British army's bomb disposal squads. His handiwork had accounted for the deaths of two senior disposal officers, had brought buckets of sweat from others and had created many a morning or evening traffic thrombosis in the city. He had filled many pages of the little diary he carried in his breast pocket with the record of official estimates of damage caused by the bombs he had made. No names, dates or money symbols appeared on the pages; simply the cash amount of each official estimate, in figures only together with a similarly stated estimate of his own for broken glass, etcetera, in premises within damageable range of the explosions. Each page was totalled up and the amount carried forward to his current grand total of £3,611,000.

Chuck Duffy, a milk roundsman and ex-British Army sapper, was also in the room. Chuck helped his late pupil, Rice, in preparing some of the bombs but was especially useful in repairing and maintaining weapons as well as 'delivering' some of the bigger bombs. He was regarded as a good all-rounder in the company: knowledgeable, a good shot with the M.I. carbine and thoroughly reliable in a tight corner.

Spence, Morrison and Lindsay sat together on the couch. they were all around twenty years of age and one of them, Martin Lindsay, had seen service with the Irish Army, from which he had deserted to return to his native Belfast after the troubles of August 1970. The three men kept very much to themselves, sharing their own jokes, confidences and conversations and sharing equally the enmity and even mild distrust of the rest of the Company. Their language, their coarseness and their attitude to members of the Cumann na Bhan, the women's section of the I.R.A. - whom they referred to as the

Cumann na Flap-Doodle - were resented by their puritanical comrades but they were protected by Quinn's favour and their undoubted fighting qualities.

Peter Adams was seated in the corner by himself. His eyes were closed and the others knew he would be praying - not because he was afraid (indeed he was always the least afraid of any of them) but because he was a passionate believer. Quinn had quipped about him one day: "Adams would not only believe that Jonah was swallowed by a whale - he'd believe the fucking whale was swallowed by Jonah, if the Church told him!" Adams was a fanatic; about the Church, the Irish language - which he spoke only poorly - and about the I.R.A. These were his trinity of absolutes - probably in reverse order.

By profession he was a bank clerk despite a good education which had been supplemented by a London University Arts Degree, resulting from study during his internment in Belfast prison from 1958 to 1961. Outside the subjects of his bigotries, he was an engaging and talented fellow but the ramifications of his religion and politics militated against friendship outside a narrow circle. He was, for example, desperately suspicious of Protestants and this, and the other phobias of his beliefs, inflicted him with an unworldliness and insularity that set him apart from his fellows.

Still, he was probably the best Thompson-gunner in the whole of the I.R.A. He had, by his attentions, earned the right to keep the Thompson - which he had affectionately named 'Sean' - in his private and apparently secure 'dump'. It was maintained always in excellent order and he had painstakingly filed down the mainspring boss, to allow the weapon to respond easier to trigger movement, thus controlling the concentration of fire to a greater degree than the manufacturers had provided for.

Adams always prayed before an engagement. He was not ashamed that the others should see him - no more than he would have been ashamed to bless himself in the public street when passing a chapel. In his mind the martyr's death was an open passport to heaven but even so, heaven would have the bonus of an immaculate soul.

After an engagement he prayed, too. He prayed for Ireland, he prayed for peace, he prayed for victory and once, after he and Spence, Morrison and Lindsay had attacked an army post and his Thompson had killed a soldier, he had suggested that they should seek refuge in a Catholic church and "say a decade of the rosary for that poor corporal who got it across the stomach."

Doran, the ninth man in the room in Leeson Street, was twenty-five and he was married with four young children. Sometimes he'd say he wasn't 'very Catholic' - meaning that, before the troubles, his Catholicism was the nagging of his wife on Sunday mornings to get him to mass. Doran was now a desperado; "Rob banks, blow buildings, shoot bloody coppers, soldiers or any other bastards connected with the system!" To him 'the system' was the Protestant workers in the factory where he had worked as a fitter, who had driven him and two other Catholics out of work; it was the two soldiers who had kicked him into senselessness one night, when, in his giddy inebriation, he had disputed their parentage; it was the raiding party of soldiers and police who had broken down his front door at four in the morning and invaded his bedroom, terrified his children, left him in a 'frisking' position for an hour while they pulled up floor boards and pulled down ceilings. The 'system' was ESPECIALLY the two women police who had brought his dark-haired, innocent, Margaret into the bedroom and stripped her naked and slapped their foul hands across her face and body in response to her gentle protest. That was before Doran had joined the 'Provos' - before he learnt that 'the system' lurked in every bank, every department store, every government and municipal office; 'the system' that beat in the heart of every politician, policeman, soldier and flunkey of the State. Doran was against 'the system'; he was 'for' nothing other than destruction and death.

The chatter of the men ceased when Quinn came into the room. His face was flushed, his clothes dirty and dishevelled and he had obviously been drinking.

"Sorry I'm late, lads. I went up to my place to catch Dermot - the wee bastard niver turned up wi' the stuff - and, Christ! I ran into a bag of trouble. A bloody British secret-service man waiting for me at my own bloody front door! He'll be lukin' for a job wi' oul Nick now. The bastard!"

"Did you kill him?" It was Adams, back from his prayers, whose statements were always the shortest distance between two points.

"Dead as the bloody dodo, Peter - but to business, we'll have to hurry."

It was nearly eleven-fifteen when the men left the house. Their plan was Quinn's simple strategy: get as close as possible to the two military outposts further down the street, blast them with nail bombs while concentrating a heavy fire on the main body of troops, then escape into the street on their left.

Peter Adams had the butt of the Thompson in the left-hand

pocket of his raincoat - the type which has vertical slits on the outside and openings to the same pocket on the inside. The heel of the gun itself was resting in his cupped palm, in the right-hand pocket with the foresight nestling where the coat tightened at his shoulder. He and several of the others had no difficulty in getting right up to the vehicles surrounding the army position at the corner of McDonnell Street and positioning themselves out of sight of the latter, around the corner.

Quinn was now swaggering about the road, where the crowd was now considerably thinner. He approached the army vehicles on the left and actually stood on tiptoe to look over the bonnet of one of the Saracens.

"Down, you bastard!" Corporal Buick's angry face was staring at him from behind the raised S.L.R. "Come on there - out of it!"

Quinn retreated, staring back insolently. "Like to come out a there w'out the gun and talk to me like tha' ya yella-bellied English bastard! Come on if yer such a hard man. Let's see what yer made of!"

Buick levelled his rifle, raising his body higher. Steen was now at his side, his weapon at the high-port position. Buick said, "Listen, mac, I've had as much as I can take of you fenian shit. Be on your bloody way or I'll blast you - so help me! I'll blast you!"

"Corporal!" Jackson pushed Charters aside, "That's enough, Corporal!" Jackson looked at Quinn, "Hello, lad. Looks as though ..."

"Ah, fuck you, too!" Quinn moved off, turning into the street behind Jackson's position.

"Nice fella, that. Jesus, Buick, you'll never learn, will you? And just when chow and bed is looking closer!"

"I'd a liked to give it to that fat pig!"

"We're giving it to nobody tonight, Corporal. Thank Christ! This show appears to be almost over. On your feet, lads. We'll start the journey, eh - Jesus ...!" "The two shots, dull and heavy, rang out. They were from beside their position. They all stood perfectly still, alert, while the seconds ticked. The next shot was from the same gun and then, further down the street at their rear, they heard the screaming ricochet of three rounds fired from a high-velocity rifle.

As the last of the firing died away the engines of the army vehicles at the Grosvenor Road end roared into life. They did not move off immediately but commenced revving the motors loudly, sending their great billows of noise and smoke up the narrow corridor of street.

The armoured Land Rover had moved into position behind the heavy vehicles. Its rear doors were open and Hickson, Maithison and one of the lieutenants were preparing to get in when the Thompson gun opened up from further up the far side of the Grosvenor Road.

A train of bullets crossed Hickson's back and splayed upwards across Maithison's head. The Lieutenant dropped to cover behind his two dead comrades.

CHAPTER SIXTEEN

The Ultimate Sacrifice

It was Quinn who spotted the soldiers moving quietly up either side of McDonnell Street. The time was eleven-eighteen. Adams was standing with his back to the wall just around the corner from Sergeant Jackson's position fixing the butt on the Thompson. As Quinn hissed a warning he clicked the magazine into position, moved two yards down the street, and took up a crouching position in a doorway.

Quinn raised the forty-five and fired twice down the street. He made no attempt to seek cover but stood like a man bemused, holding the gun in firing position. Whatever the chemistry of fear or anger that was active now in his system, it had allowed the whiskey to become his master - a master that made him great ... invincible. He staggered three steps down the street and fired again.

The rifle shots rang out in quick succession. Quinn fell, the sickening, unimpeded thud of one with greater pain and fear than that offered by the hardness of the ground. For a few seconds his arms and legs worked vigorously, like some fat terrified swimmer, then he rolled around on the ground and raised himself slightly from the road on his arms but before he could straighten them they folded under him and his face slapped on the hard concrete and he was still.

Peter Adams motioned to Skip Donnelly, Spence, Morrison, Lindsay and Rice who were crouching against the wall behind him, without cover. Adams was a volunteer in the Company; he had eschewed officer rank with the most elaborate excuses though he knew, privately, that he did not want to accept responsibility for the lives of any of his comrades. Now, however, with Quinn dead, the mantle of responsibility descended automatically on his shoulders and was accepted.

The black curls of Donnelly were now behind him. Like some smooth-moving, fragile lizard the boy had moved up the base of the wall, elbows and knees giving hardly-discernible traction to his slight body, his head low so that his pale face would not show in the darkness. Cradled in his arms the big Webley service revolver looked even larger than it was.

The youth continued his wriggling motion, keeping his dark head towards the bottom of the street as he ascended the step of the house and moved in behind Adams. Even then his small body remained curled up as he raised his face toward Adams, the fixed mischievous grin showing on his lips. "How many d'yi reckon they got down there, Pete?"

Adams was again peeping around the door in the direction of the bottom of the street. He said, with propriety, "I ordered these people, in the name of the Irish Republic, to put out all lights and retire to the rear of the house." He brought his head back again; he was sitting on his haunches now, and he manoeuvred himself around to face Skip, the butt of the Thomson resting on the tiles of the hallway. "I think we should try and make our way back up the street and around the British post there - if we can make it before Doran bombs it. It's either that or ..."

It was at that moment that Hagan's Thompson started its shattering on the Grosvenor Road - relieving Major Hickson of his command and his moral dilemma.

Then all hell broke loose: Shields and his section opened up from positions in Leeson Street; the main party of military at the Grosvenor Road end were returning the fire towards attackers at their rear and were, at the same time, reversing one of the Saracens to give cover from the fire of Hagan and his party. Now some of them were returning the I.R.A. fire from Leeson Street. Death was screaming up and down the street, rattling off the pavements and roadway - and yet there were womens' voices around to lend their fearful, terrified accompaniment.

Adams realised that he and his comrades were boxed in. He concluded that the others in his section had opened up on the soldiers and that the heavy firing across the top inter-section of the street was the British army's massive response. At the bottom of the street, flanking the road on either side and blocking their planned line of retreat, were the soldiers who had shot Quinn. He might have attempted to retreat with his comrades into the terrible criss-crossing fire of Leeson Street but, even as he considered the idea, he saw the soldiers at the bottom of McDonnell Street beginning their advance up both sides of the street.

He swung his body out further from the doorway and fired a burst down the street close to the wall on his own side. He moved in a little, jammed the barrel of the Thompson against the brick edging to prevent upward movement, and emptied the magazine down the far side of the street. The double echo of the shattering Thompson reverberated through the narrow streets, dying in an echoing silence, the shattering of glass and the running footsteps and curses of the fleeing soldiery were followed by a renewed burst of firing from the contending forces in Leeson Street.

Peter Adams was balancing the Thompson by its pistol grip. He put his right index finger along the receiver and forced the magazine release with his thumb using his other hand to pull the magazine free. Another box magazine had been taped to the empty one with its platform reversed and clearance allowed for entry to the body of the gun, and Adams now reversed the magazines and snapped the new one into place. He looked around for Skip before taking up his firing position but Skip had crawled out of the hallway again and Adams saw only the soles of his shoes, wriggling briskly and quietly, as he snaked his way along the base of the wall.

In Leeson Street, Charlie Shields had opened the firing from his party at the troops. The McGarry brothers, who had arrived late at Sorella Street, were with him on one side of the street and Connor and Burns were on the opposite side. Tony McGarry had a double-barrelled twelve bore shotgun and his brother, Liam, had an old American Springfield. Charlie Shields had a long-barrelled 9 mm. Mauser "Peter the Painter", and was well provided for with four clips of ammo. Their target was the military position on the right-hand side of the street which was occupied by ten of the quietest soldiers seen in any war.

This group of soldiers were in a particularly difficult position. The vehicles behind which they sheltered after their hasty retreat had, more by fortuitous accident than design, been drawn into an excellent protective tightness which had, largely, sheltered the men during the stone throwing earlier. Unfortunately for the defenders of this outpost, however, most of them had been armed with batons only when the retreat came about and their rifles had been left in one of the vehicles that helped to form the protective barrier of their comrades at the other corner. Only two rifles and two baton round dischargers remained with them and the use of these was restricted by the very tightness of their defensive position - which meant that a marksman would have had to take up an exposed position either on top of, or underneath, the vehicles.

One the other side of the street, across from Shields, Connor and Burns had taken up positions in open doorways. Both had modern self-loading rifles and were concentrating their fire mainly on Sergeant Jackson's position from which, as yet, no fire had been returned.

Liam McGarry had now given the Springfield to Shields who was motioning to Connor and Burns to stop firing. Connor got the message and, between shots, shouted it to Burns. Both men were well concealed in the doorways when the three S.L.R.'s from Jackson's emplacement started ripping at the bricks around them and yet they were able to observe Liam McGarry running quickly down the other side of the street, close to the wall, hidden from the view of Jackson's men by one of the vehicles that was protecting them.

McGarry actually stood in the angle of this truck and the wall, his arms by his sides, his body touching the armoured vehicle and the wall. In the course of his journey he was open to the view of the soldiers on the other side of the street but now, for the moment, he was probably in the safest position in the street - at least as far as enemy fire was concerned. He fumbled under his coat and brought out the two bundles and then he turned his face to the corner, placed the bundles on the ground and got down on his haunches. The light flickered for a second, McGarry lifted the bundles and pitched them high over the Saracen.

At that moment there was a crunch of metal against metal as one of the vehicles in the army position across from Jackson's moved forward about six feet into the roadway, pulling one of the other vehicles partly around with it. There was a wild scurry of feet as the frightened soldiers raced from the new opening and scurried down the street towards the main army position. As soon as they had gone a few feet, Shields and Tony McGarry, in their separate doorways on the left of the street, had lost sight of them - their view obstructed by the vehicles protruding on their own side. Immediately after the last man - the man who had moved the vehicle and then jumped from the driver's seat - had disappeared from their view Shields heard the two quick revolver shots and knew, from the direction of the yell and the noise of the falling body, that this man had not made cover. He assumed he had been brought down by Cairns' party in McDonnell Street.

He did not know that Doran, of "C" Company, First Battalion, Belfast Brigade of the Provisional I.R.A. had just scored a blow against 'the system' from the top of the narrow street, behind the military position into which McGarry had just thrown his two bombs. Nor did he know that at that very moment the tousle-haired Skip Donnelly was in the act of lighting another bomb.

That was the moment, too, when Peter Adams saw the soldiers moving again up the narrow street. His action was instinctive and predictable. His moment of sacrifice had arrived - the moment for which life had been a mere preparation. It was with him now and he was AFRAID - but it was the fear of the actor in the wings when, after all the study, all the rehearsals, the great moment arrives; the fear that he might disappoint his unseen audience of Ireland's dead who, enshrined in their heaven, were yet never far from the bleeding heart of Ireland. The fear that his death might not win penitents to the shrine of Cathleen Ni Houlihan; that he might sully the Martyr's path with a questioning of death.

It was his supreme moment of dedication; the culmination of those dreams dreamed in the felon's cell or in the moments stolen from the actuality of money changing and accounting in his mahogany cell in the bank; of his sexlessness, his abstinence from alcoholic drink and strong language. It was his song, his smile, his poetry - it was him!

The imposed inferiority of his childhood life in a Falls Road back street had been the mould of his patriotism. His mother had taught him the songs of defiance against an alien culture and way-of-life that had vanquished the bards and robbed the common people of their dignity and material prosperity; that left them soulless and barren - the mere court jesters of their ancient foe.

Patriotism was the songs and the poetry of Ireland; was cleanliness and dignity - rising superior to the "Paddy" concept of the English. It was acquiring the ancient tongue; it was education along the lines of purity and decency and dignity; it was exorcising the notions of the slave and developing oneself, mentally and physically, for the ultimate sacrifice - for God and Ireland.

Adams aesthetic features were pale, his eyes blazing, his lips moving in silent prayer. Across his mind flashed the vision of his mother - she would bear her grief with pride. His last thought, before he moved into the street, was a montage of sadness and sad curiosity: his comrades of Oglaig na h-Eireann! Was this, finally, for Ireland, the dawning of the day?

On the street he was a soldier of Ireland and his enemies were almost on him. He ran into the middle of the road, took up a left-foot-forward stance, jammed the butt of the Thompson fiercely between his elbow and side and swept the street with a raking fire, a vicious 'flat-eight' described by the contorting of his trunk and arms. Three men fell before the withering fire and Adams turned to run for the shelter of the door again, to change the magazine of the gun, when the bullet struck him. He almost regained his balance at the pavement but the soldier with the night-sight, at the far corner, was deadly accurate and his second shot removed a piece of Adams' head.

Before Peter Adams had made his stand, just as the soldiers who attracted his fire were beginning to move, in fact, Skip Donnelly had lit the nail bomb. The bomb had a five-inch fuse which would allow him some twelve seconds before it exploded. As he ran the few yards to the end of the street he heard the crunching of metal as the Saracen on the other side of Leeson Street moved to allow the soldiers to run for the cover of the main army group. Already several of the men had moved out of the gap and were running towards the Grosvenor Road end of the street. Skip hesitated, the bomb in his slightly-raised hand. The soldiers had moved too quickly to allow him enough time to mentally adjust to the idea of tossing the bomb at them instead of his intended target but, before he turned again, he saw Doran raise the revolver and fire twice at the man who had jumped from the driver's seat of the Saracen and when he was running towards Sergeant Jackson's position he heard the yell and the sound of the man falling.

Before he dropped to roll the bomb in under the armoured vehicle he saw the muzzle flashes from the three S.L.R.'s, firing obliquely across the street in the opposite direction from him and it was this that determined him to ensure that the bomb was well placed. He was on his hands and knees at the rear wheel of the flanking vehicle when the voice had shouted, "Look out, Buick! It's ..." and he had a brief look at the two spluttering points of light. Two terrible blue-white suns burned into his eyes and the ground beneath him went giddy; then there was the terrible flash beside him. He had an impression of the ground moving away to the left of him, moving fast for a long time, and there was nothing on his right to hold on to. He felt no pain other than the fearful silence and, peculiarly, he waited for the noise to break out again - like a swimmer waiting for the water to run out of his ears. But the bright, luminous, concrete still moved away underneath him; his body was suspended and there was absolutely no sound! Even the weight that fell across him did not seem to push him to the ground.

Sergeant Jackson, the gruff-voiced, brusque soldier, who boasted his sins but had never added hypocrisy to them, was decapitated. The State would bury him and his official demise might occasion some preoccupied functionary a moment's annoyance before the buff folder would be finally closed in the happy realisation that the Sergeant had, officially, no next-of-kin.

Adam Charters had lost his eyes, ripped from their sockets; part of his lower jaw was missing and his right forearm had been torn off. With the help of medical science Adam would live and might even achieve a condition of pained happiness sufficient to reflect that if only God - or the Ministry ... But such subjective wisdom would be self-pity.

Steen was alive; he was blind and deaf and would never speak of the hours of sewing that would join again the parts of his mutilated body. The remaining confusion of limbs, flesh and bone was the human debris of three other soldiers.

Only Corporal Buick had escaped unscathed. He had been thrown into the air and had fallen, unconscious, with an awesome, sinister symbolism on the dead body of Volunteer Frank Doran of "C" Company, First Battalion, Belfast Brigade of the Provisional I.R.A. Liam McGarry had run only fifteen yards after tossing the bombs into Jackson's position. It had been his intention to get back to Shields, concealed in the doorway of the house forty yards from the explosion, but his eyes, dominating his terror, had noticed a partially-opened door as he ran from the scene after discarding his lethal burden and he had crashed into the doorway and thrown himself down with his arms covering his head.

The two bangs had come crashing on top of each other and the ground had rumbled as though in a state of subterranean indigestion. But as the noise dissipated in an accompaniment of lesser noises and breaking glass, even as McGarry was withdrawing his protecting arms from his head and adjusting his panic to thoughts of escape, the third explosion occurred. For a few seconds he was overwhelmed not simply by the force of the explosion but by the sheer force of his surprise.

His legs were rubbery as he charged from the doorway and ran up the street to where he had left Charlie Shields. He had to slow up in order to find the right doorway but, still, he had passed it when he noticed Shields standing well back against one of the walls. He bounded back and jumped into the hallway flattening his body against that of his chief. "Jesus! Did you hear them? There was three explosions! Must have been their ammunition, or something."

Shields did not reply. His ashen face was drawn like a death mask and McGarry felt the tremble of his body - the involuntary shivering, a fearsome ague. Shields' eyes were straight forward in his head and his left cheek was on the wall and away from McGarry. The latter looked at him, put a hand to his chin and forced his face around towards his own.

Shields' eyes did not move in their sockets but turned, fixedly, with the face. There was concern - fear - in McGarry's voice: "You O.K. Charlie?"

Without using his hands, Shields pushed the weight of his companion off him, turned towards the wall again and, with great caution, towards the edge of the door frame. It was only then that McGarry became aware of the resumption of the shooting. The sharp crack of rifle fire mingled with the dull bangs of revolvers and, now and then, the shrill singing of high-velocity bullets ricocheting away into the night. Across the street from him he could see the muzzle flashes of the carbines in the hands of Burns and Connor.

Shields withdrew his head. His voice was low, fearsome, "My God, Liam - there's bodies everywhere down there! Good God! What are we going to do? Oh, merciful Jesus! We're done for. We can't get away! We will be ..."

He was holding McGarry now. His voice had risen in a trembling falsetto and his body was shaking desperately, beyond the control of his terrified brain. "For Jesus sake, Liam, what are we going to do? I never thought that ..."

McGarry caught a movement on the periphery of his vision. He raised his left hand to Shields' chest and pinned him harshly against the wall. His eyes strained out into the darkness: either Burns or Connor had run down the street and was now firing at the main body of troops from underneath one of the abandoned Saracens.

He turned again to Shields. The man had accepted his pinning to the wall without any resistance and now stood on tiptoe against the wall mumbling incomprehensively. McGarry' open right hand whipped his face viciously and Shields, with his right hand, forced the other's hand from his chest with ease and pushed McGarry against the open front door. For a moment he held his cheek like some overgrown child contemplating rebellion and looking as though he was going to cry but his body had stopped trembling.

"Where's the Springfield?" McGarry was searching the dark hall, "Where'd you put the bloody rifle, Charlie?"

Shields' voice was remarkably steady. "I thought it best to get rid of the guns, Liam. I flung them down there, out into the road. If we've any chance of getting away ..." Shields was recovering. "I mean ... retreating - I thought ..."

"Jesus Christ, man! WE'RE WINNING! That's THEIR corpses down there! We're winning - you cowardly bastard, Shields! Where'd you throw them?"

McGarry was on his haunches, bending forward trying to

scan the dark carriageway. Shields said, pointing, "Over there, somewhere" but McGarry's eyes had already picked out the shape on the street.

He bounded, crouching, from the doorway and Shields saw him throw himself down on the road. For ten seconds he did not move then he raised himself on his left arm, his left leg forward, the rifle, muzzle downward, steadied against his right thigh. His move had been prompted by a lull in the shooting but as McGarry rose to make the run back, two shots rang out, overlapping each other, and he pitched forward and fell over the rifle on to the ground.

Shields realised that the shots that had killed McGarry had come from further back up the street. The British had them boxed in.

CHAPTER SEVENTEEN

Despair

Throughout the entire area of the Falls people were standing at their doors in little clusters or in groups at street corners. The noise of the Leeson Street battle could be heard plainly and rumours, largely coloured in the bitterness of their origin, were being handed out, enlarged and passed on.

Thirty soldiers had been killed by the I.R.A. The British Army was pulling out of the Falls district and encircling it in a ring of steel. A British general had been shot. The two factions of the I.R.A. had united in open insurrection. Fierce battles were being fought in Derry, Newry, Strabane, Dungannon and other places. Units of the Irish army had mutinied and were crossing the Border to help the I.R.A.

Nora Quinn had risen from Mrs Fleming's living-room couch. The ministering care and concern of the big woman and her husband had been overshadowed by the excitement and they had both gone to the door to join in the animated babble of voices discussing the Leeson Street fighting.

Nora had heard the explosions as she lay on the couch but these were the sounds of the Belfast night scene that registered only superficially on her consciousness. Her thoughts were on the grim events of the evening - on Hegarty, on Johnny and the gun. Suddenly she realised, with a sharp quirk of conscience, that she felt no real remorse for her brother. She could understand and feel sympathy in the abstract... for the I.R.A., the British soldiers - she'd even hazarded an understanding of the conditions likely to create the big man who had killed Hegarty - and yet her brother, Paddy, went undefended at the bar of her understanding. It was easy to understand the alcoholic, the mentally ill, the thug, the... the anything! But not when you suffered the direct consequences - not when it was your brother!

When she did come to the front door of Mrs Fleming's house, she could hear the shooting quite distinctly; sometimes a rolling concentration of fire chased by its echo over the low lines of slum rooftops; sometimes the emphasising silence broken by a single shot or a short burst followed again by the angry overlapping of fire, all knitting their grim tapestry of horror into the night.

Mrs Fleming, her husband and those neighbours who were

standing about the door, counselled Nora to return to the warmth of the house but she argued for air; for 'company' to 'lift' her. She listened to the chatter of these frightened people; to Mrs McGrath who hoped she'd, "live to see the day when England will be on her knees", when "the Russians or the 'Chinks' kick THEM about, break up THEIR homes, insult and degrade THEM as they're doing to us." To Mrs Hughes, who was secure in the knowledge that God was "Slow but sure". To her husband, who thought the I.R.A. should start bombing the families of British Army personnel in England.

They all spoke in tones of hatred, about death and violence and revenge, punctuating their bitterness with banalities about the power, goodness and mercy of God. And yet Nora knew that these were- the poor... the poor who knew kindness, charity, generosity and mercy as a way of life. What terrible thing had happened to these people that they had become so alienated from the very precepts they had lived with ... and suffered with?

Neither the politicians nor the generals knew these people. To the gold-braided general and the silver-tongued politician these were just the mere packing of real social existence; these were the scum - the poor who are always with us; the drawers of water, the hewers of wood; the people who exist in slums to make mansions; who have nothing and make everything. To the politicians they were mere things to make promises to... to cheat, to bluff... to strut over... to allow to bow and scrape. Happily, they were ignorant, servile, submissive - but, sometimes they got out of hand; then the generals took over. The generals took some of them and put uniforms on them and guns in their hands and used their ignorance, servility and submissiveness to get them to glory in their new power and to use it, always obedient to the generals, in keeping down, or putting down, the others.

And the Johnny Cairns and Dermots and Mrs. Flemings and Mr. McGraths thought they could be opposed with the same weaponry; cultivated hope where there was no hope - because the real enemy was not the politicians or the people they served or the generals who served them; the real enemy was the ignorance of the people, THE FAILURE TO UNDERSTAND THAT THEY WERE THE REPOSITORY OF ALL REAL POWER in a world rotten with riches... riches sufficient to allow men to forge a veritable Walt Disney wonderland of material plenty.

But there was nothing romantic in exorcising the ignorance of the working people. The system has created its own values, its notions of bravery and strength and courage. It would be the task of history – in a society where there was no measurement for exchanging wealth – to comprehend why the slave continued to prattle in song and story about his dreams of freedom and wanted to fight only to change his masters ... to die in defence of his misery. All for so long ... so sadly, so tragically long before it occurred to him that he was the keeper of his own chains.

All their thinking was within the confines of the patterns laid down for them by their masters. They made virtues of necessity, talked of 'rights' that were really obligations imposed on them by the whole pattern of slavery they accepted as the only way of doing things. They 'demanded' the 'right' to work when work, FOR THEM, was an obligation. They would never have entertained the notion that it was within their power to 'demand' the condition of life of their masters – the 'right', if they required it, not to have to work.

In the early days of the Civil rights struggle, Nora had argued with some of the leaders. They had said that the Catholics were second-class citizens often denied jobs and houses simply because they were Catholics. Nora argued that the struggle for 'civil rights' was, then, no more than a demand on Authority to allow members of the working class who were Catholics an increased share of the poverty of that section of the working class who were Protestants. "If you are demanding 'first-class' citizenship for your followers, why do you hold up – the mere poverty of fully-employed, council-housed, Protestants as your ideal? Even if it were possible to eradicate ALL unemployment and ALL slums – and no government ANYWHERE has been able to fit these ideals into its market economy – would not, then, all the Catholic and Protestant workers, in full employment and in their council houses, with their larders and peace-of-mind mortgaged for Great Universal shoddiness, electric heaters and Woolworth culture, still be second-class citizens in relation to that minority of Catholics and Protestants who live by hiring labour?" But the notion of slavery was too strong within them for them to see this.

They talked of revolution – some even adjectivised their revolution with 'social' – but their minds were obedient to the concepts of leaders and led, of buying and selling, of wages and money, of those who did it and those who told them what to do. Their hope of tomorrow was an Ireland where the State would be the boss-substitute – setting their alarm clocks and programming their lives against the needs of the market.

Their scheme of 'socialist revolution' was couched in the vocabulary of capitalism ... employment, wages, exports, nationalisation - the slavish dreams of a prison free from hunger and homelessness where State governors or Party bosses would plan their ignorance, their docility and their submissiveness on their market progress charts and promulgate welfare relief to buffet them from the worst excesses of their continuing misery.

Show them the path to real freedom and they would rattle their chains and look amazed. Tell them that freedom was essentially a world concept based on the idea of voluntary human co-operation to produce the needs of the human family and free and equal access to all men in availing of their material needs - and watch the reaction of the slave! To pursue the hope - even the dream - was a treason to their knowledge of slavery - and all the social ailments of their condition, under the blanket of what the high priests of the system called 'human nature', would be trotted out in justification of the continuance of their misery.

And yet they would, with dedication, mortgage their miserable lives, offer their years to the prison or their necks to the scaffold, to change the colour of the flag that showed the location of their misery and they would add sophistry to ignorance in their misconception of the fact that man does not live by bread alone.

Give them work and a private cell to live, breed and pass on to their future generations of slaves the values of their circumstance; give them faith to understand that theirs is a pre-life, pursuant of an Eden in which things will be like for them, THEN, what it is for their masters NOW; Give them the poetry of hope, the promise of easement bound in the chosen bunting of some new master and you have patriots, idealists, poets - and slaves!

The bonded slave was a free man by comparison with these people; his master would marvel at the response to a factory horn - when he needed a spear! How had Shelley put it? "'Tis to be a slave in soul and to hold no strong control o'er your own wills, but to be all that others make of thee!"

These were the poor, the ignorant, the dispirited. The people who had erected their own prisons, their managerial trustees, their alarm clocks and klaxons, their spies, their policemen and jailers - a veritable perpetual motion of self-contained slavery outside which, the masters, cocooned by their joint-stock companies - which, even, the trustees operated for them - kept a strong hand on the faucets of freedom.

Nora fought off her despair. The sadness of the tragedy was in the present but the story of Man was his ability to overcome. The people WERE the power and they would retain that power; they could not lose it and it would be the handmaiden of knowledge – when knowledge came. They WERE beginning to rise from the sludge – they WERE beginning to throw off the old values, their priests and parsons, their belief in the dignity of labour, performed degradingly, their notions of respect for their 'betters', their belief that an end to poverty might be found in a wage packet.

They WOULD yet rise in dignity to transcend the mere problem of economic sufficiency and meet the challenge of a life where talent and industry, art and education were not simply the prostitutes of survival.

Mrs McGrath suggested that they should say a few decades of the rosary 'for peace'. It was their way ... they would faithfully enjoin in appeals to heaven – but they would pray with less fervour and expectation than their forebears and those who would now pray would not be the majority. Mrs Fleming, Mr and Mrs McGrath and a few of the older people filed into Mrs Fleming's little living room but it was no sin now to refuse and, indeed, when one teenage female slyly advised a male counterpart to join in the prayers, she drew the response "Ah wish to Jasus this bloody war was over!" and they all joined in the laughter.

Nora took the opportunity to get away. She could no longer stand the idle chatter of the doorstep – she was drawn, inexorably, by the sound of the guns. On a pretext, she slipped down the street towards her own home but she passed the door and continued down the street and around in the direction of the Falls Road.

CHAPTER EIGHTEEN

Back to the Oedipal Shell

Johnny Cairns was pleased that the occupants of the house in which he and Sean Gallagher had sought refuge were an elderly couple. When the fighting was over the military would seek fearful retribution in the area and obviously, they would be easier to convince that the old couple were uninvolved than they would be if the occupants were younger and more active people.

But the old man did not want to remain uninvolved; "Wet blankets, lad! That's what we used in the Twenties when their bloody fathers, the Black and Tans, were over here murderin' us. Get some blankets, Madge, girl! Get the furniture against the front door - best way out's through the landin' windy. You know, lad, I was in the Raglan Street ambush in Twenty-one. We dug a big hole..."

It was just then that Quinn had opened up on the military and they had returned the fire. The words had died in the old man's throat but he hesitated only for a moment before taking his wife's arm and forcing her towards the back bedroom. Johnny followed and insisted, with robust gentleness, that the old man accompany his wife and that neither should attempt to open the door of the room.

From a short distance off the Thompson commenced its fearsome chorus and Johnny knew that it was Hagan on the Grosvenor Road - but the earlier shots, outside on the street, puzzled him. It could not be Charlie Shields' party, they were to commence their attack from Leeson Street AFTER Hagan's fire. He instructed Gallagher to lie low beside the front window and made for the stairs to see what he could learn from the front bedroom window.

He was on the stairs when the short burst of machine-gun fire rocked the street and before his mind could grapple with its increased puzzlement, the gun was chattering again - this time a long burst that set the windows rattling and brought its responsive echo in a shattering of glass and running feet.

Johnny was easing himself to the window frame while Adams was changing his magazine and making the final preparations for his martyr's role. Johnny eased aside the flimsy lace curtains and peered out into the darkness. His eyes were adjusting their vision when he saw the man taking up a position in the middle of the street. Almost leisurely, he seemed to adjust his stance and his weapon to their task; then his form was lost to Johnny in the muzzle-flash as the blue-white flame sent the lead crashing on its lethal course.

It was slow motion now: the man was turning, his right leg forward; somewhere down the street a man was flinging the last moments of his pain on the night air; the man with the Thompson had taken his step and the sharp crack of the rifle was an echo when he staggered, then the crack happened again and the man was lying on the road. Johnny pulled himself back from the window and stood with his back flat against the wall.

Then the bombs had gone off. Johnny watched the curtains rise up, floating to the ceiling. Underneath him, the floor punched at his feet and even the wall at his back vibrated its protest. The curtains were nearly back in position when first one pane, and then another, cracked with brittle modesty and sent their falling pieces into the street. A cold wind swept through the room and the curtains ascended again, fell and had their ends pulled through the broken frames to flap in the night air. Again the near gunfire could be heard - dim against the echoing reverberations of the great explosion.

Charlie Shields was standing in the doorway in Leeson Street. He could see, occasionally, the flash of the rifle fired from behind the rear wheel of the abandoned Saracen at the corner of McDonnell Street. Whether it was Connor or Burns that had run to this position, before McGarry was shot, he did not know but whoever it was was changing his position every now and then, firing at the main party of military at Grosvenor Road and then, at the patrol further up Leeson Street, on the Falls Road side, which had accounted for McGarry.

Shields was not shaking now; he was thinking with grave intensity and, at the periphery of his thoughts, there was a real consciousness of his conquest of panic. Only McGarry had witnessed his fear ... his moment of panic ... and McGarry's body was lying out there on the wet road, holding fast to its grim knowledge. Charlie wondered if he was glad that ... that he would not be able to ... No ... NO! He examined the question again. No! No! No! But Charlie was disturbed at his lack of real grief. He barely knew the lad, of course ... seemed a nice enough fellow ... But real sorrow is seen in association with knowledge; he didn't know how McGarry laughed ... never knew about him ... family ... girlfriends ... grief was the transfer of their feelings - they were the tallies of remorse. He just seemed O.K. and Charlie was sorry. He'd rather he wasn't dead but, since he was dead – he didn't want to associate the two but it was a fact – since he was dead ... well ... no one would ever know ... no one would ...

From the hallway almost in front of him, three shots were fired off quickly. There had been a temporary lull in the shooting which, by contrast, made the other noises of conflict appear as silence and it was this, and the flashes lighting up the small square of hallway in which the shots were fired, that accentuated their cracking sequence. Charlie still did not know whether it was Burns or Connor who had remained in the hallway but whichever of them it was, his comrade under the Saracen, further down the street, followed the three shots with a rapid-fire fusillade up the street in the direction of the troops on the Falls Road side.

The reply took the form of two single shots fired, presumably, by an army marksman, with an interval of a few seconds between. Charlie heard the bullets sing through the night air and saw one shot spark off the brickwork surrounding the hallway. He discerned dimly the form of the man in the hallway taking up a new position and half-a-minute later he was again firing up the street from close to the ground.

It was obvious that both the man under the Saracen and the man in the hallway opposite Shields were trapped. At best they would be captured; if they were not shot and wounded or killed, then, inevitably they must be captured; – they could not escape. And yet they continued to fight, each with the knowledge that, outside death, further resistance could only aggravate their fate. It was probable that both knew, and accepted, that death was the most merciful answer. If they raised themselves to surrender it was probable that the troops would shoot them anyway but if they were taken alive, their fate, at the hands of an enemy in the throes of hate-incensed fear, would be terrible indeed.

The soldier's abiding respect for the power of legal authority was overwhelming and was reflected in his attitude to his enemy. If this was a war between two LAWFULLY constituted armies, using the most ghastly weapons of destruction, the soldier would not question the source of legality of his enemy or the purpose for which such legality was being used. His hatred would be dissipated in the fighting and when the battle was over his prisoner was a fellow-soldier who had done his duty. He would share his rations with him, exchange family chit-chat or give him a fag. If his enemy died in the fighting he would bury him with a fanfare of trumpets, play the anthem of his enemy and wrap him in his flag. It was the thing to do – the civilised thing – for lawfully constituted enemies to do.

But if the enemy was not 'lawfully constituted', then he was a terrorist. The more bravery, the more daring, such an enemy would show, the more intractable his villainy. If he was captured alive, his fate should be the boot, the fist or the torture chamber. If he was dead, he should be buried ingloriously. How else could it be? If it were not thus, might not all sorts of brave causes find armies?

Shields wondered about Cairns' detachment. He had heard the shooting behind the blown-up army position and assumed it to be the work of Cairns and his men. At the Grosvenor Road end of the street the military position had remained static with only an occasional volley being fired up the street in the direction of the man under the Saracen. Obviously they were still concerned with Hagan's party on the other side of the Grosvenor Road - it was some time since he had heard the Thompson but he had heard other shortarm fire and didn't know whether it was coming from Cairns' party or the I.R.A. group on Grosvenor Road itself. Presumably the military at the bottom of the street were going to play 'shovel' to the 'brush' sweeping down from the Falls Road side.

He had not debated with himself his own position. He had discarded both guns and ammunition - he was 'clean' and the guns had been wiped free from fingerprints before he had thrown them into the road. His alibi was sound enough - he was an officer of the Citizens' Defence group - even the military authorities knew that - and he was in the street trying to becalm the riot when the shooting had started and had taken refuge in the hallway.

Cairns watched events from an upstairs bedroom. After the explosion the troops at the end of the street had retreated. Most of them had run for the safety of the gable walls but a few had sought urgent refuge in doorways.

Across the road from the window at which Johnny watched, he could discern the form of a soldier lying inert on the pavement. The man was either dead or unconscious. Somewhere out of his vision, on the side from which he watched, a man had screamed immediately after Adams had cut loose with the Thompson. Johnny had heard the screaming but did not know whether it was the protest of terror or pain, but every now and then after that he had heard noises that told him it had been pain. In moments of quiet, when the guns were seeking their targets or being recharged, he had heard the man.

After the shrill scream had come the explosion and, then, the guns; a shot here, a volley there, a crisp shattering of overlapping sound as the grim musicians of death set forth their fearsome orchestration. In a moment of quiet, after this, Johnny had heard an English voice; the man was not shouting, he was talking, loud, but as though to himself and his voice vibrated with suppressed pain or fear - or both.

Johnny had heard the sounds of the man's body scraping along the ground. He could make out the sound of his boots, of metal, even of flesh, in pained traction against the wet pavement and the noises carried the awful substance of the soldier's plight to Johnny's inner vision. From somewhere at the top of the street the guns carried on a sharp, fearsome exchange then, again, the silence - or the lesser noises of battle - descended on the street. The voice of the wounded man rose from a crackling incoherency of pain to a pervading, eerie loudness that started a cold finger down the spine of the night and brought violence greater than the sound of the guns in the minds of the combatants. For a full ten seconds the full-blooded animal cry was in command of the battle, staying fingers on triggers, paralysing hatred ... a loud, cruel cry that hung suspended over orders and ideals, a cataclysm of sheer terror that sucked in bitterness, revenge, courage, cowardice, profanity and anger and left man in the action of death momentarily contrite, naked ... humble.

The cry ebbed from its chilling denouement to a feeble sobbing that they heard because it was accentuated by their terror. It was the adult sobbing of a baby retreating from the imposed defensiveness of life, coursing back the short years to its oedipal shell. "Ah... agh-agh-agh-agh-ha-agh... mam-my!".

The silence of attended death crashed on them. In the respite there were no longer British soldiers and I.R.A. volunteers trading death - each in the protection of his ideals or legality. The barriers were down - their purpose and instruments irrelevant in the few moments of humble unanimity and fear during which they identified with the pain, fear and defensiveness of the man who had died.

Even the resigning crack of the single shot that followed seemed lonely and apologetic and Johnny Cairns knew that his was not the only fleeting hatred of the finger that signalled the resumption of the conflict. Absently, he thought of an injured cat in a tree; he saw the soldiers and the I.R.A. volunteers, their ingenuity pooled, their resources combined in its rescue - but the desecratory shot was the harbinger of other noises of death and the thought died on the crack and counter-crack of resumed conflict.

His back was against the wall at the side of the window and

he was aware that he was shaking. He raised his thumb from the butt of the Luger by his side and scraped the nail against the rough serrations of the butt plate, absently - almost as a test of the reality of the situation. His thoughts turned to Nora. Were these the birth pangs of the new freedom? Her face was close to his, its sweet scent dominating his consciousness until her voice said, quietly, "Are they, Johnny? Is this piece of fashioned metal with the power of death, truly the instrument of freedom? How's it going to work, Johnny? Freedom... freedom... FREEDOM! Before man can be anything, Johnny, Catholic, Protestant, English, Irish, black or white, freeman or slave, he must be LIVING - not dead! In order to live he needs food, clothing, shelter, Johnny, and in order to live in freedom, he needs free and equal access to these things. Will your Luger create the conditions of abundance for freedom, Johnny? Is your gun the great revelation? The precursor of universal knowledge? Have you revolutionised the gun? Changed its historic role of enslaver to that of emancipator? Is it to be the voice of the people with the alchemistic power to make freedom, the fruit of knowledge, grow on the barren boughs of ignorance and acceptance?"

Viciously he thrust her from him; drove her harshly from his thoughts and puzzled the enigma of her parting words: "It takes a brave man, Johnny, to resist the fool's coward," "but the death cry of the soldier was still in his mind - the terrible finality of death, raised on the shoulders of doubt.

The noise of movement outside arrested him and he became aware that there was now no one shooting down the street at the soldiers. He turned his body to the window and looked out.

On the far side of the street he saw the soldiers in cautious extended file moving up the street in a quiet leap-frogging action. One of them would move into a doorway, raise his rifle to the firing position and offer cover for a plimsolled comrade who would pass him and adopt a similar stance in another doorway. Johnny held his breath and stood on his tiptoe trying to see into the pavement immediately beneath him and he heard the quiet movement of rubber soles on the pavement and, a second later, the front door of the house carried the pressure of a man's weight against it.

CHAPTER NINETEEN

Charlie Gets Out

Charlie Shields was thinking of fear. Connor and Burns were holding back a hundred well-equipped soldiers. Were they afraid? If they were, they had mastered their fear for every shot they fired was a derisive gesture at death. They must know they were living out their last moments on earth, that they were going to die - yet their unpractised hands still fulfilled their deadly function.

He wondered if they could think beyond the reality of their rapid movements - aiming their rifles, squeezing their triggers, scrambling back from the path of their enemies' fire. Were they concerned with the imminence of death? Were they preoccupied with staying alive only for the grandeur of the moment? - Did no future, no pain, no tears, no love intrude on them? Or, were they heroes? Did they transcend the carnage, hating the killing made necessary by the needs of their ideal?

He did not see them as heroes; they were two rough, uneducated fellows who showed neither dignity of speech or dress - two typical working class lads whose very way-of-life, super-imposed on the present condition of things, inevitably brought them into the I.R.A. Of course they were fighters - fighting was the norm of working-class life in ghettoland - bravery, with them, was a practised art; but ... they were pretty typical ... they'd never known much in the way of real living ... education, culture. How could they fathom the true ideals of the Republic? No, to them, this was just another Saturday night brawl in which they'd only see shame in defeat. That's what it was! They were just natural fighters, wholly involved in the fight, incapable of ...

God! Shields felt the sweat of shame on his forehead; I am thinking Anna's thoughts! I am thinking through the whole phoney, tawdry snobbery of the other me that Anna has made. The picture in the drawing room flashed through his mind; two hundred and fifty quid! He'd argued about that. Bloody blue rectangles bisected with shaded white lines! Anna gave him the salesman's spiel and he'd echoed it a hundred times to a hundred people who were not convinced by the real glory and artistic genius of two hundred and fifty quid.

Who'd believe that a man could choose a mean, narrow street occupied by a hundred soldiers and a handful of trapped rebels to stand away from himself and have a good look. To realise that he'd got lost somewhere - lost in Anna's tinsel world of empty grace and phoney culture. Systematically, imperceptibly, he had been sucked into the void of falsity ... protesting less ... accepting ... husbanding and, even, reflecting the nothingness of a respectability that was simply aversion to the valued, the earthy values, of his origin.

He was a silver tea-service man with a well-spoken wife, a Rover Two Thousand, a two hundred and fifty quid surrealistic squiggle and ... no guts! He was scared; not the honest fear of a man in an untried situation but the currish fear of a man who would read the guts of another in the other's lack of phoney social refinement ... who thought the inner poetry of idealism, the dream that demanded sacrifice in blood, effulgent only in the breast of the 'cultured'.

For a moment his brain pulsated; if he could retrieve the guns! Better that he should die now, even if he should only give inspiration to the poet or the songster, than that he should live out his ephemeral span with the memory of his cowardice. He thought again of Anna ... and the children. She would fashion his martyrdom to the needs of her pathetic drama; she'd become a tireless Maud Gonne, serene in the flamboyance of her grief. She would love the memory of her martyr more than she loved the reality of her man. The thought that war was some kind of primitive, masculine, proving ground intruded on his vision of Anna, Anna, the sweet-faced, well-spoken, cultured widow of Charlie Shields - Charlie Shields who ... died for Ireland.

He would make a dash for the gun! He could use the dead body of McGarry for cover, retrieve the rifle and go down fighting! The thought brought him intoxication. He wanted to do it! He was not afraid! That was the heroes' secret - that was the force behind Connor and Burns over there: you did it! You didn't think - you MOVED into action realising that the only thing your enemy could take was your life. You gave it to him and then you had the excitement of trying to cheat him of it!

Suddenly there was the clatter of a sub-machine gun from up the street on the Grosvenor Road side. The bullets splattered off the Saracen at the opposite corner under which either Connor or Burns was lying and Charlie realised that the firing was coming from the intersection on his side of the street. His brain was a panic again. He assumed that the shooting from that quarter, earlier, had been the work of Johnny Cairns and his party and that now the military held the position and were using it to enfilade the trapped I.R.A. man beneath the Saracen.

Cairns and the others must be ... well, if they were there - and the shooting from there, earlier, proved they were - they must be ... dead. Wiped out or, maybe, captured. But some of them would have taken their chances in Leeson Street, surely, rather than allow the avenue of fire to become a wall in a three-sided cage against an enemy approaching up the street. They were dead! They were all dead! Only Burns, Connor and he remained alive!

Now the fear was back in him. He didn't want to die - he was afraid! On the fringe of his terror he tried for apologies, excuses, for his fear; his death would contribute nothing ... someone had to stay alive for ... But the mainstream of his pulsing, terror-laden thoughts rejected assuagement and excuse and he knew that even if his death would free Ireland, he wanted to live. He retreated back into the hallway, feverish with fear. He must not be found here! They might not even listen to his explanations - they might kill him without enquiry!

The thought fathered inspiration; that was it! Of course! Why hadn't he thought about it before? He had only to close the front door and retreat into the house, in the hallway of which he was now standing! The weight of his terror lifted from his mind and some sort of dizzy elation coursed its way into his movements. He squeezed his body against the vestibule door and, with a new calmness, moved the front door forward and gently eased the lock into its keeper.

"I wudn't go doun there, luv - there's murdur goin' on!" The elderly woman had just moved back into the street from the Falls Road. Her face was flat, nondescript; wire-framed glasses were askew on her nose and her hands were tucked into the sleeves of her unbuttoned coat. The nod of her head gave gravity to her words.

Nora stopped at the corner; the shooting was close now and though there were a few people dodging about the road, there was a peculiar background of quiet. She smiled at the older woman, acknowledging her advice, and said, "I'm looking for my ... my brother. Did you hear if anyone had been killed?"

"God's sake, dear, there's bin a stack o'them kilt! Tha putt three in an army ambulance there a minit ago and flew up t'the 'ospital w' them and the say the bottom o' Leeson Street's swimmin' wi' blood!"

"Do you know if many civilians ..."

"An' the fellas has putt barricades up doun t' road an' at

Springfield an' there's fightin' there. Oh, Jesus, Mary and Joseph! What's to become o' us? An' my wee fella's out God knows where!"

The woman's voice had risen and she was walking up and down the pavement, occasionally putting her head around the corner and muttering incomprehensibly to herself as she withdrew her head and retraced her small steps up and down. "Oh, God forgive Englan' an' them cursed sudgers for the way thar treatin' the people here! Them's the Black-an'-Tans all over agin! If my Shaun ... I'll kill that wee bugger whin I git him!"

At that moment there was a burst of concentrated firing from Leeson Street. The woman stopped, momentarily, then she withdrew her hands from the sleeves of her coat, placed them above her ears with the fingers extended over her skull; her chin had disappeared into her neck and her back was bent and now, suddenly, she gyrated about in a peculiar skipping motion. "Oh Jesus Christ! Mother o' God save us from all harm! Oh, curse them bastards this night! Where's our Shaun? Wait'll I git him! Jesus! If anything's happened to the poor chile! Oh, I'm goin' to our Mary's ..."

The woman was distraught, hysterical; she was not talking to Nora, not, even, consciously to herself; but her decision to go to "Mary's" seemed final and momentous and, still with her hands holding her head, she skipped off up the street with the heels of her bedroom slippers scraping the ground.

Nora stood with her back to the wall. The shooting in the distance had turned to sporadic single shots, each echoing through the almost-eerie quiet of the night. The pavement and the road were wet and dirty and overhead dark clouds were being wafted by a strong breeze over the bright night sky. The place seemed to bulge with unseen, frightened people, behind windows, doors, walls; quiet people, whispering people, worried people, angry people - the whole great mass hiding and anxiously ear-sucking at the wind for news of the fighting; for information to believe or disbelieve, to cheer or sadden - or to fashion to one's liking.

Nora peered into the night sky - a dark-stained woollen carpet in the moving constancy of earth insulation - insulation from the infinite vastness ... perhaps a curtain of shame to hide men who could build ships to pierce the sky and plan their trajectory to the worlds beyond ... men who could multiply the capacity of their brains in metal cabinets of electronic wonderment ... men who could break things to their smallest particles and reconstruct them to their liking ... men who had taken the jungles of the Gods and fashioned them into a City from which the Gods retired in recognition of their own impotency. Men ... who were committing suicide in Leeson Street.

Oh, Johnny ... why? What is there in tomorrow's glory set only in gold lettering on cold marble for those who cannot know? What is there in this sacrifice of ... of fresh green fields with the sun shining down on them and hands touching and sending blood coursing warmly through our bodies and the supreme crystallising of those bodies in an infinity of forgetfulness and the strong smell of tea and the song that lingers afterwards and the hope of LIVING tomorrow and the walk on the road at night with the light rain brushing our faces and the fecund soil of the springtime and the flowers and the sweet singing of birds and being tired together and walking out into the waves and ... oh God, Johnny! ... and everything that is the tellable substantials ... the ladders we climbed to our happiness, Johnny! What glory is there in this death on damp, dirty streets in the foulness of the city for an Ireland that is a pale dream of yesterday in the trappings of tomorrow?

The sacrifice is for the new banks and building societies and the new public boards and the new breed of honey-tongued men who will preside over the old slums, the old miseries, the old despairs and who will enjoin your sacrifice as a testimonial to THEIR greatness. Only the marble plate, the cold, dead, eyeless bust, the name in the new song of old heroism will be different, Johnny. This is the reward of your sacrifice!

Oh, Johnny, if we could make tomorrow ... make it in the mean streets by the mingling of our blood with the rain and the dirt; if we could draw down the castles of privilege and corruption and make the fair land of freedom ... Johnny, then we could go together, love ... with the joy of our memories and our hopes and dreams compressed into a moment of supernal greatness in the joy of our sacrifice.

The hot tears rolled down her cheeks. Her heart was full to bursting, swelling in her breast, convulsing her lungs and pressing at her sides. Her back was against the wall, her hips and legs extended out, her eyes and ears were sheltered and she had no feeling beyond the utter desolation of her full heaving breast.

But the tears of her grief emptied the pressure enough to bring back the thoughts, and the dread of their content forced on her a resistance to their terror. She took her handkerchief from her pocket and dabbed at her eyes and nose, then without stopping to give grief a new initiative, she turned into the

Falls Road.

At the corner of Leeson Street a group of women were chattering in a shop doorway. Anticipating their warnings, Nora made in the direction of the door immediately adjoining the street as though that was her destination. The eyes of the women followed her but the confidence of her action forestalled them and she reached the refuge of the doorway without interference from them.

She stood with her back to the closed door. In Leeson Street she could hear the English and Scottish tongues of the soldiers shouting urgent messages, but there was no shooting. The minutes passed; then came the crack of a shot and the whistle of its echo up the narrow funnel of street. Almost immediately, three louder reports, closer to hand, rang out and before the silence had settled, the earlier crack was repeated and Nora was startled to hear the almost-accompanying noise of the bullet striking the wall across the road from her and the faint tinkling of shattered brickwork on the ground.

Then, again, silence.

Nora had not planned the move but all of a sudden, she found herself out on the pavement taking a preparatory stance for flight across the mouth of Leeson Street. She hesitated for just a moment and then she was running with her eyes downward, as fast as she could across the street. But still she heard the rough, masculine voice of the woman shouting "Look! That silly bitch is ..."

At the other corner she pulled herself into a doorway and sucked in air. It was the fear that had winded her - the fear that now crystallised in her bowels and sent a rumbling through her stomach that culminated in the sourness of her retching.

Further in the distance, but frighteningly distinct, she could hear the sporadic exchange of firing and her mind worked feverishly, conjuring its pictures of men crawling in the gutter, shooting and being shot at, killing and dying. This was one battle that would shock more than all the academic statistics of those who compiled the grim tally of death and destruction in Northern Ireland. Here the opposing forces were locked in close mortal combat, each forming its grip on the throat of the other in the narrow streets. Many men must die. The newspaper statisticians cushioned the terror of their message with time - "One hundred and fifty three civilians and sixty eight members of the security forces have died since January 1970" - but here the hour-glass had broken and the human particles of life were tumbling down, each setting up its own whirlpool of tragedy, bitter sadness and mere grief from which the wavelets would break on each other in a terrible pattern of sorrow, bitterness, revenge.

And somewhere down there was Johnny! She knew her selfishness, but Johnny was her whirlpool, the sun of her life without which her spirit would wither and decay. Johnny was down there with her love and her life, lurking in a doorway, lying in the dirty street, bleeding ... dying ...

And her brother, Paddy? He was in her mind's eye now and she felt guilty. He was the way she saw him most often in the house, without his jacket, his sleeves rolled above his elbows; but the setting of her vision was not their home - it was in the middle of Leeson Street. He was standing on a small turntable of the kind used to display goods in shop windows and his fat body was turning around slowly before an encircling audience of I.R.A. men and British soldiers who stood about in postures of ease, their rifles, sub-machine guns and pistols pointed at the turning figure. She saw her brother raise himself on one bent leg while he raised the other in a silly caricature of a cossack dancer and his arms contorted in some mad mimicry. The figure turned and she saw the V-shaped patch let into the waist-band of the trousers above his hips. The tempo of his movements increased to a wild frenzy and he was shouting, cursing, joking, while the perspiration ran down his face. The audience was laughing too; some pointed, some answered his obscenities, but she knew they would laugh on until the wild movement of the fat man on the turn-table stopped.

Then she saw the stirring among the audience. The frantic movements of the dancer were getting slower but he, too, caught the expectancy of the audience. He shouted louder, he laughed with grim terribleness, his hysterical voice rising to a macabre crescendo of terror as his legs and arms, like the limbs of some grotesque mechanical doll slowing in the lessening tension of its spring, ceased the wildness of their movement and became an easing, mechanical economy of effort.

And now the audience had become quiet - a gripping, fearsome, purposeful quiet. They all rose to a position of attention in a disciplined conspiratorial innuendo of effort. The terrible awesome silence ... their firearms extended ... their eyes fixed on the diminishing contortions of the fat man.

Suddenly, the latter stopped in an erect position of attention - stilled, fearfully in the enveloping silence of the grim cameo. All the guns roared together ... a clean crisp thunderclap that shook the street and the buildings and sent up a great multicoloured cloud that continued to rise and collect in a huge assurgent column above the place where the fat man had, a moment earlier, performed his wild pirouette.

The vision ended with the fat hissing form of her brother contracting in a wrinkled mass of bubbling flesh like a great punctured inflatable doll.

Again Nora felt the warmth of her tears. She'd never really known Paddy; she shared her childhood with him and, from the death of their parents, they had occupied the same house, but they had been strangers. Worse, his dominating manner, his obesity, his obscenity, had actually repulsed her and his flippancy and persistent bonhomie only increased her revulsion. And yet she knew that she was Paddy's constant boast - his bright, good-looking, intelligent sister ... the girl who knew it all ... who could explain everything - everything except the circumstances that conspired to put a fat man on a turn-table.

She sobbed bitterly now, caught up in a void of utter desolation. Nothing was right ... they were all dying in a madness of unreason and reason was impotent - it could not even explain away its own failure. Anger, viciousness, hatred, revenge and death had taken over in a singleness that had become an all-pervading purpose - closing inexorably on them all. Johnny, Paddy, the boy Dermot - "the talk was very interesting ... I'd like to hear more SOME TIME ... BUT I still think that we've got to FIGHT if we're going to get ANY-WHERE"! Let reason come again when we're all dead! Let it orate over our graves, its golden words explaining its cowardice ... analysing our failure ... condemning our success. We haven't time for REASON ... Time! Time! Must reason always be the unseemly guest at the wake? Always slow ... unromantic ... impotent ...

Even young Dermot, with less than a quarter of his life lived, had no time! Oh, where was Hope when Time bullied Reason? Even Dermot ...

CHAPTER TWENTY

Escape

Cairns went softly down the stairs to the living room. As he reached the bottom he was greeted by Gallagher's urgent whisper, "They've passed up the street - there was one of them in the door - what'll we do?"

Johnny's eyes were adjusting to the scene; the explosion at the corner had blown in the glass of the window, the window blind had been pulled from its fixings and the curtains hung diagonally across the window frame, broken from their anchorage at one corner. Liam Gallagher was crouched on one knee to the left of the window and Johnny saw the dull gleam of the barrel of the carbine. The broken glass cracked under his feet as he moved forward on his haunches to the other man.

"Do you think they've all gone up - that none of them remain at the end of the street?"

He raised himself to the window ledge and with slow caution bent his head through the broken frame, staring up toward the Leeson Street intersection. Two shots rang out but they were fired from some distance off and Johnny saw the silhouette of the soldiers, grouped at the top of the street, in the muzzle flash that signalled their return fire. He raised himself and, with less caution, thrust his head through the frame and peered in the opposite direction down the street. As he withdrew his head his attention was caught by the door opening on the far side of the street.

"I think they've all gone up, O.K. They're congregated at the far corner, firing up Leeson Street - listen!"

In the distance they could hear the sharp crack of the self-loading rifles - four, seven, nine, then a pause and another shot. "We've no one in Leeson Street with that type of weapon," Johnny's ears strained into the silence and his voice was a whispered articulation of his thoughts; "The army must be in at the Falls end of Leeson Street. Shields and his party are bottled in! We'll have to try and dislodge that lot from the corner, here. Look, we can't try from the house, Liam, we'll have to ..."

Johnny's voice trailed off, his attention held by his two comrades now clearly discernible and obviously awaiting his lead in one of the doorways opposite. He drew Gallagher's attention to them; "We can't fire from here, Liam, not with those people in the back room. Use the front door and don't crowd. Got your stuff? Good lad! Now use the doorways and remember we have the advantage of surprise."

As they opened the door they saw one of their comrades in the opposite doorway quietly breaking cover and moving up the street to the next doorway. Cairns squeezed Gallagher's arm and motioned him in the other direction to widen the angle of expected fire. He changed the Luger to his left hand thinking, fleetingly, of Gallagher's difficulty with the carbine, and took up a crouching position. As he raised the weapon he noticed the stooping form two doors up from his doorway and realised that the younger Gallagher had stayed to fight.

He squeezed the trigger of the Luger, repeating his firing until the blue flame seemed a constant fire, but after his first shot the noise was lost in the vibrating clamour of the other guns. The group of soldiers at the corner were in disarray - yelling, cursing, falling and now ... moaning.

Five pairs of hands were feverishly reloading. Johnny had dropped the empty magazine into his right hand pocket and rammed the spare magazine up the butt. He changed the gun to his right hand, raised it towards his chest and with his left hand holding the cocking-piece, brought the gun down sharply and allowed the breach-block to push the bullet into the breach. He did not need to change his position; the attack on the soldiers had been so successful that they were unlikely to have pinpointed him.

He did not know just how successful their action had been. The soldiers at the top of the street, largely protected from the fire of the man under the Saracen in Leeson Street and his comrade further up the street by the damaged vehicles which had lately protected Sergeant Jackson's position, had been firing occasionally - more to show their presence to the surrounded I.R.A. men than for effect. On three sides the military were drawing the fire of Connor and Burns; they did not need to take chances. Inexorably, the ring was closing little by little but the final snap would only come when the trapped men had run out of ammunition. So the group of soldiers at the corner were relaxed, awaiting the end, when the unexpected attack came from Cairns' party more than half-way up the street at their rear.

Eight soldiers in the group were hit even before they broke in hysterical disorder - and that disorder went unchecked by Captain Clark and his sergeant who were among the first to fall and among the three who died. Some of the others just broke and ran, others froze, yelling piteously, and one unarmed soldier ran down the street towards his attackers. He succeeded in passing all the doorways in which his assailants were positioned before Liam Gallagher drew a bead on him with the machine carbine and sent two quick shots into his tottering body.

In Leeson Street, the man below the Saracen saw the chaos and broke cover, making for the street in which Cairns and his men had carried out their attack. His comrade, further up the street, hesitated, then he, too, broke and ran but he had only taken a few paces when he was cut down by a hail of fire from the Falls Road side.

Bullets peppered the path of the other as he ran towards the mouth of the street but his comrades' diversion had drawn the fire from his left and, even as he gained the relative security of the street, he had raised the rifle and was firing from the hip at the disorganised soldiers who had borne the brunt of Cairns' attack.

He careered on into the street, half turning to cover his own retreat, but as he was making for one of the doorways, one of the soldiers at the top of the street had recovered, raised his rifle and sent the dead form of the man stumbling across the pavement.

The I.R.A. men in the doorways had held their fire before this new drama and now, even as the man fell to his death, they could hear the long, loud whistle blast. Cairns leapt from the doorway and, before squeezing the trigger, he shouted at the top of his voice, "Out! Out!"

His comrades were on the street now firing back at the soldiers as they ran. Johnny could hear the sound of men and machines as the various army groups converged on the mouth of the street and now the whine of bullets passed him, coursing their way down the street.

He flattened himself in a doorway. On the opposite side of the street one of his comrades had fallen and the other was pulling his body along the ground. The firing from the top of the street was constant now and suddenly there was new menace in the chattering of a sub-machine gun. The cracking and thumping of bullets against masonry, wood and metal was interspersed with the noise of falling glass and now, in the background, the yells and squeals of terrified residents of the street. On the pavement opposite Johnny saw his comrade collapse over the form he was dragging and even in his terror he saw the ridiculousness of the position in which death placed the two corpses.

Up the street, between himself and the military, he saw

the younger of the Gallagher brothers break from a doorway and start a mad, zig-zagging course that carried him past Johnny, off the pavement and down the street. He ran with the energy of a sprinter, his arms pumping vigorously at his sides, and all the time the bullets splattered around him. Suddenly his legs lost contact with the ground, his body somersaulted and his head hit the ground with a sickening thud. Still his arms and legs thrashed madly, propelling him over the ground like some grotesque crab, then he fell and in a hoarse shout he cried "Liam! L..i..a..!

Momentarily the firing had ceased - the silence amplifying the terror of the youth's cry. For five horror packed seconds the soldiers, the I.R.A. and even the panic-stricken inhabitants of the houses, seemed to hold their breath as though some new dimension of terror had been revealed to them in the youth's voice - five seconds given only to the noises of the inanimate things contracting to their peaceable ways in an accompaniment of gentle noises.

Then, as Liam Gallagher ran past Johnny in the direction of the troops and threw himself down heavily in the firing position, the sub-machine gun started again but Gallagher's first shot ended its lethal chattering. Johnny, too, raised the Luger and fired from a standing position, easing his finger only for a couple of seconds before emptying the magazine.

The bullet caught him on the left thigh. At first he thought it was a knock or a graze, for there was no great pain, but then he felt the warm trickle coursing down his leg. He had the Luger under his left arm with the hand holding the magazine and his right hand filtering the steel-jacketed bullets to his thumb and index finger for insertion in the magazine, when he felt the heat at his instep. Instinctively he wriggled his toes and felt the squelching in his shoe and now there was a knife in his leg, turning viciously and sending shock waves of pain through his body.

He steeled himself to the completion of his task, took the Luger from under his arm and pressed the magazine-release, allowing the empty mag to fall to the ground. With some difficulty he pushed the re-loaded spare into the butt, cocked the weapon and again eased his head out. Liam Gallagher's body lay stiff and inert over the carbine.

When Johnny made his break he was surprised at his ease of movement. He knew that the pain in his leg would have broken him in other circumstances but now it retreated before the greater terror of his need. He had fired four shots up the street before breaking away and now he was running down the street with surprising ease. Behind him he heard the angry cries of the guns, he heard the lead breaking on the road and on the walls, but his eyes were on the big grey rectangle of light between the houses at the bottom of the street that represented escape.

The bullet thudded into his left shoulder, propelling his body forward faster than his legs could bear it and he lost his balance and fell headlong on to the pavement. His arms were above his head when he fell and, for a few seconds, he lay with his cheek against the damp square-setts. A bullet splotched off the ground three inches from his head and, instinctively, he closed his eyes to the shattering concrete.

When he opened his eyes again he could see the wound in the pavement and his eyes gazed at it hypnotically - his whole consciousness dementedly preoccupied with the missing sliver of concrete. On the periphery of his consciousness he was aware of the noise that signalled the cautious advance of the soldiers but he could not focus his thoughts away from the hole in the pavement. Around him was silence, a luxuriant silence that seemed to stand respectfully off - conscious of its revelation. The hole was widening ... deepening; now it slithered gently under him and increased its depression until it enveloped him ... covered him ... shielded him.

At the bottom of the street, across from where he lay, the blunt muzzle of a Thompson belched flame. With a great effort Johnny lifted his head - his freudian vision gone before his returning consciousness. He was wracked with pain but now he was fully conscious, measuring with his eye the six yards to the end of the street.

The soldiers advancing down the street had turned and run for the protection of the corners, leaving two of their comrades moaning on the ground. Only for ten seconds was the Thompson quiet and then again it was barking out its furious anger into the night.

Johnny had raised himself above waist level when the shoulders of the man interposed themselves between him and the ground and he found himself raised high in the air on the other's back. His body was careered around and he was moving rapidly in the direction of the corner.

The Cortina was driving furiously up the Falls Road. Hagan was at the wheel, his face set to the work. Speers and Boyle were beside him. In the back of the car Johnny Cairns was sprawled against the rear seat, his face white, his eyes half-shuttered. Danno was kneeling beside him holding a home-made tourniquet firmly on his thigh. Beside Johnny was

Dermot, wide-eyed but calm -sometimes drawing a handkerchief over the brow of the wounded man.

"Aye, you can thank this lad, Johnny - says he's a Provo." Danno's voice was soft. "Apparently the Provos had business there tonight, too, and he was to join them. He could not get up the street because of the soldiers - before the banging started - and, later, when he tried to reach his unit by a roundabout route, he saw the situation of you lads in McDonnell Street. He remembered the firing from the Grosvenor Road and, very fortunately, made his way through the streets and, through a mutual acquaintance, was able to contact me. I got the handyman, here, with his Tommy and we collected a car - luckily! But I shouldn't be talkin' to you. How's the shoulder?"

Johnny opened his eyes wide, "Not so bad now, Danno. Anything about ... about Char ... Shields and ... and the lads with him?" He screwed his face as his voice trailed off and Danno evaded the question with a tightening of the tourniquet and Johnny winced. The pain passed from his face and he turned and smiled weakly at the youth. "Dermot - it is Dermot, isn't it?" Dermot nodded and wiped the perspiration from Johnny's brow. "Would you like me to get in touch with Miss ... with Nora, for you?"

Johnny closed his eyes. Poor Nora! Poor Nora! She would seek no martyr's widowhood - she would suffer the more. He opened his eyes again and looked with a strange earnestness at the youth. "Dermot ... the things she ... said to you ..."

"Yes, Johnny." The boy's voice was hesitant but he was calm. "I didn't grasp all the implications of what she said but ... well, I can't think ... I mean I have thought about it. It sounds silly - at first, like ... but you can't argue with it ... it's too simple really, and yet it's, well ..."

"It's right, Dermot - sense ... reasonable. I understand now. She's ... right. Sometimes you travel ... far ... quickly - too quickly. Too ... too preoccupied with the journey ... and ... and when the road ... ends, Dermot, you have ... you've got to think about it. About the journey ... the purpose ... the end. You begin .."

Danno was looking up into Johnny's face. The eyes were closed again, the cheeks white velvet - ruffling only slightly with the slight movement of the drawn mouth. "Journey?" "Road?" He was approaching delirium, he thought. He gave Dermot a reproachful look and said, with a harshness he did not feel, "Alright now Johnny; no more talking. There's a good lad."

Johnny's pale lips bent in a smile and he lifted his right arm laboriously and put it on Danno's shoulder. "Yes, Dermot. Tell her ... I ... said ... she ... she is right!"

CHAPTER TWENTY-ONE

The Reporters Will Come

Nora was still standing in the doorway. The cold had eaten through to her flesh and flushed out the sobriety of her thoughts. She was conscious now of the approaching noise that sliced bluntly into the eerie silence and only now she realised that the silence had been there for some time - that the shooting had stopped.

She looked up at the rumbling armoured vehicles coming up the road on both sides and she saw the extended file of soldiers, rifles poised, close to the wall on the opposite side. She turned her head sharply; a similar column of rifle-poised soldiers were approaching, close to the wall, on her side.

She heard the sounds of breaking glass. The soldiers were kicking in doors and breaking windows with the butts of their rifles. The premises on the front of the road were mainly shops and business premises, closed for the night, and the military made no attempt to enter them; but interspersed with these were some houses, and groups of soldiers were breaking off from the main party and entering these. A pyjama-clad man, his face running with blood, was being hauled through a doorway into the street.

One of the soldiers had opened the rear door of a Saracen and the man was trying to climb in but the kicks and the blows of the soldiers around him kept him on the ground, vainly trying to defend himself with his upraised hands drawn across his head. Nora did not see the woman before she had broken away from the troops but now she was running across the pavement in her flowing bed-robe, plastic curlers dancing in her hair. She beat with her fists on the backs of the soldiers surrounding her husband, all the time shouting dementedly - incoherently. The soldiers who had been holding her were now at her side and one of them struck her viciously across the back of the shoulders with a wooden truncheon. Then Nora heard the terrified voices of the children. "Mammy ... Mammy! Oh, Ma..my!"

"Oei! Look at this gorgeous fenian bitch!" The men were around her, standing off, staring. She was shivering now but her body was warm and perspiration ran down her forehead but, still in her terror, she stared at them, her eyes ablaze with anger and indignation. "What sort of creatures are you?

179

How could you do that to another human being?" Her voice was just above a whisper and even as she spoke, she was aware of the naivete of her words - but impotency and indignation had scrambled her thoughts.

"Oh! Fucking Miss La-Di-Da, if you don't mind!" The youth had put his flushed angry face close to hers; his breath stank and she mentally related it to the evil in his eyes.

"You're a nice lot of bloody human beings! You've just murdered a dozen or more of our chaps. Bloody Irish shit!" The tall man's accent was Etonian, his demeanour, cinema-officer. "Search this bitch!"

Eager hands grasped her and turned her face to the wall then she was lifted bodily and her feet placed some eighteen inches from the base of the wall. They were meticulous in their arrangement of her: her legs were kicked apart and her hands so arranged that her fingertips bore the weight of her body. Then came the hands around her, her legs, her thighs, her waist, then the rough hand squeezing at her breast viciously until she cried out in pain.

"Right, chaps, that will do." She was wheeled around to face old Etonian. "Right now! The truth! What are you doing here?"

She stared at him, shaking, afraid of the hands that could strike her and the feet that could kick her but even more afraid of submissive surrender to indignity. When she replied her voice was even but with a diamond edge. "I was on the road because I wanted to be on the road, not to impede or intrude on anyone. I am at this corner because gunmen endangered my life and I had to seek refuge and now I am being impeded, assaulted and degraded by you. More men ... more guns! You are all the same - yes, you are!" She took a halfstep forward and shot her words into the officer's laughing face. "Little men with big guns - in uniform and out of uniform ... dangling little puppets dancing on the strings of your masters. I.R.A., British Army - just men with guns forcing the servility of your own souls on others!"

"Shut your bloody mouth, you fenian bitch or I'll shut it for you!" The red-faced youth had his hand raised.

The faces were merging into a shimmering mass in her vision and she knew they must see her trembling. She felt faint but she must hold on. She must hold on! Deliberately she eased her back to the wall and, when she spoke again, her effort of control strained through her voice. "You know you ARE just like the I.R.A. - only it could be said in mitigation of their viciousness that they are motivated by lofty, altruistic dreams while you ... you are attracted by advertisements appealing to your self-interest. But neither you nor they ever had an original thought in your lives. You both accept the old fiction and it justifies anything - doesn't it? Put the kids in the trucks and bring them to the seaside - do it! It's an order! And you like it. Shoot the kids, gas the kids! Go on - do it! It's an order! And you don't like it but ... you MUST do it! You've mortgaged your brains!"

The red-faced soldier was looking quizzically at the impatient, half-interested face of his superior. Nora had stopped speaking and her eyes searched each of the half-circle of faces. Her look was emphasizing the sarcasm of her words when she spoke again. "No - you are not looking for me. I could not support the I.R.A. for the same reasons I could not support you. You are both lesions on a sick society. If I wished you harm, I'd cheer you as a soldier, but ..."

The man who struck her hard across the face - a wide, swinging blow with the inside of his fist - came from the back. He did not speak and, in the confusion of her falling, he stepped back again to the outside of the pack.

Nora lay in a forest of camouflaged legs. Again the trembling was on her but her eyes were on the heavy boots under the legginettes and her head pulsed with the urgency of remaining conscious. Some of the soldiers were laughing and she looked up the long funnel of light between the giants whose great heads bent towards her. The officer's posture had given him a double-chin that was vibrating with laughter. "O.K. chaps. Come on - up with the rest now!"

She closed her eyes as they were moving off and then she felt the arms under her shoulders helping her to her feet. Three of the soldiers had remained behind and two of them were now holding her erect while the third was brushing his hand down the mud-stained skirt of her coat.

One of the soldiers who had lifted her up was at her side steadying her with a hand on her elbow while the other hand fumbled awkwardly at her right hand. She looked at him. He was a tall, well-built youth with large eyes that dropped before her gaze. "I'm sorry, Miss. Genuinely. Some o' them are rough when they're scared - an' we're all scared, aren't we, Miss?"

The other two were standing in front of her now. The older man who had been dusting her coat fumbled in a pocket and brought out a handkerchief which he offered her, without words. She knew he wanted to speak but that shame and remorse had crowded out his words and she smiled at him. The man replied with a flat, mirthless movement of the lips and Nora was overwhelmed with compassion to the point where she put her hand on the man's shoulder and said, with thick-throated earnestness, "Thank you." She looked at the other two, to include them in her gratitude; "Maybe we'll ALL learn ... sometime - eh?"

The Etonian-tongued officer was on the outer edge of the pavement, walking backwards, looking down at them. The soldiers fixed their equipment and moved off silently but as each moved away they patted her on the arm or the shoulder and she was touched with the moving eloquence of their regret.

She relaxed against the wall and closed her eyes. There was a strange quiet abroad now, broken only by the steady, receding drone of the army vehicles. But already the denizens of the area were emerging, hungry for news of the battle. Nora opened her eyes, still standing with her head erect against the wall. Yes, they were gathering again; the tired, aged faces in the tired setting of slumdom, tirelessly taking the blows, tirelessly and impotently venting their protest with bricks and bottles - and prison sentences and death.

Now the reporters would come and talk and chortle, pressing their incisive questioning in a masquerade of sympathy and understanding. "What's your occupation, Sir? ... hm ... your age?" Tomorrow the NEWSLETTER would tell them about the trouble - through the filter of its editorial prejudices; "Mr. O'Neill, a forty-six year old labourer said ..." But it would be the British Army's statement, backed by the authority of the absent police, that would make the headline and the heavy print and there would be 'soldiers' and 'gunmen' and even the dead would be categorised. The press would be writing history for the better-off in the bungalows and the semi-D's, to read with their fruit juice and argue over in the offices - some with the added drama of noises actually heard, far off in the night.

She thought of home and, in response to her thoughts, the screen of her mind was filled with the picture of the living-room. Her body convulsed involuntarily; the big man who had ... JOHN HEGARTY! Now the sad, vacant smile was etched in her consciousness and it emptied her of everything but the hammer blows in her chest. Even the undemanding life of Hegarty! The discarded jacket ... the second-hand trousers ... the grateful, inconsequential bite ... Even small grains of life ... forfeit!

Then she thought with a start of Johnny; but the thought of

Hegarty had drained her feelings and concern for Johnny was now only an added ache.

CHAPTER TWENTY-TWO

The Portals of Martyrdom

Danno's was a difficult decision; Johnny Cairns was in need of urgent medical attention but the question was, where to bring him. Hospital meant handing him over to the authorities and Danno was not in a position to know if the wounds were sufficiently serious to trade life for a lengthy prison sentence - or worse. Perhaps a friendly doctor could arrest the bleeding and patch him up but the army would seal off the entire Falls area, impose a curfew and ransack the houses.

Johnny himself resolved the problem; he had regained consciousness for a few minutes and Danno had asked him if he wanted to go to hospital. The question had alerted him and Danno was pleased at the indication of regained strength. He had not moved, even his lips were immobile, but his answer was clear enough: "The garage, Danno ... keys in my pocket ... the garage." Only then had he made a movement, around to the right, silently indicating his left jacket pocket. Danno steadied him with his right hand and it was then that he felt the Luger, still in Johnny's left hand.

Danno could not leave the tourniquet but with one hand he helped Dermot to free the gun from the gooey mass of congealing blood that had run down Cairns' arm, cementing the gun to his fist.

The street off the Shankhill Road was quiet enough and they had little difficulty getting the injured man out and into the garage, even though he was unconscious again and a dead weight on Speers and Hagan who had supported him under the arms while Danno had moved awkwardly in front, still retaining pressure on the tourniquet.

Boyle had lit matches before he found the switch and, in the first spluttering light of the neon tube, Dermot was already looking for a place for the injured man.

The garage was an old structure reclining between the gables of two houses. The floor was an uneven expanse of cracked bricks set on their edges and covered with a black film of dirt and dried up oil. At the rear of the building, running from wall to wall, was a workbench cluttered with an assortment of tools and discarded vehicle parts. Close to the bench was a small lorry from which part of the front had been removed and, suspended immediately in front of this on a block-and-tackle hoist, was a partially-assembled engine. Behind the lorry was a small Ford van and, nearer the gate, Cairns' ancient blue, two-tone, Humber Hawk.

Close to the bench was a rough office constructed of timber and hardboard. Dermot pressed the switch and a single unshaded light revealed the small room, its floor covered with a thin, oil-impregnated carpet. To one side was an old roll-top desk and a car seat raised on a wooden trestle, to act as a chair. In a corner beside the desk was a hessian sack filled with rags.

Outside the office, the men were still holding the wounded man. Dermot said, "In here," as he passed them. He went to Johnny's Humber and, a minute later, followed them into the office with the rear bench seat under his arm and a folded tartan rug.

They had made a bed for him out of the bag of rags and the car seat and placed the rug and two of their overcoats over him and Danno had secured the tourniquet with a knot. The paraffin heater had been lit but was emitting a foul black smoke so Dermot had carried it out into the garage to burn away the excess oil.

Cairns' face was a white cast; the skin was drawn tight over his nose and cheeks and the immobility and the pale blue threads of veins on his eye-lids gave him the appearance of cold marble. Even the lips had paled and looked fixed and undisturbed by his breathing.

Hagan wanted to get away. He was a big, gruff man in his mid-twenties and a veteran of the troubles. As a fighter he was fearless - an obedient journeyman with a Thompson; he could kill and had himself touched hands with death on more than one occasion but he could not cope with dying. Now it was not fear of detection that provoked his restlessness, nor yet was it lack of concern; it was his impotency - his utter uselessness to meet the exigencies of the situation and, too, his fear of death as a deliberate, steadily-encroaching thing that could not be held off and might expose the weaknesses of the dying.

They discussed in whispers. Danno was insistent that the first priority was skilled medical assistance and he even suggested that Johnny should be taken out again in the car, left somewhere, and a few shots fired to draw attention and the inference that he had been shot in mysterious circumstances. Speers and Boyle shared the opinion that the coagulated blood could save the injured man's life and moving him again could be dangerous. Dermot was staring at Johnny's face; he was thinking of their earlier meeting at Nora's house and he said, absently, and only loud enough to be heard in the lull in the whispered conversation, "He was full of life this evening in Quinn's house and now ..."

The sombreness of his words caught the others and they looked from the youth to the face of the wounded man. Danno's broad face puckered; "Quinn ... Nora Quinn! That's Johnny's girl-friend ... she's a nurse! She's the one could help!"

It was relief from their impotence; not only was it a practical suggestion, but it involved them IMMEDIATELY in its implementation. Danno suggested that Hagan and Speers go for the girl but they objected that they would have difficulty finding the house and anyhow, Hagan thought the arms would have to be dumped first and that it would be dangerous to bring the blood-stained, stolen Cortina back into the Falls area.

Finally they decided that Hagan should take the arms away in the Cortina and that Boyle should take Dermot, who knew the house, in Johnny's old Humber to fetch Nora. Danno and Speers would stay with Johnny.

Nora had not spoken to Boyle when she got into the car. Dermot had called at her house twenty minutes earlier - for they had not been able to get the car into the Falls district which was swarming with British troops - and Dermot had made his way on foot to her house.

The youth had told her that Johnny was hurt and had added quickly that he was "safe" and out of the area. "How badly - is he shot?" Dermot had been remarkably collected; yes, Johnny was wounded in the leg and shoulder - he couldn't say exactly where but time was important - she should not ask questions ... she should hurry. She was excited, desperate with concern; tears had shown in her eyes and the muscles in her throat were contracted, but he would not let her break. She must think clearly now - for Johnny's sake. Had she dressings? Antiseptic? Anything to kill pain?

She had taken her big handbag and had disciplined her concern enough to collect the items she might require - and she was silent.

Now, in the car, she was thinking. If the bleeding had stopped ... get him away. A couple of days maybe, and he would be mended enough to get him over the Border into the Republic of Ireland. He was strong ... the thigh was not the worst place - if ... the shoulder? In her mind she mended him and walked with him along the golden strand in West Mayo, knowing that the Atlantic breezes would resuscitate him; conspiring with the August sunshine to put new strength in him ... a strength safe from dissipation in the squalor of the city. And the lunacy would pass in the time of his recuperation and he would have survived it.

Dermot was sitting low in the back of the car, from which the seat had been removed to make a bed for Johnny. He was sitting, silent, with his own preoccupations, concerned lest he intrude on her grief. Boyle was manoeuvring the big, unfamiliar car through the narrow network of streets, his mind fully occupied in his task. They were now on the Shankhill Road, in trouble-free Belfast - where the ghetto Protestants had been conned by their political overlords into the belief that they were the favoured children of the State - the poor who protested, with the rich, that the poor were no longer with us.

Even in her sorrow, Nora could not elude the depression that the Shankhill provoked in her. Catholics were tilting at windmills, following a dream that carried them, through suffering, death and destruction, back to their misery. They were slaves, desperately tugging at their fetters to break free - even if they sought only new fetters. They were following their leaders who had never glimpsed freedom - who were less concerned at the fact of slavery than they were with the condition of the slave. But the Protestant poor ... they only made self-deceiving noises with their claims to warm the hearts of their masters.

They were disciplined to the slum and the factory hooter and their masters did not need to send the soldiers after them. They were rewarded with warnings that the Catholic poor were endangering their way of life.

It was the poor who took the knocks; the poor who were Catholics, the poor who were Protestants and the poor who had been given ambition in a military uniform and a gun. Let them run their own rat-trap, disciplining one another with their imposed prejudices, their bigotries, their patriotism and, when they became really unruly, let them beat hell out of one another. The masters and their political flunkeys will stand on the touch-lines, tut-tutting, wondering, overcome with indignation at the weaknesses of human nature that have somehow, escaped them.

The car stopped at the narrow gate and Nora was back in the present - angry at the treachery of her thoughts which had taken from the urgency of her mission. Dermot was already out of the car and opening the door for her and Speers was holding one of the gates of the garage open.

She looked down into the white face, devoid of any expression of pain or remorse or any of the other indications of conflict or emotion within that the face mirrors. It was a baby's face, stark and beautiful and frightening and, even ... inhuman - in that it bore no mark of human experience.

Johnny!

Her knowledge and experience deserted her and, for an eternity, she stared at him, capsuling her love of this man ... his kindness ... his frailties ... his dreams - along with the dirt under his nails ... his passion for walking ... his romanticism, and his tenderness, his laughter and his doubts ... into a single agony that tore at her stomach, set a hard ball in her throat and confounded her understanding.

She raised his arm and took his wrist in her fingers. Somewhere within life was still struggling and sending its weak message of hope to her fingers. She was not conscious now of the others; there was only Johnny and herself. She stared at the black hairs on the calloused hand, at the powder burns and the dark etchings of his trade in his capillaries - the hand that had cradled her head while he spoke his poetry and talked his dreams. She looked again at her watch and the pain of its message piled on her sadness.

Danno helped her to tear away the trouser leg. The bullet had gone through and the blood had sealed its passage but not before it had drenched his leg and trousers and coursed its way around his foot. She adjusted the tourniquet and covered the leg then she turned to the shoulder, trying to ease away the blood-satiated overcoat and jacket while Danno gently eased the wounded man's back on its makeshift bed.

Johnny gave a low moan and his body stirred. Danno gently relinquished his pressure and Nora turned her eyes to the white face. The slight convulsion of the mouth told his pain and she left the shoulder and took a white cloth from her bag and mopped away the cataracts of crystalline beads from his forehead. She was close to his face, fighting a compulsion to gather his head to her and place her cheek against his and send the warm life of her body through him. Instead she watched the struggle in his eyelids as life contested easement and death.

At first it was the mere pulsation of the almost-translucent lids; the movement of pale veins and contraction of the little creases in the corner of the eyes, but, as Nora watched, the movement became more regular as consciousness percolated through and marshalled a dwindling stamina in the performance of an activity normally instinctive and untaxing. The lids parted slowly, the man's efforts now concentrated in raising the lashes that yet formed a curtain on his vision. She watched his efforts, constricting her breathing, willing the opening to his consciousness – and the eyes opened ... staring sightlessly at her – and her vision, too, was blurred with protecting tears.

Danno looked at her and he knew that her whole senses were on the glazed eyes. He hesitated for a moment before he lifted the handbag closer to him and removed the tiny bottle of whiskey from the opened bag. He put his hand under the sweat-matted head but he had not removed the cork; he put the bottle to his mouth and locked his teeth on the cork and screwed. It came away and the noise curiously embarrassed him but he put the bottle to Johnny's pale, cracked lips, forced them apart and eased a little of the whiskey into his mouth.

Very slowly he raised his eyes to her, but even when they were focussed on her face, there was, for a moment, no hint of recognition. She heard the whiskey pass over his tongue and into his throat and now his body was wracked with coughing and she held him gently, fearful of the effect of his efforts on the shoulder wound. His eyes were still on her, wide now, with fear and puzzlement in them.

"Johnny! It's Nora. Johnny!"

Then the small light flickered in his eyes and he marshalled his strength in a vain effort to raise himself.

"No, Johnny! Keep still!"

Nora fought back the tears for his eyes were still on her face – speaking to her now ... loving her ... and his message stuck in her soul, tearing at her and forcing out hope.

The big man, Danno, had moved away, his back now turned to the others in surrender to his private anguish. He had never seen a man die; death to him was heroic – the sad screen through which the patriot must pass to the portals of martyrdom to be canonised in verse and in legend and inspire the continuance of the process. It was a noble and a holy thing, visualised as a SUDDEN cutting of the link with life. The reality of blood and pain and the cold sorrow of parting was a bitterness he could not take.

Death was not the stuff of poetry; the songs and the poems came afterwards ... afterwards ... when time has hallowed the memory, washed away the blood and the echo of the pain and dimmed the bitterness of parting ... afterwards.

Boyle was standing very erect, a pace away from the makeshift bed. He was pale and his eyes sought refuge from the scene in their movements away from the face.

Speers, the Catholic, was on his knees, his rosary beads in his hands, praying for his Protestant comrade. Unlike Danno, Speers had been the harbinger of death and he had prayed for the repose of the soul of the man he had killed and for the recovery of the two he had wounded; but, like Danno, he had never stood by while death, with slow inexorability, contested with life. Now his eyes were closed as he searched in the empty turmoil of his mind for a vision to pray to - not for life ... but for merciful death ... and the assuagement of memory.

Dermot was at Nora's right shoulder, his hand on her arm. His face was pale but there was an earnest isolation in his eyes. He was facing death, honestly; unshielded by sentiment - thinking only of its irony ... the irony of its fleeting pain on this man who saw in its pain a path to freedom, and the permanence of its agony on this woman who saw in it only sadness and tragedy. He watched the dying man's face, watched the receding responses of life in his eyes and in the tremor of his mouth and he knew that it was his battle too - his struggle with a decision that could not be made simply in fear of death.

He had made his decision when Johnny's eyes looked away from Nora and slowly, his head still, turned his gaze on him. For a moment the eyes of the dying man locked with those of the youth - the pained, troubled eyes of the dying man craving understanding ... there is no glory in death, Dermot; it is the brave man's response to tyranny when he is without under-standing ... without understanding, what can a man do? When authority kicks him and degrades him ... if he doesn't know ... what can he do? He must tremble in his dead spirit or fight back ... either way he must lose. With understanding, with knowledge, he is impervious to degradation - even in his chains - and his enemies are ensnared in his pity.

Dermot smiled at him and his lips parted, but the words would not come; but his eyes were softer, less troubled, when he looked at Nora again.

She was still holding his hand when the eyes closed and she knew his memory of her, his love, his pain and his sorrow, were forever shuttered. The icy pain of her grief expanded itself in her breast, hurting her breathing, shaking at her, holding her throat and welling up in her head demanding the relief of her tears. But tears were a luxury for after ... Now it was only sadness, loneliness, bitterness and pain.

For a long time she knelt beside him, his dead hand in hers, her mind meandering down the stream of memory and it was the high points of their happiness that were now pulled into the vortex of her grief and sent coursing through her being in bitter shafts of sadness. And still she stared at the dead face, composed now in its last setting - without laughter or anger ... without sadness or pain.

Johnny! No ... Johnny was dead! This composed dead face was that of the truly anonymous dead soldier - without cause now ... without country ... without flag. One of the dead who had died for ... for the peace and opinionless serenity of death.

Dermot's urging hand was on her arm. She looked around to face him and his young face somehow induced the first slow trickle of her tears. She held his arm, the tears coming freely now; "Oh Dermot! Oh, why ..." but the tears stopped the words in her throat.

When he spoke, it was a man's voice, quiet and confident. "You know 'why', Nora. Johnny knew at the end and now I know, too. It's part of the sad problem we must face - without tears ... without glory."

Now she saw that this man was fighting his tears and she knew he shared her grief and his words and his unshed tears eased her pain.